M000237278

Madness in Brewster Square

A Brewster Square Mystery

Narielle Living

Cactus Mystery Press
An imprint of Blue Fortune Enterprises, LLC

Cactus Mystery Press Titles by Narielle Living

Brewster Square Series Cozy Mysteries:

Madness in Brewster Square
Birding in Brewster Square

Paranormal Mysteries:

Signs of the South
Revenge of the Past
Children of the Tribe

MADNESS IN BREWSTER SQUARE
Copyright © 2018 by Narielle Living.

All rights reserved. Printed in the United States of America. No part of this book may be used or reproduced in any manner whatsoever without written permission except in the case of brief quotations embodied in critical articles or reviews.

This book is a work of fiction. Names, characters, businesses, organizations, places, events and incidents either are the product of the author's imagination or are used fictitiously. Any resemblance to actual persons, living or dead, events, or locales is entirely coincidental.

For information contact :
Blue Fortune Enterprises, LLC
Cactus Mystery Press
P.O. Box 554
Yorktown, VA 23690
http://blue-fortune.com

Book and Cover design by Wesley Miller, WAMCreate, wamcreate.co

ISBN: 978-1-948979-00-9

Second Edition: April 2018

DEDICATION

To all of my aunts:
Violet Marino, Rose Lagasse, Terri Nigro, Nancy Slavin, and to Linda
Bunker and Nancy Ciaramella, the real Claudia and Estelle.
You helped me become the person I am today because of your love.

Chapter One

I USUALLY AVOIDED THOUGHTS ABOUT whether or not ghosts really existed, because it's not like there was going to be a test. I should have known better, at least with my family.

I counted three hundred and thirty-seven steps from the bakery where I got my breakfast to my job at my brother's store. I count things when I'm bored, restless, or trying not to think about something, and I was trying not to think about the current direction of my life and the never-ending Connecticut winter. The cold would go away, eventually, but I was also bored with my work and my life. Jumping into something new wasn't so easy, though, since I had obligations—family obligations—and I couldn't just dump them and follow my dream.

Not that I even had a dream.

A nameless dread began to fill me. The back of my neck tingled, and I was certain that something bad was about to happen. I'd had these feelings before, but they weren't specific and I never knew exactly what was coming. *Burnout. I've read about this.*

With my hair blowing into my eyes, I made sure to look both ways twice so I wasn't flattened by some commuter in an SUV, and hurried across the street. I didn't want to be late for work. *Maybe Scentsations is going out of business.* I was the assistant manager for my brother's store, so I knew that wasn't possible. Business had been good in the little aromatherapy store. *Besides, my good luck would be my brother's bad luck. I can't think those kinds of thoughts.*

Juggling a muffin, cup of coffee, oversize purse, and book I reached for the door handle. One quick glimpse inside stopped me in my tracks. I took a step backwards, hoping to get away before either of them saw me... Two heads inside the store swiveled, looking out the window. Crap-a-roni, I was too late. They saw me. Now I had to go in.

The gentle tinkling of the wind chimes attached to the door was a direct contrast to the fight brewing inside the store. Taking a breath, I forced myself to step over the threshold.

"Ava Maria Sophia Cecilia, how are you?" The voice greeting me was trying for maximum warmth, drawing my name out like butter on a hot pan. But I knew better. Plus, he used my full name, a sure sign he wanted something. He winked at me before turning away, a gesture I found repulsive. Ex-boyfriends should not wink at ex-girlfriends. Ever.

Turning back to my brother, the sleazy ex moved a step to the right. Doing this positioned him in front of the mirror better, a habit formed in high school enabling him to make sure his slicked back hair was still slicked back and his gold medallion still sparkled from the confines of his hairy chest. For the millionth time, I wondered what the hell I'd been thinking when I dated him.

"Joey, you gotta listen to me." His sharp words were a contrast to his attitude toward me. I stood in front of the door and closed my eyes, wishing that for once I'd been late. I needed a new job.

My brother stood on the other side of the counter with his arms crossed over his chest and spoke through clenched teeth. "My. Name. Is. Giuseppe."

My creepy ex, Kenny, smiled. I'd known Kenny for most of my life, and I knew what a rat he could be, but whenever he smiled he had this ability to appear warm and sincere. Even though I should have known better, I relaxed for a moment, hoping everything would be all right. Until Kenny opened his mouth again. "You'll always be Joey to me. I can still remember little Joey O'Dell cryin' for his momma the day he lost his lunch box."

Ouch. It looked like this fight was shaping up to include past insults all the way back to elementary school. Clearly I needed to step in and defend my brother. "Kenny, I don't—"

Giuseppe cut me off. "First of all, that was a long time ago. Second of all, you're the one who stole the lunch box. Now, what do you want?"

My head swiveled back to Kenny. Giuseppe had a legitimate question, especially since we weren't on the best of terms with Kenny. What did he want?

"And then, wasn't it just last week I saw you crying, again, down at the beach? What were you crying about then? Maybe something to do with that sweet little wife of yours."

"You're an idiot, Kenny, a big, stupid, idiot. And you can shut up about my wife. I don't even want you thinking about her, you hear me?"

Crossing between them, I set my coffee and muffin on the counter. "Kenny, what brings you here?" I asked, hoping he'd leave soon. My coffee was getting cold, and I really wanted to eat my carrot muffin. With my Italian heritage reflected in my shapely figure, I probably should have just had carrots without the muffin, but I liked to eat when it was cold outside.

"Yeah, don't you have *work* to do?" My brother was not helping the situation.

Kenny strode over to the counter, trying to act casual. Pretending to examine the array of organic lotions and soaps, he put his arms behind his back.

"I came to make you an offer."

Did he really say that? I always thought if you wanted to do business with people, you made an effort to be nice to them. Silly me. But Kenny has always talked to others as if he were a very important person.

My brother didn't stop to think about it. "No."

"Hear me out, then you can say no." Kenny's voice continued to ooze charm, but it was wasted on us. "I would like to offer my services to you." He raised a hand in protest before Giuseppe could say anything. "It would be mutually beneficial to present a united front to the community tonight."

"What's tonight?" I asked.

"We'll talk about it later," Giuseppe answered me before turning to Kenny. "No."

"Talk about what later?" I asked. My voice was low, but not because I didn't want Kenny to hear me. With him standing right there, I knew he could hear every word. My voice was low, which is what happens when I get mad or upset. I don't scream, I whisper.

Plus, I had a bad feeling about whatever my brother had planned for me, but not from worry about the actual event. Something felt wrong. Maybe the tingling anxiety thing was about tonight. Why would Kenny want to tag along on whatever my brother was doing?

"Ava, we'll talk about this later," Giuseppe whispered back.

Sometimes when Giuseppe has something in mind for me it isn't anything I want to do, but for whatever reason he decides it's an absolute necessity. Like the time when we were kids and he decided we needed to see if aliens really existed. He convinced me it was important to all of humanity for us to stay up all night to see if we could send or receive some sort of communication. He rigged up something on his short wave radio that he was convinced would work and to this day I have no idea what it was. He was the person in charge of the radio, and I was the person in charge of "direct contact." That meant I spent the night on the roof, and he spent the night in his room. When it got to be around four in the morning and I could hardly stay awake and had to pee, I climbed back into the house through the upstairs window and found Giuseppe sound asleep.

In his bed.

Snoring.

You'd think I would've learned from that experience, but through the years I have found myself being somewhat forgiving toward my brother. Even though he's a few years older than I am, he acts like the second or third born child. Creative, disorganized, and charismatic. He is the type of sensitive man who women always claim to want, but most couldn't handle it when he cried about famines in distant lands or the demise of the spotted toad. Thankfully, he met his match in Janine, an equally sensitive and all around good person. Even better, he married her. Unfortunately, Janine shared most of his views regarding the paranormal. And even more unfortunately for me, he talked a lot about those views.

Frankly, he scares the bejeesus out of me when he brings up ghosts, aliens, and demons.

But it's not like I believe in any of that stuff.

"You guys are doing a ghost hunt tonight," Kenny told me.

"No," I said.

"Apparently you two need some family time right now," Kenny said. "I'll come back later." As he turned and walked out the door, it briefly flashed through my mind that Kenny's diplomacy was uncharacteristic. I didn't really care, though, because at the moment my focus was on making sure my brother understood when I said no, I meant no.

I must've told him a thousand times I'm not doing ghost hunts with him anymore. Period.

"What the hell are you wearing?" Giuseppe demanded.

Momentarily thrown by the abrupt conversational switch, I didn't know what to say. "Good morning to you, too. Yes, I'm fine, how about yourself?" *Keep a Zen attitude, stay in the moment and maintain balance*, I told myself.

"How many times have I told you that color is not good for you? You can't wear black, it's all wrong for your skin tone and it throws Janine's aura off. You have to wear positive colors, reflections of the energy of life."

"I have to wear what's clean and will keep me warm." Janine was the main reason I worked at Scentsations, and she and I were friends, but I never once heard her talk about her aura. She talked about other people's auras, but never her own.

Giuseppe shook his head, clearly disgusted by my lack of understanding when it came to auras. "You can throw the day into chaos by not being careful about these things, you know." He looked at me thoughtfully for a moment, before adding, "Although it might work for tonight. Yes, that would be good."

"I told you, I'm not doing it," I said, glad I hadn't gotten him a muffin from the bakery. I'd almost ordered him his favorite, lemon poppyseed, but Janine had him on a diet and I didn't want to get on her bad side. And right about now I had a feeling Giuseppe was going to say something I didn't want to hear, so I was glad I hadn't wasted the money.

"I have you scheduled to come out with us tonight on our latest paranormal event," he said, turning away to open a box. I knew he was so busy unpacking inventory right now because he couldn't look me in the eye.

"What if I don't want to?" So much for my Zen attitude. "You know I hate doing those things. I can barely stay awake, and nothing ever happens."

"We have an investigation, and I'm short an investigator. I need you to come to the house with us. I have a few new investigators, and they don't understand the intricacies of all the equipment."

"No." I wouldn't do it, no matter what he said. He couldn't make me be part of that group if he offered me a million dollars.

I really should look for a new job instead of putting up with this manipulation.

"I'll pay you fifty bucks."

I hesitated. I hadn't expected him to offer me money, so now what? Fifty dollars didn't sound like a lot, but I was trying to save every little bit I could for a vacation. Of course Giuseppe used that to his advantage.

"It's not a lot," he said, looking up from the box, "but some extra cash will get you a little closer to buying the plane ticket you want."

Damn him. He knew how much I wanted to go to Ireland, but working with those people always tried my patience—made me want to scream, actually. Ghost hunters can be weird.

"Tell me again why you're doing this."

"Why I'm doing what?" he asked.

"This group you've put together. You must be losing money on this business. I've seen all the advertising you've done, and it's not cheap."

Giuseppe straightened to his full six foot height and rolled his shoulders. "We are truth seekers. We are investigators, and we have standards. Which is more than I can say about some paranormal groups."

My brother's paranormal group, or ghost hunters as they were commonly called, was known as AA Energy and Spirit Investigators. He started this little side business only after Kenny started his, which was called AAA Paranormal Investigators. And anyone who knows anything about alphabetical listings in the internet yellow pages or old fashioned phone book would realize why my brother chose AA, even if it did mean he got more than a few phone calls from drunks looking to stop drinking.

I wasn't finished. Other issues were bothering me. "Seriously, G, when are you going to ban Kenny from the store? Asking him to stay out is the best thing you can do. You don't like him, and people don't want to shop in a place where you guys are standing around arguing."

Giuseppe scowled at me. "First of all, don't call me G. You know I hate that almost as much as being called Joey. And second of all, it would be bad for business to ban him. How would it look to the rest of the town if I forbid him from coming in here for no good reason? Kenny has his own business venture, I have mine. I can go into his if I want, he can come in here. That's it. The end. Period."

I put my hands up in front of me to ward off any more ranting. "Okay, fine, whatever you say. Where's this thing going to be tonight?" I needed to change the subject if we were going to make it through the day working together. If anything caused a fight between us, it was Kenny.

"At the old McAllister place, the one over on Chartres Drive."

I was shaking my head and backing away from him before he even finished his sentence.

"Have a good time," I said.

"You agreed. Fifty bucks."

"Sure, before I knew where you were going. Sorry, G, but there is no flippin' way you're going to get me to go into that house. Ever."

Chapter Two

I WAS TEN YEARS OLD when the old McAllister woman died. Until now her house had remained unlived in, completely deserted with dusty old furniture. I'm sure mice, raccoons, or squirrels were crawling around and making a home in there. For whatever reason, no long-lost relatives came forward to claim the house, a major mystery since you would think a big old house in Connecticut was prime real estate. I always assumed the relatives didn't want to brick up the entry to hell in the basement or whatever supernatural ick that made the house so darn creepy. It sat empty for years and gained a deserved reputation as a menacing place.

In fact, the reputation of the house was so solid not even area drug dealers or criminals used it as a hangout. Nobody wanted to go there.

Rumor had it the house was built over an ancient burial site and it was haunted even before the old lady kicked off. To my adult self, the rumor sounded lame. As a kid I'd believed it with my whole heart. I didn't know the history of the house, but I did know I was not inclined to step anywhere on, near, or in it.

I wasn't a big baby or anything, but the distinct memory of my thirteen-year-old self running out of the yard after hearing very clear snarls and growls coming from the basement made for an easy decision. And they weren't earthly snarls and growls, I'd like to add. They were demonic, definitely not-from-around-here sounds. I might claim I didn't believe in the paranormal, but I wasn't stupid, either. I knew when to leave things alone, and this house needed to be left alone.

"I'll give you sixty dollars."

I shook my head. "Dude, that place is scary. You don't have to go in there looking for things, everyone knows it's haunted."

"Exactly," Giuseppe said. "This is our chance to get some real proof of ghost activity, which could be groundbreaking. Don't you see what an opportunity this is?"

"Nope. I see what a mistake this is."

"It's not scary anymore," he wheedled.

"Really? It suddenly got un-scary? I didn't know that could happen." My brother was always good at making things up to fit any situation to his needs. This time it wasn't going to happen. Whatever he said would not change my mind.

I am not going in there. Period.

"The old house has finally been sold to someone, and the new owners have been in and started to clean the place up. They've done a bunch of renovations."

My silence was all the answer I would give him. I said no, I meant no.

"It looks nice in there," he said. "They put in a new garden, and the inside has fresh paint and period furniture, with the hardwood floors all redone. The place sort of reminds me of that television show, what's it called? Oh, yeah, *Make It Pretty.*"

Only my brother could so consistently manipulate me. He knew he had me as soon as he mentioned *Make It Pretty.* The show was one of my favorites, where the hosts went into crappy old houses and made them look elegant and sophisticated. It always amazed me how they could work magic with a little fabric, paint, wood, and tools. I loved the entire design process, and I especially loved the ending where they unveiled the new look of the home.

"It's really cool in there," my brother continued. "With all the work they've done the house looks like the end result of the show. Amazing, really."

He was devious. This was so unfair.

"Okay." My hand covered my mouth a moment too late. *I can't believe those words came out of my mouth. What the heck was I thinking?* Although, now that I thought about it, the old house had probably cleaned up pretty well. If they knew what they were doing, it might look darn good in there, and they'd probably sealed up the entrance to hell in the basement or fixed whatever had made it scary in the first place.

"I'll do it, on one condition."

My brother knew he had me then, so he waved a hand in my direction. "Sure, what do you want?"

"I want to be able to take a friend with me tonight."

The bell on the door jingled and a new customer stepped in, meaning I was going to have to wait a few minutes before convincing my brother to let me have my way. Since I was helping him out with the evening's events at the house of hell, the least he could do was give me the couple of things I asked for.

The customer, tall, silver-haired, with a military bearing, strode in, blue eyes scanning the room until he saw Giuseppe.

"I'm here for a... marble," he said.

I looked at him, wondering what he meant. Linwood Cosgrove, a retired Army Colonel, was always very pleasant. I usually saw him around town with his wife, Valerie, who had the same polite-yet-distant demeanor as her husband.

"She changed her order and decided against the marbled design," Giuseppe said. "Here, they just arrived yesterday." Reaching under the counter, Giuseppe pulled out a box and set it next to the cash register. "Three beeswax candles with grapefruit and lemongrass essential oils." Giuseppe smiled at Linwood. "I think this is what you're looking for."

Linwood hesitated, eyeing both Giuseppe and the box with suspicion. After a moment, he nodded. "Okay. How much do I owe you?"

Giuseppe rang the order up and looked up at Linwood. "That'll be ten dollars and seventeen cents. Do you need this gift wrapped?"

Linwood stared at him for a moment, then reached into his wallet and extracted some money, handing it to my brother. Giuseppe stood, waiting in silence. After a few moments ticked by, he said, "Ten dollars, Linwood. You gave me a five."

Linwood nodded. "Right." Reaching back into his wallet he pulled out another bill, which I could see was a twenty. Giuseppe gave him the original five dollars back and made change.

"Gift wrap?" I asked, wondering if maybe he hadn't heard my brother. Linwood looked at me and shook his head slightly, so I grabbed some of the new deliveries and started to unpack. Might as well get some work done while I thought about why I put up with a brother who insisted on dragging me to the funhouse of evil.

"Tell Valerie we said hello," Giuseppe said, handing the change back.

Linwood smiled for the first time, making him look distinguished. He was a handsome older man, and I'd bet in his younger days women were falling all over him.

"I will. For now, I'm on a mission to carry out my day's assignments," he said.

My brother nodded. "Good move. It's always best to do what the wife wants." I gave a half snort at his serious "man-to-man" tone. Giuseppe's wife Janine was a real sweetheart and I never once saw her harass him in an overbearing of way. She was lovable and kind and supportive and had produced the most beautiful baby boy ever for him. Of course my nephew, Baby Danny, tended to throw up more than most kids, but Janine's wasn't at fault. It was the organic baby food Giuseppe insisted the kid eat. I'd throw up if I had to eat that, too.

Linwood nodded, stepping away from the counter. For a moment, he stood in the middle of the store as if he were lost.

"Don't forget your package," Giuseppe said, grabbing it off the counter and handing it to him.

"Thanks," Linwood said. "And say hello to, um, everyone."

As soon as Linwood was out the door, I turned to my brother. "So, who bought the house?"

"Huh? Oh, the house," he said, unpacking a new box of organic essential oils. The faint scent of sandalwood drifted through the store. "Well, remember how the land north and a little bit behind the old house got sold to the development company?"

Did I ever.

Brewster Square was a quaint New England town with a bustling center green, replete with shops and churches. Spreading suburban landscape and forested areas created a highly desirable community for folks who preferred to live outside the city. My parents lived on a farm in the farthest northwest corner of our town. Driving west down the road past my parents' house very quickly led out of Brewster Square. To the south of their farm were acres and acres of forest, an amazing place to hike and bird watch and catch frogs. In my mind, it was magical, probably because my parents always taught us to be respectful of nature.

I guess all good things come to an end, because last year the bulldozers came in and cut down all that magic.

We learned too late that the family who owned the land didn't even live in Connecticut. When the town finally got sick of them not paying their taxes, they decided to unload the property to the highest bidder. Quick as you could say "suburban sprawl" a developer snatched it up and started to plan out a lovely little community.

My parents were furious, as were a number of townspeople. Maybe we should have all read the classifieds a little more carefully to see if large tracts of desirable land were being sold at public auction, but nobody noticed until too late for this little piece of utopian woodlands.

"What's the new development have to do with us going there?" I said. I knew there was probably a good story here, but I wanted my brother to get to the point. He was tall, dark, and sometimes referred to as handsome, but he was never silent. Giuseppe liked to pontificate, while I was more of a "get on with it already" sort of woman.

"When the family who bought the old house first came to town, they met with a realtor to look at a house in the new development. According to them, when they toured the new home they hated it. The ironic part is they hated it because it was so new. But to get to the new neighborhood they had to drive down Chartres Road and past the McAllister house. It was love at first sight."

"Then they must need glasses," I muttered.

"I think it's wonderful they were able to purchase the house," Giuseppe said. "That thing has been sitting empty for too long now, and it's about time someone went in there and made it a home again."

I knew he was right, but I didn't like it. Especially since this particular chain of events meant I had to go into that house tonight.

"I don't know, G, sixty dollars isn't enough. I still won't do it."

"Don't call me G, and yes you will," he said. "You're going to go with us tonight, or don't come back to this store."

"What?"

"You heard me. I need you. I need to know you're with me all the way. You might think this is some silly little side business, but it's part of everything I'm creating. You do an amazing job here, and I'm grateful to have your help."

Giuseppe paused, putting on his stern face and looking me dead in the eye. I knew that face well; he'd used it on me his whole life. "I want this to be a family-run business, and I want you to be a part of the whole thing. But, if you don't do the ghost hunt with us tonight, you're fired."

Chapter Three

GIUSEPPE ALWAYS THREATENS TO FIRE me. He's not always fair about it, but I believe him. I don't know for certain if he'd really do it, since he's my brother and all, and he doesn't have anyone else to work with him, but I don't want to take a chance. Without this job, I have no money, and even though I'm bored and want to do something else I still don't know what I want to be when I grow up. I need this job while I'm figuring my life out. Plus, his wife and kid were counting on me to help out, and I wasn't going to let them down.

One day soon I'd have a different career, but for now I had rent and a phone bill to pay.

When Giuseppe first opened the store, Janine was the one who worked as assistant manager and general helper. It was a great situation for both of them, but things changed drastically when she got pregnant.

I remembered the day a year and a half ago when everything fell apart. That sunny Tuesday was a beautiful fall day. I had barely registered the explosion of color on the sidewalk trees when I wandered into Scentsations. There were no chimes on the door back then, so nobody noticed my entrance. Wrapped in a fog of depression, I didn't see the state of everything around me at first.

"Miss, do you have any more of these soaps?"

"Janine, is there any more of this gardenia spray?"

"When are you going to get more books?"

The questions were being hurled at Janine from shoppers all over the store. I made my way around unopened boxes in the aisle to where Janine sat at the counter, rubbing her belly and reading a book.

She didn't even look at me as she read out loud. "It says here pregnancy drastically changes our hormones, and most women get a little crazy even though they don't know it." Looking up from the book, Janine's eyes filled with tears. "I'm not crazy, am I?"

"No, no... um, no," I said.

Grabbing a box from the aisle, I moved it behind the counter so people could get by. "I'll go check on those products you all asked about," I said to the customers, grabbing the portable phone and answering it on my way into the storage room.

By the time Giuseppe returned twenty minutes later, I had some semblance of order restored. I'd found what the customers wanted, gotten the boxes out of the way, and answered all the questions as best I could.

"How did you do that?" he asked.

I shrugged. "I just did."

"I'm going upstairs to take a nap," Janine announced, lumbering off the stool and heading for the door. "You should hire your sister, she's really good at this," she called over her shoulder.

Giuseppe sighed. "She can't help it, it's the hormones."

"I know." I didn't, really, but I knew this pregnancy had changed my sister-in-law.

"She can't seem to focus on anything outside the baby," Giuseppe said. "The kid's not even born yet, and she's a really good mother already. Too bad she's not so good at retail anymore."

"What are you going to do?" I asked.

"I don't know," he said. "Want to quit your job at the library and work here instead?"

"I don't have to. I was laid off today."

Giuseppe's eyes widened. "What? Why?"

"Budget cuts."

He put his arms around me. "I'm so sorry, sis. I know how much you liked your job."

I did like my job, and I had planned on working at the library for a long time. I loved being around books, and I loved helping people. But economic times were difficult, and my position had to be cut. We stood for a moment, me feeling a little better now that my big brother had shown his support. He stepped back and looked at me. "You heard Janine," he said. "Do you want a job here?"

Sometimes my brother might push me around, but in the end he's always there for me. The least I could do was be there for him once in a while, even if it was in a demon-infested house.

"Fine, I'll go to the ghost hunting thing," I said, not caring that I'd caved to his demands so quickly. Like he said, it was part of the business, and I should probably be there anyway. "But I want to bring Charlie with me."

He nodded. "Okay."

"And I want you to give Charlie fifty dollars, too."

He gave me a dark look, but this time I held my ground.

"Fine," he said. "Charlie gets fifty dollars."

"And we get to leave early."

"How early? You can't cut out too soon, or you won't be any good to me."

"I want to be out of there by one a.m."

He pretended to think about it, then nodded. "One a.m."

One other thing bothered me about all this. "Why on earth are these people letting you do this? If they've just redecorated the house, don't they want to, I don't know, enjoy it without strangers traipsing through, knocking stuff over and videotaping a whole lot of nothing?"

"We won't be knocking stuff over, and hopefully we'll be videotaping a whole lot of something tonight," he answered. I shivered as images of basement doors leading into hell floated through my mind.

"We won't see anything," I said, more to myself than my brother.

"They're thinking about opening a bed and breakfast in there," he said. "Can you watch the store while I go take care of some paperwork?"

I knew that meant he was going to go to his apartment upstairs and take a nap. "No, I'm not finished. What does opening a bed & breakfast have to do with finding ghosts in the house?"

Giuseppe looked at the ceiling, as if he needed answers. Or strength. "Sister, everyone would rather pay money to stay in a haunted house rather than a boring old house with no spirit activity."

Not me, I thought. I would rather not have weird sounds and apparitions appear when I vacationed somewhere, or worry about what was watching me while I took a shower.

"Do they know there's already a bed & breakfast in town?" I asked. The Lilac Inn, the other bed & breakfast I was referring to, was on the corner adjacent to Giuseppe's store. Both were located on the town green, a big square of grass common to most small New England towns. A gazebo sits smack in the middle of the Green, and each corner of the square has a very large bronze statue of a horse and rider. I think they were supposed to be soldiers or something, but to me they looked like the four horsemen of the apocalypse. Buildings and businesses crowded around the Green, including old apartment houses with tons of character and charm. My aunts own one of those beautiful old buildings, and I live on the top floor and do my best to take care of the place.

Our little downtown area includes Scentsations and The Lilac Inn, as well as a Catholic church, town hall and coffee shop called Big Beans. Kenny owns Big Beans, which meant I had to inconvenience myself to get my coffee and muffins at the deli on a parallel street. Since it meant I didn't run into Kenny in the mornings, I was fine with that. Besides, he wasn't in there at night, so I could always go there after work if I wanted to hang out and listen to the open mic thing they had, with sort of good acoustic folk music.

The bell on the door jangled. I turned to see who was coming in, and my heart did a flippy-thing.

"It's not a crime to have more than one bed & breakfast in town," Giuseppe said. "And with that gorgeous old house renting out rooms, I'll bet even the townspeople will want to stay there."

"Hey, Stanley," I said, aiming for a nonchalant, cool sort of tone. Guys really like it when you don't fawn all over them.

My brother frowned at me. "Are you okay? Your voice sounds weird."

"I'm fine," I snapped, wishing he would go take a nap already.

"I caught the tail end of what you were talking about when I came in," Stanley said, walking over to the counter where I stood fiddling with a box. I looked down at a miniature pile of shredded cardboard, wondering how much damage I could do if this guy stayed for any length of time.

"The old McAllister house has been bought," Giuseppe said.

"Yes, I heard."

Of course he had. Stanley was the mayor of Brewster Square, so it was his job to know what was going on around here. Slightly older than me by a few years, Stanley was the kind of mayor who took his job seriously and worked hard for the town. I always thought we were lucky to have him, and not just because I had a big crush on him. Stanley came across as someone who put ethics and justice before his own personal agenda, a rarity in politics from what I could see.

"Did you know they were thinking of doing a bed & breakfast sort of thing?" I asked.

"Yes, they talked to me about it. I told them about the Lilac Inn, but they didn't think it would matter. Looks like they've got a pretty good marketing plan, and they're ready to go."

Stanley and I stood there for a minute, looking at each other. I had a major crush on this guy, and I was pretty sure it showed, but I couldn't seem to stop myself from acting like an idiot. I could feel my face turning red as I frantically tried to come up with something intelligent to say.

"So, I guess it's going to be baseball season soon." Baseball seemed like a safe topic, guys love baseball.

"It is? Oh, right. I don't follow baseball much. I'm not really a sports person." Now it was Stanley's turn to become red in the face, but I didn't know if he was embarrassed because he didn't like sports or because I was an idiot for asking. Time to change the subject again.

"How's the mayor thing going?" I asked. My mother's gentle voice echoed in my head. *The mayor thing? Very eloquent, Ava Maria Sophia Cecilia. Try to speak in a manner befitting your degree in English Literature.*

I tried again. "I mean, do you feel comfortable in the position?" Did I really just say that? Seriously, I should give up, because clearly I couldn't talk to this guy to save my life.

"I hate to interrupt this riveting conversation," my brother said, "but I've got to go upstairs and get a few things together. Ava, if you need me just ring the apartment. If I don't see you, lock up at the end of the day and meet me at the investigation tonight."

Giuseppe nodded to Stanley, turned, and left. Stanley looked at me, his face serious. "He's going to take a nap, isn't he?"

I shrugged. "Not for the whole day. He'll probably read a little, too. But in his defense, he's got to rest up for tonight."

"Ghost hunt?"

I nodded, not sure if I was supposed to talk about it. Sometimes Giuseppe didn't want word getting out about where he would be investigating until the investigation was over.

"The McAllister place?" Stanley asked.

I nodded again, wondering how he knew.

"I heard a rumor that you guys were going to be there tonight because the new owners thought it might be cool to see if the place is haunted."

Small towns amazed me. There wasn't much going on that everyone didn't already know about. I looked up at Stanley, who was now looking at the floor. His lanky frame appeared awkward, as if he wasn't quite sure how his arms and legs should go with the rest of his body, and he kept pushing his square black glasses up his nose. True, he was a geek, but he was one of those geeks I found extremely handsome. Behind his glasses were smoky gray eyes, with his mop of adorable blond hair kept flopping into his face. He looked smart because he was smart, and I loved that in a guy.

"Well, I guess I'll see you later," Stanley said, starting to edge toward the door. "I just stopped in to say hi, see how things were going."

"Thanks. See ya." Clearly my conversational skills were lacking. What the heck was I thinking? How come I never asked this guy out?

Girls don't call boys. Again, my mother's voice floated through my head with her words of wisdom imparted to me when I was a teenager. Like most kids, I had ignored my mother and made sure my parents didn't know when I decided to call a boy. Now it was a nuisance thought in my head.

Maybe one of these days Stanley and I would actually go on a date, but for now I needed to concentrate on running my brother's store and figuring out what I was going to say to Charlie later tonight. It had to be something good, too. I knew I would pay for involving her in this later, but I had to think of something to entice her out to the scary old house. I needed her with me if I was going to make it through the night.

Chapter Four

"WHAT DO YOU MEAN WE have a little 'thing' to do for your brother tonight?" When Charlie was upset, her voice tended toward shrill. Right now it was piercing.

"I told him the only way I would help him was if I could take you with me," I said, trying to sound like this was the best idea ever. "It'll be fun. Plus, he's going to pay us."

"You can have the money, I don't need it," Charlie answered without thinking. My friend was beautiful and generous, plus she had an amazing job in some sort of advertising or promotions or something where she made gobs of money.

"I can't take your money," I said. "It's yours just for being there. Plus, the fact is, I really need you."

Charlie arched a perfectly waxed eyebrow at me. "Please don't tell me you're scared of ghosts. You know every time you go on one of these things you never see anything anyway."

"It's the old McAllister house."

Charlie sat on my couch and let a long breath. "He must've talked the new owners into letting him go in there."

I wondered if the whole town knew the details of the people who bought the decrepit old building. As usual, I was probably the last to know.

"I don't know if I should go in there," Charlie said. She twisted a piece of her blonde bangs around her finger, a sure sign she was nervous. Charlie was always well put together and never appeared disheveled. Hair twisting meant something was bothering her, something big.

"Giuseppe said it's really nice in the house now, and they've made it look like one of those houses on television."

"I'm just not sure it would be prudent for me to join you," Charlie said, almost as if she hadn't heard me.

"He said it looked like the end result of *Make It Pretty*." I knew I was getting very close to sounding whiny, and I tried to stop myself. Nobody wanted to hear my complaints, including me, but I really didn't want to do this without her. Sometimes being with Charlie gave me a kind of false courage, an ability to do things I might not normally do. She was sleek, fun, and always willing to try a new adventure. I was cautious, precise, and usually thought things through very carefully before making a decision. Charlie, on the other hand, was the kind of caution-to-the-wind girl you see on television shows. We're even somewhat opposite in looks, my long red hair and voluptuous figure a direct contrast to her short, blonde, and ultra chic skinny look.

None of that mattered, because we were best friends.

"I have to be more careful of outward appearances," Charlie said, looking at the floor.

"Is your future father-in-law harassing you again?" I asked. I liked Charlie's boyfriend, Fred, but his father was an uptight pain in the patootie.

"He's not my future father-in-law if Fred doesn't ask me to marry him," she said.

"He will," I reassured her. "He's just waiting for the exact right time." I sometimes wondered if he was waiting for his father to kick off, then I felt really bad for thinking that. I knew Fred truly loved Charlie, and everybody who saw them together knew they were a perfect match. Fred's mother loved Charlie, and often spent time with the two of them dropping broad hints about grandbabies, stopping just short of buying baby clothes. But Fred's father was an entirely different story.

Fred's family has lots and lots of money, which around here was considered "old money". "Old money" meant they'd been rich since they stepped off the Mayflower and claimed all the loot for themselves. Fred's father, Win, took their station in life very seriously, and had long ago decided his son needed to marry for strategic reasons. Empires uniting, that sort of thing.

Good old Win (short for Winthrop) might have had his way, too. When Charlie met Fred he was dating someone who was his social and financial equal, a very nice but boring woman whose name I could never remember. But Charlie, as I've said, is gorgeous and sweet and funny, and Fred couldn't help himself. I think he was in love with her before he even asked her out.

"Win said he knows a good plastic surgeon, but I don't know if he meant I should see one or if he was just making conversation," Charlie said.

Everything was almost perfect, except Win was always looking down his nose at Charlie and making comments about how she should act and dress and behave at all times. He was an annoying ass.

"Stop listening to him. He has no connection to reality," I said. I tried to steer the conversation back to where I needed it to be. "So I was thinking we could go out for a drink or something after this thing with my brother tonight. Girls' night out. We'll be done early, so we'll have some time to ourselves." By speaking with a positive tone of voice I hoped it would encourage her to say yes, a technique I'd learned from watching one of those videos about self-empowerment.

"I'll do it," Charlie said, "but not because you're using the 'positive voice' thing with me. I'll do it because I know you're scared."

"Am not." A little, but if I acted unafraid maybe I could trick my mind into believing I had no fear.

"Do you really think he'll ever ask?" Charlie said.

I tried not to sigh. As I've said, my friend is sweet and gorgeous and she really is smart, except for this one little area. She doesn't realize how much Fred loves her, and constantly tries to analyze what he's going to do next. This wasn't typical behavior for her, so it always made me a little irritated when she started playing this game. But she was my friend, and she had agreed to go along with me tonight, so I really had to do my part.

"I'm sure he'll ask you to marry him when he feels the time is right," I told her, like I told her every time she asked this one question.

"It's been three years. I'm ready. Do you think I should push the issue?"

I didn't think she should push the issue at all, but I did think she should talk it over with Fred and let him know how she felt. I'd already said this to her a gazillion times before, so we were going over old ground at this point. Why was it so easy to hand out advice to others about dating when I couldn't even be in the same room with someone I liked without acting like an idiot?

"Never mind," Charlie said, "I know what you think. You're right, I'll talk to him." I leveled a look at her, knowing what that meant.

"Soon," she added. "I'll talk to him soon. What's going on with you and Stanley?"

Nothing was going on. I couldn't even speak normally in front of the guy, and I needed her to give me advice on how to act sophisticated. I figured it was as good a time as any, since we didn't have to be at the house for a couple of hours and I wasn't expecting anyone else at my apartment.

As I opened my mouth to tell her what an abject failure I was at flirting, a sharp knocking interrupted me, making me jump.

The impatient rapping did not stop. *Who the heck is so anxious for me to open the door?*

Chapter Five

I DON'T KNOW WHY I was so spooked. *Must be because I agreed to help my brother's lame group again.* Deep inside, I knew who it was before I even opened the door.

"You really should ask who it is before you open the door," my aunt Maria said. She walked into my apartment carrying a large plate of cookies. "I brought these for you and your friend."

"Thanks, auntie, what's the occasion?"

Aunt Maria walked into my kitchen, presumably to put the cookies away. I had three maternal aunts—four when I counted Claudia— all of whom lived in the same building as me. Aunt Estelle, Aunt Maria, and Aunt Sophia lived on the first two floors of the building. Aunt Claudia was Estelle's partner, although they'd only recently come out, a source of great amusement to my large family who had never once believed they were just friends. I loved Claudia, and I always thought she and Estelle balanced each other.

"You didn't have to come all the way up here, you could have called me to come get the cookies." I was the only person in the family able to take the third floor apartment because there was no elevator and nobody else wanted to walk up three flights of stairs. My mother came from an extended Italian family, and my name, Ava Maria Sophia Cecilia, reflects that. My first three names were family names, the fourth name, Cecilia, was because my parents were big Paul Simon fans.

My mother, a bit of a free spirit, had done the one thing she and her sisters had been explicitly warned not to ever, ever do. Being the headstrong girl she was, she went ahead and defied her parents and did this one thing, leading to a life changing event.

She dated an Irishman.

Then, she took it even further, and married him.

In Brewster Square, families who have been here for generations tend to isolate themselves into ethnic enclaves. The Italians, Irish, Jews, Poles, and Swedes stick with their own kind. It's not a very big town, but we lean toward socializing by ethnicity. It might not be as true today as it was when my parents were young, but it's still whispered about if an Italian girl, say, has a crush on a nice young Swedish sort of man.

When my mother married my father you would think she'd destroyed any hope for mankind the way my grandparents carried on. At least, that's the story I've been told. My aunts, her sisters, were very supportive since a) my dad is such a nice guy, and b) they were obviously in love. Who can argue with love?

Eventually all the hoopla died down and everyone got over it, but my parents never forgot my aunts' support. Hence, my name.

"Those smell so good," Charlie said, sniffing the air like a dog.

"Eat!" Aunt Maria said, shoving the plate at Charlie. "You need energy for tonight."

Charlie shrank away from the plate as if it were a writhing mass of venomous snakes. "I can't, I'm on a diet."

There was a moment of absolute silence as my aunt and I looked at her, my friend who had no obvious weight problems and would probably disappear if she turned sideways. I squinted my eyes, trying to see something. Nope, no fat rolls, the couch didn't sag, and she still had one chin, meaning only one thing.

"What did he call you?" I asked.

Charlie tried to look everywhere except at me. My aunt's eyes narrowed, and she started muttering in Italian. We didn't know exactly what she was saying, but we didn't have to. Some languages are universal.

"Nothing," Charlie hedged, watching my aunt.

"He told you to lose weight, didn't he?"

"He said only common people gained weight, and people of a higher class have to make sure they look good."

My aunt said more of something, and louder. I cringed, thinking it was a good thing I didn't know what she was actually saying because I was probably too young to hear it, even at the age of twenty-eight.

"Stop letting him run your relationship and your life. Your future father-in-law is a bully. Stand up to him—make him stop," I said, knowing she wasn't ready to hear it, but compelled to say it anyway.

"She's right, and he's no one to talk with his background." I wondered what my aunt meant, but before I could ask she continued talking. "Are you girls ready for your night at the Laurence house?"

"I think Giuseppe must've told you the wrong house," I said. My aunt wasn't usually wrong about anything, but there's always a first time. "We're going to the creepy old McAllister house tonight."

"It's not the creepy old McAllister house anymore," Aunt Maria said. "The Laurence family bought it, and I heard it looks really nice inside. Kind of like one of those television shows."

"*Make it Pretty?*" I said.

"No, the other one," she said. "Anyway, you'd better get used to calling it the Laurence house, because that's who lives there now."

"How do you know these things?" I asked.

Aunt Maria shrugged. "It's a small town. Anyway, be careful, and don't get scared."

"I'm not scared." I don't think either Charlie or my aunt believed me, based on the looks they gave me. "I don't believe in ghosts, so there's nothing to be scared of. C'mon, let's go. I don't want to be late."

Although the house was well within walking distance, we decided to drive since we would be going out later. Charlie drove, mostly because she has a nicer car, but a little bit because I'm not always the best driver.

I get distracted easily, which can affect my driving. At least, that's how Charlie phrases it. I know she's just trying to be nice, but I'm not a good driver. Sometimes I forget to watch the road when I'm behind the wheel.

Not watching the road can be a problem, which is why my friends drive whenever possible.

For the short amount of time it took us to get to the house, I had checked and double-checked my cell phone reception, wondering if I should just go ahead and call Stanley. Did the "don't call boys" rule still apply when you're in your late twenties? I wasn't sure, so I put the phone away.

Charlie drove the speed limit in her shiny new red mini cooper while I sat back and watched the familiar buildings roll by. I'd grown up in Brewster Square, and although I'd gone to college in the neighboring state of Rhode Island my heart has always been here. I've travelled to a good number of places, and although my destinations have always been English-speaking—mainly because I'm too chicken to travel alone to a foreign language place—I can honestly say I've always been glad to come home. I never planned on escaping Brewster Square, I never saw any reason to get out, and I've always thought this was a darn good place to live.

Maybe all this makes me unusual, but I like it here. I like the New England style of the architecture, the no-nonsense, practical approach of the people, the rocky shoreline, the golden air of autumn and the smell of lilacs in early summer. There's a half magical feeling in this part of the world, a sense of living in an enchanted land that I have never experienced anywhere else.

Soon—maybe too soon— the old house loomed before us. It looked as creepy as I remembered from my childhood days. "I thought they fixed this place up," I muttered. A couple of cars were parked on the side of the street, and I saw someone carrying boxes inside.

"Why are the police here? Wait, they're leaving," Charlie said.

"Keep driving," I said. Maybe the owners had changed their minds and called the police to have everyone kicked out.

"Good idea. If we delay a little they'll have everything all carried inside and wired up by the time we get in there."

Charlie drove around the block a couple of times, staying well under the speed limit. When we finally pulled up and parked in front of another car on the street, Giuseppe was standing in the driveway with an impatient look on his face.

"Why were you driving in circles?" he demanded as soon as we got out of the car. "There's work to be done, let's go."

Usually I had a smart retort for my brother, but I didn't say anything. Instead, my attention was riveted to the person standing behind Giuseppe, the last person I'd expected to see on a ghost hunt.

Chapter Six

MY HAND INSTINCTIVELY REACHED FOR my cell phone when I saw him, as if my thoughts of calling him had conjured his presence.

"Hey, Stanley. What are you doing here?" I hadn't meant to sound confrontational, I was going for more of an interested tone. Good thing for me he didn't seem put off by my words.

"Hi, Ava, I just thought I'd stop by and see if there's anything I could do," he said. "To help."

"I'm going to help your brother with the equipment," Charlie said, disappearing like any good friend would at a time like this.

"So, this should be an interesting night," Stanley said, shoving his hands deep into his coat pockets. He wore a lightweight jacket, and I couldn't help but wonder if he was freezing. I was, and I had a fleece pullover under my jacket. "This house kind of reminds me of a book I read a long time ago. Daphne DuMaurier."

I knew what he meant immediately, because I'd been thinking the same thing when I saw the house. "Rebecca."

He smiled. "Yeah, but I don't know why."

"I know," I agreed. "The house doesn't look anything like the description of the one in her book, and there isn't enough land, but still..."

"Maybe it's the architecture, but there's a mysterious quality here reminiscent of that book," Stanley finished for me. For a moment we stood and simply smiled at each other. "Would you like to go out with me sometime?"

I was frozen to the spot, and I couldn't speak. At least his asking me out took care of the question about whether or not I could call him. I wanted to say yes and was horrified I hadn't jumped at the opportunity. But maybe it was better not to appear too eager. I'd never been good at dating rules or games.

Giuseppe staggered by with a suitcase full of equipment. "That looks heavy," I said. "Do you want some help?"

"No, I want you to say yes to Stanley and go out with him already." My mouth dropped. *How the heck did he hear what Stanley said? Giuseppe wasn't anywhere near us when he asked me out.*

"I mean it, little sister," Giuseppe called over his shoulder as he walked toward the house. "Go out with him or you're fired."

What an ass. "I was going to say yes," I told Stanley.

He smiled at me, reminding me he had the cutest dimple on his face, and looked like he was getting ready to reply when he was interrupted by some woman with big gray hair, a purple tunic, and a long orange skirt. "I can feel them already," she spoke loud enough for people in the next town to hear her. "Can't you feel them gathering?"

"Maybe we can have dinner this week?" Stanley was ignoring the crazy lady, but she'd already distracted me.

"I'd really like that." There was a long moment of silence while we stared at each other. Finally, I broke the spell. "Who is she?" I asked.

Stanley turned and watched the woman walk into the house, hands waving in the air as she talked about seeing spirits. "I don't remember her name, but she's one of those weird new-age health people."

"Looks like she's seeing things before the show even starts," I said.

"Listen, I'm sorry, I should be nicer about what I say," Stanley said.

A young couple floated by, eyes bright with excitement. "Can't you feel them gathering?" the woman asked her friend. I didn't know these people, but I watched them carefully. The man's eyes glistened, and I wondered if it was moonlight or if he had a fever. "We've been waiting for this... look, on the porch!" He pointed at the porch, but I couldn't tell what he was talking about. It looked like the same old crumbling porch to me, except... I squinted. Yep, sure enough, new rocking chairs and tables were up there. The new furniture was a start, but I didn't think that was what everyone had been waiting for.

"I didn't mean to be insulting, it doesn't really matter to me whether or not people are into the whole New Age thing." Stanley's countenance was serious, as if we were discussing matters of world diplomacy.

"Does it seem like there's something wrong with them?" I asked.

Stanley looked taken aback by the question. "Um, no," he stammered. "I mean, they might believe in some strange things, but they're basically harmless—"

"Not the New Agers," I said. "Them." I pointed to the crowd gathered on the front porch, animated about something. "They're all talking about seeing ghosts or something gathering. They seem a bit..." I searched for the right word.

"Frantic?" Stanley suggested.

"Maybe," I admitted.

"Worked up? Excited? Foaming at the mouth?" The corners of his own mouth turned up a bit.

"On the edge of lunacy?" I added. "Rabid?"

We smiled at each other, sharing a moment of connection. "Seriously," I asked. "Being the mayor, you must know lots of people. Do these people seem a little off? More than usual?"

Stanley's eyes darkened for a moment and he seemed to struggle with what to say. "Ava, I've got to tell you something."

My heart sank. I knew that tone, and it usually meant I was about to hear something I didn't want to hear. He had a girlfriend, he had a wife, he had a boyfriend, he was actually a woman trapped in a man's body... the list was endless. And I'd already heard a lot of it from others.

"It's about being mayor," he continued.

"You're doing a good job." I could at least be encouraging.

"The truth is, the only reason I'm the mayor of this town is because I sprained my ankle."

Okay, honestly, this was so not what I expected to hear.

"C'mon you guys, let's get this thing started," Giuseppe called from the porch. "I've got your assignments ready."

I shuddered, wondering what my assignment would be. Hopefully I wouldn't be stuck watching the computer monitors, which usually put me to sleep. I couldn't help it; watching empty rooms was boring.

Nothing ever happened during these ghost hunts besides the usual petty arguments and disappointment at not seeing anything.

"Ava, you've got to come in here," Charlie called from the front door. "You were right, it is totally gorgeous inside. The outside is still all yucky, but they did an amazing job inside." I cringed, hoping the new owners weren't within earshot of her statement.

Stanley and I walked to the front porch. We weren't holding hands, but we were shoulder to shoulder. I liked being near him. "I'll tell you about it later, but I wanted you to know," he said. I nodded, wondering what sprained ankles had to do with being mayor.

As we climbed the steps, everyone started streaming through the front door into the house. A soft glow came from the overhead chandelier, a whimsical piece of lighting that sparkled from the many drops of glass suspended around the bulbs. The hardwood floors had a high sheen, and oriental throw rugs were scattered about. The foyer was huge, comfortably holding the twenty or so people gathered there, and it looked like the hallway in front of us led to a kitchen at the back of the house. To the right was a tastefully furnished sitting room with a fire in the fireplace, and to the left was an enormous dining room that looked like it could seat about forty people. A grand staircase rivaling the one from *Gone with the Wind* invited us upstairs.

"This place is huge," I said to no one in particular. I looked around carefully, trying to orient myself before Giuseppe turned all the lights off. At least there was a fire burning, adding a little light near the computer monitors.

"I love what they've done with the walls," Charlie said, looking around with wide eyes.

"I think they restored what was already here," Giuseppe offered. The walls were elaborate panels of mahogany, with intricate patterns detailed onto some of them. The effect was luxurious, and all I could imagine was how much money people were going to pay for an overnight stay here. The new owners were going to make a fortune, which was good, because it looked like they'd already spent a fortune.

"As you can see, we've set up the monitors in the room to your right," Giuseppe said. "It made the most sense to be in there because they've already lit a fire. Rather than put it out, I decided it would make it cozy."

Okay, my brother had a point. At least if I was going to be bored tonight,

I'd be bored in a nice setting.

"I want Sarah, John, and Rebecca to be on the monitors tonight," Giuseppe said.

Hmmm. Maybe it won't be so boring, but hopefully he won't stick me with one of those people I saw walking in earlier.

"Remember, this is an old house, and it's a big house, so I'm sure there's something here. We want to be very thorough and get readings in all the rooms, cover as much as we possibly can." When my brother talked about getting readings he was referring to the equipment they carried around, like digital recorders and energy sensitive reading-thingys. I wasn't entirely sure how it all worked, but since nothing ever happened on these ghost hunts I wasn't too worried about it. I've never once had any type of reading on anything he made me carry around. At least, I didn't think I had any readings.

As Giuseppe kept talking, I started to worry. His assignments so far had not mentioned me, and he had covered the front and back of the house, the first, second, and third floors. Maybe I could just sneak into the computer room and sink into one of those comfy looking chairs.

"Ava, don't worry, I didn't forget about you." Giuseppe smiled at me. "I know how bored you tend to get on these evenings, so I've given you the best room in the house tonight." I did my best to look as innocent as possible, shaking my head a little at the suggestion that I'd get bored. Who, me? Never. I'm sure nobody was fooled by my attempts at disguising my true feelings.

With a broad sweep of his arm, Giuseppe gestured to the hallway behind him. "Back there is the door where you'll go."

Now I was confused. "Where am I going, the cupboard under the stairs?" Sometimes my brother had a twisted sense of humor.

"No, you're going in the basement."

Chapter Seven

"NOT GOING TO HAPPEN." I was shaking my head before the words were even out of my mouth. "There's probably all kinds of rats and bats and snakes and spiders down there. Nope, I'm going in the computer room." I'd rather be bored than bitten.

The woman I'd seen earlier with the big gray hair looked at me like I was crazy. "Bats don't live in basements, they live in attics. Everyone knows that." And everyone knows there's no such thing as ghosts, but I wisely kept my mouth shut.

Another voice piped up from the back of the crowd. "There's definitely going to be spiders down there, though." People nodded in agreement. Were they on my side or were they just making observations? I had no idea what to expect from these people, even though I'd known some of them since elementary school.

"Don't know about snakes, might be too cold in the basement for them," an older voice drawled. Who said that? He sounded familiar. My head swiveled around as I tried to locate the speaker. It sounded like an older person, but it could've been anyone.

"Probably mice, I doubt there's rats," Big Gray Hair added. Who was this woman, some sort of wildlife expert?

"I don't care about the specifics of what's down there, I am not going," I said as succinctly as possible. It was time for everyone to stop speculating about wildlife and find me a new spot to investigate.

"I'll go with you," Stanley offered. I smiled at him. *What a sweetheart he is to offer.* I was fairly certain he didn't like creepy crawlies any more than I did, but he was willing to put up with it for me.

"Here, take this with you," Giuseppe said, shoving something into my hands. I looked down at it, not remembering the name of this piece of equipment I was sure I'd used before. It was a handheld plastic thing, with a series of different colored lights across the top, from green to yellow to red. "It's the EMF meter," he added.

"I know," I said. He didn't need to know I couldn't remember what it was called. "EMF. Stands for electromagnetic frequency."

Giuseppe looked impressed. "I'm surprised you remembered. Do you know what it does?"

This part was easy. Everything sort of did the same thing in one way or another. "Of course. It detects the electromagnetic frequency of ghosts." Every time Giuseppe asked me if I knew what a piece of equipment was used for, I answered the same way: '*Insert name of equipment*' detects the frequency of ghosts. Easy to remember, and usually correct.

"Good. Now take this with you, and Stanley can take this notebook, and you can work as a team to record any unusual readings you get." He looked at me closely, probably trying to decide if he could trust me with this job. "Remember, it's the basement, so I'm expecting some sort of energy fluctuations down there. Basements are prime locations for activity."

The basement was also going to be a prime location for me to hang out with Stanley and get to know him better, despite the spiders and ghosts. This might work out okay after all.

"I'm on it, don't worry about a thing," I reassured my brother. With the EMF thingy in one hand and Stanley walking behind me, we headed toward the area Giuseppe had pointed to before. It took a minute to make my way through the crowd, as it seemed like everyone there was just standing around watching me. I was definitely feeling paranoid. Stanley and I reached the middle of the hallway and stopped.

"Keep walking," my brother called out. "The doorway is on your right."

"It looks like a closet door," I mumbled.

"It looks like a regular closet door," Giuseppe called out. "You can go on down as soon as we turn all the lights out."

I'm not usually afraid of things, but I didn't think it was a good idea to go down basement steps in the dark. People started moving around us, some of them going to the back of the house while I assumed others went upstairs and into the much desired computer room. Lights were being turned off throughout the house.

Stanley stepped closer to me and leaned in. "How are we going to be able to see if the lights are out?"

"I usually bring a small flashlight, but I forgot this time. It comes in handy so I don't bump my head or trip and fall. Do you have anything?" I asked, hopeful that his job as mayor made him as prepared as a boy scout.

"I've got one in my car in case of emergencies," he said. "I'll be right back."

He turned and walked away, moving with purpose. I stood there for a moment, feeling like an idiot. Sure, I wasn't crazy about the idea of going into the basement, but I also hated standing around looking like I was slacking.

I remembered I had my cell phone in my pocket. I have a flashlight on the phone, which the salesman had used as a selling point as to why I needed that model. Looked like he was right.

Assuming Stanley would catch up with me, I pulled my phone out of my pocket and turned on the flashlight. The LED light was brighter than I expected, which Giuseppe wouldn't like, but I wouldn't have to use it for long because Stanley would be right back.

The door opened without a sound, and I started down the steps, determined not to think of things jumping or landing on me, like spiders, mice, rats, or mutant ninja turtles. *Weird things can happen at a time like this.*

I walked carefully down the steps, a little worried about tripping and falling. I probably should've worn sneakers, but my cute red heels looked so much better with jeans and I hated wearing sneakers.

When I got to the bottom of the stairs, I realized two things: first, it was a darn good thing I had a flashlight. Second, none of my previous fears mattered. Snakes, spiders, and flying ninja bats would be preferable to what I was looking at.

A person was lying on the cellar floor, twisted at a weird angle and lying in a pool of dark liquid.

I was all alone in the basement with a dead body.

Chapter Eight

I COULDN'T BREATHE. THIS WAS a major problem, because I needed to scream. But I couldn't get any air into my body, so I couldn't scream. The light from my cell phone illuminated enough of the corpse for me to know this was real, not some leftover mannequin from Halloween past.

From what I could see of the clothing and shape of the body, it looked like a woman. *Poor thing, she must've fallen down the steps.* I inched closer, wondering if it was possible for her to still be alive.

A thumping noise upstairs startled me, dragging my gaze to the darkness hovering over me. I heard it again, only this time it sounded like it was in the corner of the basement. The dark corner.

Maybe she didn't fall. Maybe she'd been pushed.

My thoughts were scattered and rapid, like my breathing. *I think I see a lot of blood.* Then another thought, even worse...

Is it possible whoever did this is still here?

That's when I screamed. The thought of being in the basement with a murderer scared the bejeesus out of me. I stood there screaming and shivering, both scared and cold. It seemed like I was standing there forever but it was probably only around five seconds.

Someone must have turned the light on right before the crowd swarmed around me. I pointed to the body on the basement floor, and the crowd grew quiet.

"What the heck is going on down here?" my brother demanded. "Can't I trust you for one—oh." He cut his sentence short when he reached the bottom of the stairs and saw why I was screaming. "Are you okay?" I was touched at my brother's concern, but at that very moment I couldn't tell how I was. Obviously I was way better than the person on the floor.

"It must have just happened," Big Gray Hair said. "The spirit is hovering behind the body."

"Shut up," I said. Honestly, I was all done with her and her lunatic ideas of seeing ghosts. We had a real problem here and we needed help, not some crackpot spouting spirit nonsense. "We've got to call the police," I said. I looked down at my phone, and of course there was no cell phone signal. Good thing I didn't have to use it to call someone for help.

"Everybody out, now," Giuseppe ordered. "I want you all upstairs, and make sure you call 911. We need emergency personnel ASAP." I was impressed at his authoritative tone.

A commotion at the top of the stairs made me finally tear my gaze away from the body. Stanley was pushing his way through the people, trying to get by. "Ava, are you okay?" he asked.

I nodded, feeling kind of weird that it made me happy Stanley was concerned about my welfare. Shouldn't I be more worried about what happened to the person on the floor than whether or not some guy cared about me?

"Does she need help?" Stanley asked.

"Who?" I said.

"The woman on the floor, is she dead or injured?" Stanley said.

Based on the amount of blood around her, I was fairly certain we were too late, but Stanley had a point. She might have just been unconscious. I stepped carefully toward the body, not wanting to ruin my shoes in a pool of blood. Leaning over, I touched the side of her neck to see if I could find a pulse. Her skin was warm, not cold like I'd expected. I poked around her neck, trying to find some sign of life. After almost a full minute, I stood and shook my head. "Nothing. I'm pretty sure she's dead."

"Is she cold?" a voice from the stairs asked.

Giuseppe whirled around to face the crowd. "Has anyone called the police yet? I told you all to go upstairs. We have to be careful not to contaminate the scene here."

"What are you saying?" Stanley asked.

"I'm saying that I'm in charge of this group, and I want you all out," Giuseppe said. I had to agree with my brother, if this was anything other than an accident all these people needed to leave right now. At least with the lights on I felt better about being able to see if anyone was trying to sneak up on me.

"G, I'm going to stay down here with her," I said.

"Don't call me G," my brother said.

"I don't want to leave her alone, whoever she is," I said, ignoring his comment. It felt disrespectful to leave this person all alone, and with the lights on I was fairly certain nobody was hiding down there. Plus, I couldn't help but note the way the position of the body and the massive wound on the side of her head.

Maybe I'd been watching too much television, but it didn't seem normal to have the side of your head bashed in after a fall down the stairs. Then again, I was no forensic expert, so maybe it was an accident. Still, my brother was right. Everyone needed to leave.

There was a shuffling sound as people filed up the stairs, and I could hear some people talking about the spirit of the body. *What the heck is wrong with those people?* Thankfully I only had to deal with most of them for these ghost hunting nights.

I crouched down to examine the woman in front of me. She had short, graying hair and was dressed in a conservative plaid skirt and matching jacket, with her face turned away from me. I tried not to look too hard at her hair, since it was a real mess. Judging from her clothes and sensible shoes, I guessed she was older, although I suppose someone my age would wear that sort of outfit. I looked at the floor around her, wondering if anything down here could tell me if this was an accident or not, although I wasn't sure why it mattered to me.

This wasn't the first dead body I'd seen. Coming from a large extended family, I'd been to my share of wakes and funerals. I'd never, however, seen a dead body that was dead from an accident. Or whatever she was dead from.

I hope I never see this again.

A chill permeated my body, feeling like it came from my core. I was shivering. I stepped away from the body and sat on the bottom stair. Tilting my head, I squinted a little. Something about her looked familiar. Then it clicked. I knew who she was.

Voices at the top of the stairs told me the police had arrived. I stood and turned, relieved to see the uniformed man walking down the steps. He smiled at me as he wiped his hands with one of those wet wipe things.

"Ava Maria Sophia Cecilia, how's it goin'?" he said.

I smiled. "Rob, I'm glad you're here." I'd gone to high school with Rob Genova, and although we never really hung out with the same people he was always nice to me. I wasn't surprised he was now a police officer, since it had been his goal to be in law enforcement since the seventh grade. He was average height, but built like a football player. Not overweight, but with a stocky build that would be hard to knock down. His dark hair shined with the gel he put in to hold up the short spikes, exactly as it had for so many years.

He stood one stair above me, looking down at the body. "What happened?"

I shrugged. "I don't know. I came here tonight to do a ghost hunt thing with my brother, and he assigned me to the basement. She was here when I got here."

There was a commotion at the top of the stairs, and Rob put his hands in his pockets and looked at the ceiling. I looked up to see a man storming down the stairs at me, a thunderous expression on his face. He was handsome in a Tom Selleck kind of way, with the sort of dark, brooding looks that works well on the movie screen. His jeans fit nicely and he wore a pink, button-down dress shirt. *Must be one of those guys who doesn't care what anyone else thinks.* His eyes were blazing, and I could tell he was upset. I wondered who the heck he was, as I didn't recognize him. And, with Brewster Square being such a small town, I was surprised I didn't know him. Maybe he was related to the person on the floor.

When he opened his mouth to say something, his first words were not nearly as polite as they could have been. "What the hell do you think you're doing?"

Chapter Nine

THE ONLY PERSON IN THIS world who can push me around and get away with it is my brother, and I'm working on not letting that happen too often. This guy was way out of his league.

"What does it look like I'm doing, waiting for the ice cream truck to roll by?" I said.

He appeared to be grinding his teeth, and I swear his entire body tensed. "You are contaminating my crime scene."

"How do you know this was a crime?" I asked, more to antagonize the jerk than anything else.

He spoke very slowly, as if I were an idiot. "Any time a death is an accident, suicide, or homicide the area becomes a crime scene. And right now, lady, you're in the middle of my crime scene. You're going to have to move."

I didn't like the way he was talking to me, which probably contributed to me mouthing off. I'm usually much more reserved, but this time I couldn't stop myself. "For your information, I was extremely careful not to contaminate anything. Give me a little bit of credit. In fact, you oughta be thanking me."

He put his hands in his pockets and looked at the ceiling, exactly the same way Rob had just a minute ago. I wondered if there was some sort of clue up there, and couldn't stop myself from checking out the rafters. Nope, nothing but cobwebs.

"Officer, will you handcuff this woman, take her upstairs, and Mirandize her?"

I jumped up from the steps. "What are you talking about?" Rob stood looking from me to him, obviously torn.

"You are not cooperating in a police investigation, and right now you are a prime suspect in a murder," he said.

I knew a scare tactic when I saw one, but I wasn't stupid, either. "There's no need for that, Rob," I said, stomping past both of them to the top of the stairs.

Rob, who is a big sweetheart, didn't know what to do. From the top of the stairs I could hear him talking to the big idiot. "Um, do you want me to, I mean, should I..."

"No need to handcuff her, just make sure someone sits with her so she doesn't leave. I want everyone in this house rounded up and put in one room, and I want them to stay put until we have a chance to question every single one of them."

Rob came upstairs and I could see he was all business. Gone was the sympathetic high school friend, and instead he became the police officer sworn to do his duty. I tried to remember something from my college psych classes to bring the sympathetic friend back, but I don't think we covered that sort of thing. *How to Make People Be Nice To You After Finding A Dead Body 101.*

Taking me by the elbow, he began to steer me back toward the front of the house. "I need you to come into the front room with the rest of the folks and stay put." He stopped in front of another police officer, this time someone I didn't recognize. "Detective Rialto wants everyone in one room until we can question them. Let's put them in the room with the fireplace, keep them comfortable while they wait."

"Robbie, what are you doing?" Charlie's voice rang down the hall. Rob looked up and blushed, an immediate reaction he'd always had around Charlie, and unfortunately one that had not faded with time. I looked at his left hand and didn't see a wedding band, so maybe this would work in our favor.

"Just doing my job, Charlie," he answered. "I need you and Ava to go into the front room and wait for us to ask you a few questions."

"But we don't even know what's going on," Charlie wheedled. "We were going to go out to grab a bite to eat. Maybe you could meet us at a restaurant later and ask us whatever you wanted to know?" Charlie was good, but I don't think she realized Rob's code of honor would never allow him to screw up investigating a crime. His face hardened, signifying this was not an option.

"Sorry, but you'll have to wait in the room with everyone else," he said.

Charlie leaned in close to Rob, whispering so only he and I could hear her. "But these people are really, really weird. Can we at least sit in another room while we wait for you so we don't have to hang out with them?"

"No." The answer was short and clipped, but Rob was just doing his job. I had to admit, if I were him I wouldn't let Charlie and I slink off to another room, either.

"It's fine," I told him. "We'll wait there. Will we be talking to you, or do I have to talk to macho man?"

Rob tried to hide a quick smile. "I think Detective Rialto would like to speak with you himself, but I'm not certain. Someone will be with you as soon as possible."

"Who's Detective Rialto?" Charlie asked.

"Detective Oliver Rialto," Rob answered. "He transferred here a few months ago. He can answer any other questions you have."

Resigned, we went to the designated room where everyone mingled and stood at the edge of the doorway. I didn't want to be part of that circus, as I could already hear the rumors, speculation, and downright bizarre theories floating around. All I had to do was hang in there, answer a few questions, and then I'd be on my way.

"Are you okay?" Stanley was behind me, hand on my shoulder. "We're not used to seeing this type of thing here. This doesn't happen in Brewster Square."

I shook my head. "It's sort of unreal, you know? One minute someone's alive, then they're not. I've never seen a body... dead... from something else... before." I was about to start babbling, but I couldn't help it. "I mean, I've seen dead people, but not people who have just died... only a little while ago... it's creepy, and why can't I stop talking?"

Stanley reached out and took my hand, offering his support. There was no place left to sit in the room we were assigned, so Charlie, Stanley, and I found a spot on the floor and leaned against the wall. I wasn't sure my legs could hold me up much longer.

I thought we might be there for a few hours, at the least, but it was only about twenty minutes before tall, dark, and obnoxious came into the room and gestured for me to follow him. I didn't appreciate the way he summoned me, but I wasn't given any choice in the matter. I was starting to feel a bit grumpy about the entire situation.

Following him back into the kitchen, I couldn't help but notice he was a well-built man. A little over six feet tall, I had to admit he had a really nice butt. I didn't like him, but at least I had something to look at for the moment. When we got to the kitchen, he pulled out a chair and gestured for me to sit.

Sitting across from me, he pulled out a pair of reading glasses and a folder from a briefcase on the floor. I waited while he made a few notes, determined not to squirm or let his tactics bother me. Finally, he looked up at me. "So, tell me something. You are Ms. Ava O'Dell, correct?"

"Almost," I said.

His eyebrows raised as he continued to stare at me. "Ava Maria Sophia Cecilia O'Dell," I corrected. "In case you need my entire name."

He nodded. "Duly noted. Now, tell me, why should I thank you?"

Confused, I tried to figure out what he was asking. "I don't know, why should you thank me?"

"Downstairs you said I should be thanking you. What did you mean?"

I smiled as I realized I had information he would need for his investigation. "Because I know things."

Again, his eyebrows raised as he looked at me. "And what, Ms. O'Dell, do you think you know?"

This time I was smug. "I know three things. First, I know your officer who was first on the scene, Rob, didn't finish his dinner before he came in here; second, I know you are in the process of getting divorced; and third, I know who the body is downstairs."

Ha, take that Mr. Smug Detective. Let's see what he thought of me now. I was no idiot.

Leaning back in his chair, he pulled a business card out from under the folder. "Okay, let's start from the beginning. My name is Detective Oliver Rialto, and I'll be the person lucky enough to talk to you to figure out what happened. Here's my business card. Now, why don't you tell me all about how you know these things?"

"Easy," I said. I was warming up to the idea that it really was easy, and maybe my career choice had just presented itself. Brief images of me as a private investigator floated through my head, as well as the interviews I would give to the press after solving each case. "First, when Rob came to the top of the stairs, he was wiping his hands on one of those wet wipe things people use when they're trying to clean up. Since he's working the night shift, he was most likely in his patrol car eating his dinner. Plus, ever since I've known him he's been messy with his food. Second, you have a tan line where your wedding ring used to be, telling me you only recently took it off, meaning you're in the process of leaving your wife. And third, I recognized the woman downstairs. Her name is Ethel Harwich." I leaned back and smiled. I was a natural at this.

Detective Rialto ran a hand over his face, as if he were tired. Of course, he could have just been embarrassed because I'd figured out so much in such a short period of time.

"Okay, presuming you're right about the identity of the victim, I'd say that's not bad."

I felt a moment of triumph. I wondered if I should think about renting a space to run my business or if I should work from home. "Thank you."

"Most citizens think they can be private investigators, but they really don't have any idea what goes into it." I smiled and nodded, waiting for the inevitable praise and suggestion to go into this line of work. "I think you fall into that category," he said.

Wait, what?

"You were correct about maybe one out of three things. Maybe none, we'll see."

Chapter Ten

"**WE HAVE REASON TO BELIEVE** the incident tonight was not an accident," Detective Rialto said. I was having trouble listening to what he was saying, as I was still trying to figure out what I'd gotten wrong. "Do you know anyone who might have wanted to harm Ethel Harwich?"

I shrugged. "Take your pick. Nobody liked her. In fact, I'd have to say she was the most hated person in Brewster Square."

The detective stared at me for a moment, his face unreadable. "What do you base this opinion on?"

"She was a very controversial figure in this town. She had a way of making people mad at her on a daily basis."

"A daily basis? That would require a lot of effort on her part."

I nodded. "I agree, but I don't think she had a big family or anything so she had time on her hands. I mean, she never had kids, and she was widowed, so she spent most of her time ticking people off."

Detective Rialto's eyes never left my face. "Did she tick you off?"

"Me?" I was surprised at the question, but gave it some thought. "Not recently, no. But she was the driving force behind getting the new development out here built, and that made a lot of people mad."

"Walk me through tonight's events. What was your purpose in being here?"

I told the Detective all about my brother and his paranormal investigation group, which was probably more than he wanted to know. But I was trying to be thorough, so I made sure to tell him all about Kenny and Kenny's paranormal investigation group, and how there was an ongoing rivalry between the two groups. I started at the beginning, which was when we met in elementary school.

Telling all the details took longer than I thought it would.

"Why don't we fast forward to the time you got here? What happened when you arrived tonight?" he said.

Right. So then I told him all about seeing Stanley outside, and how happy I was to see him, but I chose to leave out the part where Stanley asked me on a date because it probably wasn't relevant, and I didn't want Stanley to be unnecessarily questioned.

By the time I got to the part where I stood at the top of the basement stairs ready to do my part in the investigation, I could see my story was wearing on him. I paused for a moment, grabbed a bottled water in front of me, unscrewed the cap and took a long drink.

"You don't have to tell me every tiny detail," he said.

"But you never know what could be helpful in the end," I said. "Sometimes the small details can make or break a case."

"It's not like books or TV," he said. "This is real life."

Seriously, where did this guy learn to be a detective? Everyone knew how important the details were. It took me another ten minutes to tell him about walking down the stairs and finding the body. I needed him to understand my hesitation about basements, but not think I was some kind of scaredy-cat. I finished my story at the point where he threatened to have me arrested, looking at him and shaking my head. I hoped to convey my disappointment in him and the entire police department. Disappointment was a guilt trick I'd learned from my mother.

Detective Rialto didn't answer right away. Instead, he sat silently watching me. I knew he was waiting for me to blurt out some sort of confession, but I had nothing to say. I stared back at him, wondering if he was one of those guys who needed to shave every four hours or if the stubble on his face was the result of not shaving for more than a day.

"Officer Rob was cleaning his hands because he'd been checking his vehicle's oil. As for me, a divorce is about the furthest thing from the truth." His voice was stern and a little bit low, so I had to lean forward to hear him well. "You cannot figure out what's going on in people's lives just by looking at pieces of events. Get the idea out of your head. Detective work is slow and painstaking and takes more than a casual observation."

"O-kay," I said. "I'm sorry?" I knew he had the power to arrest me, so I thought I should say something.

With a sigh, he leaned back in his chair. "You and your friend are free to go. You have my card if you remember anything else."

"What makes you think tonight wasn't an accident?" I asked.

He twirled a pen around with his large hands, scowling at the table. I wondered if the scowl was because I'd asked the question or because he was tired. I'd given him a lot to think about.

Finally, he spoke. "Do you have a cell phone?"

"Yes." I wondered where this line of questioning was going.

"May I see it?"

Digging in my jacket pocket, I pulled my out my phone and handed it to him. I didn't say anything as he began to scroll through the screen, knowing he would eventually explain. After a minute, he stopped his scrolling and handed it back to me.

"We received a phone call to our 911 dispatch center from someone in this house earlier tonight," he said. "The call might have been placed prior to the, um, event, but we won't know for certain until after the medical examiner gives us a more clear time of death. The caller said death was lurking in this house."

That explained the police car we'd seen earlier. "Don't you have the phone number of the person who called?"

"Yes. I'm just covering all the bases," he said.

"Must've been the gray-haired crazy," I said. When he lifted his eyebrows at me, I launched into yet another detailed explanation of what I'd witnessed earlier and all the people who had been standing around. This time he listened more closely.

"So you think the woman with the big gray hair may have been our caller?" he asked.

I nodded. "Like I said, people have been acting loony all night."

"At the risk of sounding flippant, the fact that you have gathered here to hunt ghosts is a little bit loony," he said.

He was right. I smiled at him before remembering he was a jerk. He smiled back, and I wondered if my first impression needed amending. He was sort of cute, in a macho kind of way.

"Like I said, you're free to go, but if you plan on leaving town let us know." He stood and gestured toward the door.

I guessed I'd given him enough so he could figure it out from here, so I walked to the front of the house where Charlie was waiting for me. "I'm starved, let's go get some food," she said.

"Starlight?" I said. The Starlight Diner was located on Route 1, about a mile from where we were. It was open all night, and had the best greasy food in the state of Connecticut. Charlie and I always went there for our serious discussions.

"Do you want some company?" Stanley asked. I hadn't realized he was standing near us and jumped a little at the sound of his voice. Charlie shot me a look, which I wasn't sure how to interpret. Stanley, however, took a step back. "Girls night, I know. Be careful, Ava. I'll catch up with you later, okay?"

I nodded, grateful he understood without having to be told. As Charlie and I walked toward her car, I saw Giuseppe jogging toward me. My brother was not a jogger, or a runner, so I wondered if there was a fire somewhere.

"Ava, you've got to help me."

"I think I've helped enough for tonight. It's bad enough I came here because you said so, but then I had to go find a body and deal with Detective of the Year."

Giuseppe's brow wrinkled in confusion. "Who?"

"Detective Rialto," I spit the words out. "He was incredibly rude, threatening to arrest me."

"You were obstructing justice," Charlie said.

"Let's not remind her right now," Giuseppe said. "Ava, I need you to do something for me."

I sighed loudly. One of these days I was going to be able to stand up to my brother and tell him I would not do his bidding. This was not one of those days.

"What do you need?" I asked.

"I need you to figure out who killed Ethel Harwich."

Chapter Eleven

DESPITE THE FACT THAT IT had been there longer than forever, the Starlight Diner had relatively new booths and a modern, clean look. Although they'd redecorated over the years, the color scheme had never changed from the original maroon and white, a fact I found comforting. There's something to be said for continuity.

Although this was supposed to be a girl's night out, my brother had insisted on following us to the diner and now sat across from me. We had all ordered different omelets, and they were delivered with the usual speed and efficiency. Against the wall was the metal container holding salt, pepper, ketchup, napkins, and halleluiah—hot sauce. I loved adding spice to my food.

Giuseppe sat poking at his spinach and feta dish. He was so nervous I wondered if he was going to hurt himself as he twitched his right leg up and down. I watched his hand shake while he used his fork as a spear.

"If you don't help, I don't know what I'm going to do." Giuseppe sounded whiny, which was very unlike him. My brother rarely turned into such an emotional wreck.

"First of all, I don't understand what you need from me. Second of all, what does Ethel's death have to do with you?"

"I'm connected to the world of the spirit, I am able to live in the in-between," he said. Charlie and I exchanged a look, and I knew she was wondering if he was going to go off on one of his rants about parallel dimensions and spiritual connections.

"You are connected to the linear world of logic," he said. "You have abilities I don't have." At least he admitted I was capable of doing things he couldn't do, or didn't want to do. "Besides," he continued, "Kenny is going to use this in any way he can."

"How can Kenny possibly use this against you?" I asked. "You and the group cannot be blamed for what happened." Although, after a moment's thought, I had to admit, to myself at least, that this whole thing did, in fact, look sort of bad. "Why don't you wait and see, maybe the police will be able to determine the time of death. Then it will be obvious you didn't have anything to do with this," I added, deciding not to mention the phone call Detective Rialto had told me about.

"Yeah, it probably happened before we even got there," Charlie piped in. She and I exchanged looks, and I knew she was thinking the same thing as me. Giuseppe was right, it didn't look good.

"I know you both understand the public relations ramifications," Giuseppe said. "It's not just about our paranormal group, it's about the store, too. Who wants to buy anything from a murderer?"

I was outraged on my brother's behalf. "Nobody could possibly accuse you of doing this."

"Not even to produce a ghost?" he asked.

My mouth dropped. Who the heck would kill for a public relations stunt? Besides, everyone knew my brother had more integrity than to concoct some half-baked ghost thing to spur business.

"That's the kind of thing Kenny would do," Charlie said, sounding disgusted.

"I don't think Kenny would actually kill someone," I said.

"No, but if he knew someone was going to die..." Charlie let the sentence hang.

Giuseppe's eyes lit up. "Sweet mother Goddess, he came into the store today to try to tag along on tonight's investigation."

"Do you think he knew?" Charlie asked.

I shook my head. "No way. He's annoying, yes, but I can't see him being involved in murder."

"Sometimes Kenny has a really mean streak," she added.

"If we are going to accuse people with a mean streak of murdering Ethel, then we should take a good long look at your maybe-future father-in-law," I said to Charlie. "He's about as mean as they come."

"I don't think they knew each other," Charlie said. "They weren't in the same social circle so they wouldn't have crossed paths."

"Are we sure it was murder?" Giuseppe asked. "If the police come right out and tell everyone it was an accidental fall, I'm clear."

I hesitated for a fraction of a moment. I didn't know if Detective Meanypants wanted me to keep quiet about what he had said, but I didn't want to get on his bad side again. "I think maybe the police will investigate this as a murder," I hedged.

"So, if it wasn't Kenny, who got rid of Ethel?" Charlie asked.

"She wasn't very well liked," I said. "It really could've been anyone who ever knew her."

Charlie shrugged. "I didn't mind her. I think she was a lonely woman who got a little set in her ways."

"She was part of that wretched development," Giuseppe said.

"She was the president of the homeowner's association for the development," Charlie argued. "How does that make her in any way responsible for the development being built?"

Giuseppe wasn't giving up. "She was a mean, nasty woman who went out of her way to make people's lives difficult."

"She took her responsibilities seriously," Charlie said.

"She was power hungry."

"I liked her."

"I didn't."

This was worse than a tennis match.

"Enough," I said a little too loudly. The people sitting at the table across from us looked over, and I offered a bright smile to let them know we weren't going to cause any trouble. My smile must not have been very convincing, because they looked away from me and wouldn't make eye contact.

"Obviously people had very strong feelings regarding Ethel," I said. "But arguing about her won't help."

"People didn't like her because she didn't break the rules," Charlie said. "Some people think rules were made for everyone else, but Ethel knew once you crossed that line there's no telling what would happen."

"The rules she was asked to break were absurd," Giuseppe said.

"What are we talking about?" I asked.

Charlie and Giuseppe both answered. "Solar panels."

Then I remembered the controversy. There had even been a brief article in the newspaper about the whole thing. Apparently, a couple of people in the new development had started the process of installing solar panels on their house, and Ethel had halted all construction. The homeowners never got a chance to install their solar panels and had lost a ton of money they'd already spent on supplies. Needless to say, the newspaper was filled with editorials from both sides of the matter.

"She was only following already established guidelines," I said. "I'm sure those people weren't happy after spending the money on the solar panels, but they should've known to check with the homeowner's association first anyway."

"You're given the list of do's and don'ts when you buy a house with a Homeowner's Association, and the list of what you can and cannot do is very stringent. It's all spelled out in black and white in the CCR—convenants, conditions, and restrictions," Charlie said. "I thought about investing in one of the homes, but I read the document and it was extensive, so I decided not to buy there."

"Your reason had to do with restrictions?" Giuseppe said in disbelief. "Not the fact that they raped the land to build those monstrosities? Not the fact that the town didn't want it built in the first place?"

I shrugged. "Not everyone feels the way we do, G. Some people saw it as an opportunity."

"Don't call me G," he said. "So, will you help me?"

I knew I didn't have much of a choice in my answer, but I wasn't sure what I could do to help. Obviously, I didn't know the first thing about being a detective, as was pointed out to me earlier by certain professionals.

On the other hand, I wasn't going to work in my brother's store for the rest of my life. Since he had things under control there, I had been thinking about a career change. Maybe this would open doors for me, or at least help me find some direction. Maybe I really could become a private investigator, or someone who did the research for the investigators. It would, at the very least, be interesting.

"I'll think about it," I hedged. "I'm not sure I would be able to find anything."

Charlie yawned. "I don't know about you guys, but I think I'm done for the night."

I nodded. "It doesn't really seem respectful to go out dancing or anything right now, does it?"

We indicated to the waitress we were ready for the check and waited in silence for her to come back. Strains of music filtered out of my pocket.

"Again with the guitar music ring tone," Giuseppe said. "When are you going to get a new one?"

"What difference does it make?" I asked, glancing at the screen. It was Stanley. "Hi," I answered.

"Hey, just thought I'd check in. Are you okay?" he asked.

"I don't know, we were just talking about what happened. I'm getting ready to go home now. We don't feel much like staying out tonight after all."

"Why don't I meet you at your house?" he said. "I can make sure you get in safely."

"You don't have to, I'll be fine," I protested.

"I'm not going to stay, I just want to make sure you're okay. This may have been a murder—I'm concerned. Statistically, this is not an expected event."

I relented. He was very sweet to offer me protection, plus I wouldn't mind seeing him again. I smiled in anticipation of our first date. Ending the call, I put the phone in my jacket pocket. Charlie was shaking her head.

"What?" I asked.

"He's meeting you at your house? I'm not sure that's such a good idea," she said.

I was going to have to make sure the volume was down on the phone when she was around. "Why not? I thought you liked Stanley," I said.

"I do, but how well do we really know him?"

"He's the mayor, for heaven's sake," I said.

"Yeah, but isn't it a little weird he was there tonight?"

"Isn't it a little weird we were there tonight?" I retorted. "What do you think?" I asked my brother.

He shrugged. "I think you should trust your instincts," he said, putting some money on the table. "I'm going home. I'll see you tomorrow."

So much for brotherly protection.

"All I'm saying is you've got to be careful," Charlie said. "What if Stanley is the killer?"

Chapter Twelve

WE DEBATED THE CONCEPT OF Stanley being a killer the whole time she drove me home. It was a short ride, but Charlie was persistent for the entire ten minutes. I didn't see Stanley as ever being able to commit murder, but Charlie insisted I needed to keep an open mind. She said it was hard to read what was in a person's heart. I took that to mean she was reflecting more on her relationship than mine, but I supposed she might have had a point.

It was well after midnight by the time her car pulled up in front of my house. Stanley was sitting on the front steps and stood when he saw us.

"Just remember, he wasn't supposed to be there," Charlie whispered.

"Neither were you."

"Don't let your emotions distract you. People always have hidden agendas, and sometimes they'll string you along for their own purposes."

"Are we still talking about Stanley?" I asked. "Never mind. Go home and call Fred, he's probably wondering where you are."

"Let him wonder," she said. "Call me tomorrow, 'kay?"

I bounced out of the car, happy to see Stanley. He approached me with a smile and wrapped me in a hug. I inhaled his scent: part shampoo, part fabric softener, part Stanley.

"C'mon, I'll walk you in as promised and check the place out. I won't stay."

Walking up the steps into the darkened building, I was glad he was with me. The dark of the night wrapped around me, and shadows loomed across the front porch. I couldn't tell if my aunts were up or not. I assumed Aunt Maria was still awake, but with her apartment located in the back of the building I couldn't see if her lights were on.

"Do you think your Aunt Maria is still awake?"

I laughed. "It's funny, I was just wondering the same thing. Probably."

"How's she doing?"

I hesitated, not sure how to answer. Three years ago Aunt Maria's only son Victor had died from pancreatic cancer. It was a terrible time for everybody, and my aunt never got over losing her boy. "She's still taking care of all of us, cooking and checking in. It's hard to tell sometimes, because I think she just doesn't want to talk anymore."

"Why not?" he asked.

"She admitted to me that she was sure everyone was tired of hearing about how much she missed Victor. She thinks she should be over it by now."

"Grief doesn't exactly have a timetable," Stanley said.

"I know, and I said the same thing, but I think she's channeled a lot of her sadness into staying busy."

We climbed the steps to the third floor with Stanley leading the way. The stairway was dimly lit, and it took all my willpower not to jump at the creaks and groans the building made. *I saw a dead body tonight*, I reasoned internally. *A murdered dead body. Of course I'm a little jumpy.*

In front of me, Stanley stopped so suddenly I smacked into him.

"What do you think you're doing here?" he said, his voice a low growl. "And how did you get in?"

My stomach dropped, momentary panic taking over. Who was he talking to?

"I'm here for Ava," a voice said.

My heart rate returned to normal. I knew that voice, and for some reason I wasn't surprised he'd shown up. Tonight was the night for weirdness. Stepping out from behind Stanley, I looked at the visitor sitting, knees bent, in front of my door. "Kenny, you're going to have to leave now."

"That's what you always say," he whined. "You should spend some time with me, I think it would be good for you. We used to have something special, you know."

"We dated for one month in high school, and nothing more. Thanks for the offer, but once again I'll have to decline."

"What are you doing here?" Stanley said.

Kenny stood. "I came to visit. I started a conversation this morning with her brother about his paranormal group, and I was hoping she could help him understand my point of view." He looked Stanley up and down. "I guess she's spending time with the mayor now, huh?"

"Giuseppe does not want to work with you," I said. "He doesn't want you coming with us on our ghost hunts because he doesn't like you, so you should stop bugging him. He said no this morning, and he'll say no again."

"Where were you tonight?" Stanley asked.

"Who wants to know?" Kenny said.

"I'm sure the police will want to know," Stanley said.

Kenny stood and brushed imaginary dirt off his perfectly pressed jeans. "Yeah, I heard you guys found a dead person. Don't worry, Mr. Mayor, I have witnesses who can attest to my whereabouts for the whole night."

I was tired, and it was time to end this. "Goodbye, Kenny."

"Someday you'll come to your senses and see what I've been telling you all along," Kenny said. When he began to walk by, he stopped and looked down at me. "You've really got to make sure you lock your door, especially since there's been a murder here in town. You don't want someone to come in and hurt you."

"Are you threatening me?" I asked.

"No, of course not," Kenny said. "It's common sense. Everybody knows you're supposed to lock your door, you never know who's gonna try to get in."

Stanley cleared his throat. "Kenny has a point, Ava. And remember, when you find unwanted visitors you should call the police and report a breaking and entering crime."

Kenny's face turned red. "Ava and I are friends, and I didn't even try to get into her apartment. I came over tonight to make sure she's okay. What's your excuse?"

I stepped in between the two men. "Stop it, Kenny. It's been a long night for everyone. Stanley is just making sure I'm okay."

"Kind of like what I'm doing," he said.

"Does he always come here unannounced?" Stanley asked.

I shrugged. "Yes, but only because he knows if he asks I'll tell him no. He usually leaves right away." I often wondered why he bothered. I never encouraged him, and at times I had been downright mean to him. I didn't like the guy, but I did think he was a little bit lonely and a whole lot unhappy with his life. And even if I was stupid enough to get back into a relationship with the creep, my loyalty was to my family. I would never befriend someone who was so mean to Giuseppe. "Stanley's right, Kenny, you can't keep showing up here."

"Why, because your brother wouldn't like it?" Kenny said.

"No, because normal people call first," I said. I squelched the desire to tell him we weren't ever going to be a couple, even though I wanted to say it. I would not resort to being a bully.

Kenny shook his head. "After everything I've done for you, Ava, I cannot believe you have hardened your heart against me."

"Are you done?" I asked. Kenny always managed to get on my very last nerve.

Kenny nodded. "Yeah, I'll go now. Hang in there, kid, it'll get better." Finally, he left, descending the stairs without a backward glance.

Opening the unlocked door, I stepped aside to let Stanley in first. Following, I flipped on lights in the living room area and hoped I hadn't left anything embarrassing lying around, like underwear or bags of opened potato chips. I was aiming for a different sort of impression than housekeeping slob.

My apartment takes up the entire third floor. The space is large and light-filled, plus I have the bonus of my aunts living downstairs. My front door opens into a small entry leading to the living room/kitchen combination. The living room to the right is a wide and spacious area with floor to ceiling windows providing a view of the town green outside the building. To the left is the kitchen, separated from the living room by a breakfast counter with stools. Directly in front of us a hallway led to the back two bedrooms and bathroom.

Stanley looked at me, and an uncomfortable silence stretched between us. I knew this was about Kenny, and even though I didn't like the guy sometimes I admit feeling the tiniest bit sorry for him. I often thought that underneath all his hair gel and cologne he might not be a bad person, if only he bothered to see things from other people's perspectives.

Finally, Stanley threw the question at me. "Does Kenny show up here a lot?

He looked pretty comfortable sitting there."

"We've known each other for a long time," I said. "Since kindergarten, actually. But it's not like we're close friends or anything. I think he comes over here because he's lonely."

Maybe I should try to say it differently. "We don't, we're not—we don't do anything, we never did. I mean, we used to date, but I wouldn't, not with him..." Charlie was right, I should have come home alone. Then I could have kicked Kenny out by myself and that would have been the end of it. I'd been dealing with him since elementary school, so telling Kenny to get lost wasn't new to me.

"Even if you're not sleeping with him, I was wondering if I have any competition," Stanley said.

I hesitated. Sure, I really liked Stanley. And yes, we'd been flirting with each other for months. But his question took me by surprise, and left me wondering if I should play hard to get. I'd never been sure about the rules of dating. I wasn't a person who liked to play games, but then again I hadn't had a steady boyfriend since college, when I decided I couldn't be with someone who constantly criticized my hair and clothes. Leaving him was easy, but I never felt like I'd learned anything about this dating game. Did men like it better when we weren't as available, or did they get scared off easily?

"Do you think I'd go out with you if I was seeing someone else?"

"No... maybe. I don't know, sometimes women date more than one person at a time." Stanley ran a hand through his hair, causing it to stick up on top. "I don't believe you would intentionally hurt anyone, but I've been surprised before by what people will do. I'm sorry, I didn't mean to offend you, especially since we haven't even had our first date yet. I guess I'm just trying to figure out where I stand."

Stanley started pacing across the living room, a habit I'd seen him lapse into at public meetings. It tended to make the others on the town council nervous, and I wondered if anyone really heard what he said once Stanley started pacing. It was hard to focus with him moving back and forth.

He stopped, looking directly at me. "You're a very attractive woman, and I guess I've had a bit of a crush on you for a while. I was just trying to assess the probability of this relationship developing into something more."

Geek-alert, sensitive guy, or budding serial killer?

"Sometimes the things I say don't come out quite right," he said.

I could certainly identify with that.

"So let's just pretend I didn't ask, okay?"

I relented. I liked him and wanted to see what this attraction was between us, and I really couldn't blame him for asking. But I had to wonder about the question. Usually guys asked those types of questions when they've been burned by other people. The thing is, sometimes you gotta take a chance on a relationship. Not that I'd had much dating experience, but I'd read it somewhere.

I flipped on more lights, illuminating the hallway. It only took Stanley a couple of minutes to check the entire apartment and declare it intruder-free.

"Make sure you lock your doors tonight," Stanley said. "Do you have to work in the morning?"

I shook my head. "No, I'm planning on putting my notes in order so I can figure this out."

"Figure what out?"

"G wants me to look into this murder. He thinks Ethel getting killed is going to be bad for business," I said. "Any thoughts or ideas to get me started?"

Stanley shook his head and pushed his glasses up as they slid down his nose. "No, no, and no," he said. "And for the record, I cannot in any way help you."

Chapter Thirteen

"BUT YOU'RE THE MAYOR," I said. "You must have some kind of connections."

"It's not what you think," he said.

"I think you're the mayor," I answered, "and you know everyone there is to know."

"I'm not the mayor for the reason you think," he said.

I hadn't given much thought to Stanley's position as mayor; I'd just assumed he wanted to be in politics.

"The only reason I ran for mayor is so I could have health insurance," he said. "And now that I have it, I can honestly say I can't imagine why anyone would want this job for any other reason."

"Are you sick?" I asked.

"No, but it's part of being sick."

"What's part of being sick? You just said you weren't sick."

"I'm not, but I ran for mayor just in case. You know I have a business as a computer consultant, right?" he said.

I nodded.

"As a self-employed person, I never bothered to buy health insurance. I figured I was young and healthy, and statistically speaking I wouldn't need it until my mid to late forties." Shaking his head, his face reflected incredulity.

"Mathematics can usually give us guidelines for our lives, but not this time."

Having been an English major, I had no idea what he was talking about but wisely kept my mouth shut.

"A couple of years ago, I sprained my ankle. It was a really bad sprain, and made me realize I couldn't rely on any statistical formulas for this. I mean, what if I got hit by a bus? What if I fell into a ravine?"

My mind frantically scrambled to remember if there were any local ravines. I drew a blank. Next I wondered if he was going to tell me he actually calculated the probability of having an accident. No doubt about it, Stanley was a planner. Did he even realize there were days I left the house without a coat because I didn't know a blizzard was coming?

"So, I did what I had to do to get health insurance," he said.

"You ran for mayor, instead of changing jobs?"

"It was a kind of a job change, and I didn't have to give up my business in computers."

"True," I said. "But what if you'd lost?"

"Don't you remember when I won the election?"

I tried to think back to when Stanley was elected. It was only two years ago, and I was usually scrupulous about voting, but for some reason I drew a blank. "How come I don't remember?" I asked.

"Because I ran unopposed."

Oh boy, now I remember. No wonder I didn't bother going to the polls. The former mayor, Tony Vienzo, had decided to retire. He was well into his eighties and had been mayor for as long as I could remember. For a little while, nobody wanted to step up and take on the job. Tony had actually tried to retire in the election four years prior, but everyone in our small town was busy then, too. Finally, Stanley said yes and was hailed as a hero for running. He would have won even if his was the only vote. Even though he was the only person running for Mayor I think people liked him, and still do. Stanley comes across as genuine and sincere, despite Charlie's warnings and dire predictions.

"Why can't you help me?" I tried to keep the whine out of my voice but I don't think I succeeded.

"Because my role as the mayor has to take precedence. I have a responsibility to the people of this town, and I need to make sure if a murder took place that justice is served in the most expedient way possible."

My eyebrows raised at his statement, and I crossed my arms over my chest.

"I'm sorry, Ava, but I don't see you launching an investigation into what happened tonight as turning into something expedient." At least he had the decency to look sheepish about it, even if his words cut straight through me.

"I understand, you have to work within the law on this one," I said. "Don't worry about it. I appreciate you meeting me here, though, and making sure I'm okay."

"It's not like I live far from you." Stanley lived on Cedar Street, within walking distance of my house. If I stepped out of my front door onto Elm Street and turned left, Cedar Street was the next street on my left. His house was the second one on the left. It would probably take about two minutes to walk from my house to his, maybe four if it was snowing hard.

I could tell Stanley was getting ready to leave. Panic flooded through me. Should I hug him? Kiss him? Would he get the wrong impression if I did?

He took a step toward me, and I froze. I hated this, feeling like a gawky teenager again. Needing to take control of the situation, I stepped forward and put my arms around him for a hug. We did that awkward pat on the back thing and stepped apart.

I wasn't ready for anything more at the moment. My head was swimming from the night's events. I wasn't used to finding dead bodies and being treated poorly by the police. Usually, I was on the right side of the law, and my experience with law enforcement was positive; I had never been regarded with suspicion in relation to a crime.

"I'll call you tomorrow," Stanley said.

"Tomorrow, or today?" I asked. The clock on my stove read two a.m.

He smiled. "Today."

After Stanley left, I tried to go right to sleep, but I kept replaying the night's events in my mind. I tossed and turned, falling into an uncomfortable dream-filled state. Dead, bloated faces of not just Ethel but other people I know drifted by. They were all trying to tell me something, but the words slid into a vacuum of sound, distorted and unintelligible. I ran, getting nowhere, believing I could save at least one of them but not saving anyone. The bodies kept piling up in front of me, making a pounding noise as they landed one on top of the next.

I struggled to pull myself out of this place, fighting my growing panic. The pounding of bodies grew louder. I sat up in bed with a gasp, fully awake, my whole body trembling. Whispered words shattered like broken glass, dissolving the stillness of my bedroom. I looked around my room, trying to place the source of the voices. I could no longer hear any voices, but the pounding continued.

Someone was at my door.

Chapter Fourteen

"AVA MARIE, LET ME IN!"

Pound, slam.

Lord almighty, the sky was still smudged with gray and my sister-in-law was going to break down the door. It took all my remaining strength to unlock and pull the door open. My head was throbbing and everything looked a little fuzzy around the edges. I had the classic symptoms of a hangover, but I didn't drink last night.

Maybe I should have.

Without a word, I turned and headed into the kitchen. This was not a time for talking, this was a time for coffee. Strong coffee.

Janine's voice chattered as I took two mugs out of the cabinet. I could practically hear each drip as the coffee brewed. "Omigawd, I cannot believe what happened last night."

I loved Janine like she was my own sister but sometimes her voice cut like a buzz saw. This morning was no exception. At the sound of the blessed beep signaling the coffee was ready, I poured it into the waiting cups.

"Do you have any creamer?" Janine already had the refrigerator door open and before I could answer she pulled out the plastic container of Peppermint Mocha flavored creamer. Without a word, she poured some into my coffee before flavoring hers. I wrapped my hands around the mug and took a sip, picturing the caffeine flowing through my body and enjoying the warmth of the cup.

"No offense, but you don't look so good," Janine said.

"It's sort of early," I croaked.

"Sorry, I wanted to talk to you before the baby got up. I didn't want him to hear about this."

I wasn't sure it really mattered if my nephew heard us talking, since I was pretty sure he never listened anyway. But, to my credit, I knew better than to point out he was only six months old. Plus, I didn't feel up to hearing the "he's so advanced and can pick up on things" lecture this early in the morning.

"Aren't you working today?" Janine asked.

I shook my head. "I worked last Saturday, so I get this one off." I wondered what kind of business my brother was going to have today and whether or not people would stop in out of morbid curiosity. With us finding a dead body last night, it would probably be a busy day at Scentsations. Everyone in town would want to hear the details from Giuseppe and then talk about what it could all mean.

"What do you know about the murder last night?" Janine demanded.

I shook my head. "We don't know for certain it was a murder."

"Of course it was murder, why the heck else would she be lying in a pool of blood in the basement?"

While Janine's logic was far from irrefutable, I decided to refrain from comment. Letting Janine rant and get things out of her system was sometimes easier than a debate. Her post-pregnancy hormones were in full force this morning, meaning there was plenty of ranting and tears. A sort of double-whammy thing, not fun for anyone, including Janine. She really did get herself worked up, and I had to do something to calm her down.

Before I could open my mouth to speak, her words came rushing out. "I know what's going to happen, and we have to do something."

I raised my eyebrows, taking a huge gulp of coffee. *I need the caffeine to work, now.*

"Whoever did this is going to come after us next," Janine said. "I can't let that happen. I have a child to protect."

Sometimes Janine's reasoning was flawed, but pointing this out required delicacy. I didn't want her to think I didn't believe her, but the odds were against her and Baby Danny being in any danger. "Lots of people were there last night," I said. "I can't imagine we're all in danger."

"Of course not," Janine agreed. "Just you and Giuseppe."

O-kay... maybe Janine knew something I didn't. Maybe it was still too early in the morning for me. "Why just us?"

"Because you're the one who found the body and my husband is the reason you were there."

In my head I knew she was overreacting, but Janine's ominous words were contagious. I couldn't help but wonder if we'd seen something that might put us at risk. "I'm sure the police are doing everything they can to figure this out."

"No, it's up to you to help the police."

I knew I was making a scrunchie face, but I was confused. What was I going to do to help the police that I hadn't done last night?

Reading my mind, Janine said, "They don't know what they're doing. You're smart and analytical, you can figure this out and save us from the madman who is killing people." Realizing what she'd just said, Janine amended her statement. "Killed a person."

"Right, one person," I argued. "How can we be sure it wasn't an accident? If it was, I'm sure the new guy will have a blast figuring it out."

"You mean Oliver?"

"Yes, I mean Detective Rialto," I snapped. "How do you know him?"

"He stopped by the house last night with a few more questions."

I wasn't sure if I should be upset because he disturbed my family, pissed at him for putting these ideas in Janine's head, or happy he was doing his job. Obviously she never would've imagined she was in any danger if the good detective hadn't hinted as much. "Did he bother you? You don't have to let him in, you know."

Janine shook her head. "No, he was fine. I mean, the situation sort of bothered me, but after a while I started noticing how hunky he is."

"Hunky?" What the heck was she talking about? He had a nice butt, end of story.

"I might be married but it doesn't mean I can't look, right? Don't you think he's got that macho, handsome thing going on?"

I shook my head. "No, I think he's a jerk."

Janine nodded. "This is going to be one of those kinds of stories."

Sometimes I had trouble figuring out what she was talking about. "What are you talking about?"

"I can see the whole thing now, how you're denying your attraction to him, but eventually you'll start a relationship with Oliver and you'll marry him and become wife to a detective."

Janine's sigh was a direct contrast to my choking on my coffee. "I don't see it, Janine. He doesn't really strike me as good looking, and he's probably married." A vision of his newly bare left hand floated through my mind.

Janine shook her head. "Widowed."

"How do you know this?"

"Because he has a tragic air about him."

I waited for a moment, almost afraid to answer her. "That's it? A tragic air?"

"And he's too thin."

I sighed. A tragic air and too thin could mean he was a street person, a homeless bum who couldn't pull himself together. Or it could mean he gives all his money away to worthy charities and doesn't have enough to subsist on. Or he could have a great metabolism. Whatever the reason, it was time to find out. "Okay," I said.

Janine looked startled. "Okay?"

"Yes, okay."

"Oooo.... kaaaayyy..." She drew the word out, looking at me like I had just grown a new body part.

"I'm going to find out what's going on," I said.

"You're going to ask him how he became a widower?"

"No, I'm going to ask him what he's learned about the case. Giuseppe wants help, you want help, so help is what I'll give you. Especially if you think there's a safety issue and you and baby Danny might be at risk." I might think Janine was a little flaky, but there was no way I was going to ignore what might be mother's intuition on her part. Like any good Irish-Italian girl, I knew better than to ignore a hunch. Plus, it really meant I would get a chance to investigate being an investigator, to see if I liked doing this kind of work.

Janine stood, ready to go now that her mission was complete. "So, what are you going to do first?"

I would be logical in my approach. "I'm going to see Detective Rialto first."

"You going later today?"

I shook my head. "No point in waiting. I'm going right now."

Chapter Fifteen

RIGHT NOW DOESN'T REALLY MEAN right now when it's first thing in the morning. By the time I'd showered and decided what to wear it was already seven o'clock. My choice of outfit was important—I needed to look intelligent and serious to offset the impression the detective had of me being just another ghost-hunting wacko.

Rather than drive my old Honda that sat mostly unused in the garage behind my house, I walked to the police station. It was only a few blocks, and I was still tired enough to know I probably wouldn't focus well on the road. No different from any other time I drove, it just seemed important not to show up at the police station after having knocked down a few pedestrians along the way.

Brewster Square is pretty in a small, New England town sort of way. When I came out of my front door, I walked around the Green down Elm, Church, and Academy Streets, and took a right onto Pine Road. I had dressed in layers, meaning I had on two T-shirts under my fleece pullover with a pair of jeans. I suppose I should have worn sneakers for my walk, but my shoe weakness dictated I wear something cute. I'd pulled on a pair of short black boots, since they'd keep my feet warmer than sneakers anyway. The heels were small, so it wasn't like I was walking in high heels for several blocks. Although, if I had to walk a long way in heels in order to avoid wearing sneakers, I would.

As I walked I noticed only a small amount of snow still covered the ground. For the most part, it was dirty and gray, the type of snow most of us can't wait to get rid of because winter was too long and the snow no longer held any appeal. I counted the number of steps I took down Church Street, mentally comparing the numbers to my other walks. Birdsong punctuated the chilly air, and the bare trees were another reminder that it was not yet Spring. Both the Episcopalian and Catholic churches were shuttered and locked, leaving everyone on the outside, a symbol perhaps for the changing times. The doors were open on Sundays and by invitation only.

Kenny's coffee shop, Big Beans, already had a few customers. The bakery next door was open as well, and as I took a left onto Academy Street the delicious smells of coffee and baked goods wafted around me. I might not like Kenny, but he sure knew how to brew a good cup. I started my step-counting again and made a mental note to stop back at the bakery on my way home for something sweet. I wanted to visit my parents this weekend, and I thought it might be nice to bring them some pastries.

After passing the bakery I turned right onto Pine Road, where the police station was housed a block further down. The building was one floor, a square and ugly brick building with stern angles and a utilitarian look. The building next door mirrored the police department. I sometimes wondered if the town got a discount for using up all the ugly materials to create these two buildings, but I guess the police, dispatch, and social services didn't really need to be housed in anything fancy. It would have been nice, though, for people who had to visit these buildings to find a little corner of comfort.

Not all of us were criminals.

Usually when I took a relaxed walk I spent time looking at the details around me, the houses, yards, and decorations that created the look of the place. This time, in addition to counting my steps, I couldn't stop my mind from spinning in circles around last night's events.

The suspicious circumstances of Ethel's death were almost a cliché. True, lots of people didn't like her, so the suspect pool would be large. But nobody deserved to be killed, and I couldn't get the sight of her bloodied head and crooked body out of my mind.

Marching through the door of the police station, I approached the front window where a large male police officer sat. I guessed he was the keeper of the gate, only letting innocent people and employees through. The window was shielded by glass, which must have been bullet proof, and there was a small, vented opening to speak through. I didn't see any buttons, so I guessed I just had to lean down and talk through the thing.

Feeling idiotic, I hunched over and spoke loudly into the opening. "*I need to see Detective Rialto immediately. Now.*"

"He's not in," the officer behind the window answered in a normal tone.

"You can hear me?" I asked, surprised. I'd assumed the thick glass deadened sound.

"Loud and clear," he said, deadpan.

Well, geez, he should've told me before I made myself sound like an idiot.

I hesitated, wondering about my next step. I should have called the number on the detective's business card, but I'd assumed because of last night's big case he'd be tireless, working around the clock. After all, that's how they did it in the books I read.

"Can't you call him at home or something? This is important."

"It always is," the officer said. "I can take a message and make sure he gets it."

A door to my left opened, and I jumped. The combination of finding a dead body and not getting any sleep was making me jittery. When I saw Rob, relief washed through me.

Rob is my friend, Rob can help me.

He walked over, not smiling. "Ava, is everything okay? Why are you here?"

"I came to see Detective Rialto," I said.

"He's not here."

"I know, the guy up front told me. Maybe you can help." I was hopeful this wouldn't be a wasted trip on my part.

Rob took a step backward as if trying to distance himself from me. Raising his arms in front of him, he said, "I don't know nothin' about what happened last night. I don't think I can help you."

"Rob..." I edged closer to him. "I'm not looking for you to tell me anything. I just..." Suddenly I was lost. I had planned on using a little harmless flirtation to get information out of Rob, to try to see if they had any clues or suspects or information, but I couldn't. I was overwhelmed with a sense of loss, that this macabre death was a grave injustice, and the fact still remained: Ethel was dead. There were no more second chances for her, no more opportunities for anything. She was gone, left the building.

Dizziness washed through me, making me wish I'd gone back to bed instead of marching over here. Rob grabbed my arm, a steadying force against the tide of sadness I was feeling.

"Let's step outside," he said.

The sharp March air made me feel better. "Thanks," I said. "I don't know what came over me."

Rob studied me for a moment before speaking. "Ava, you've never witnessed this type of crime before, so it's only natural to have a reaction. You saw someone who died as a result of a violent event—not an easy thing to deal with. This might take some time to get over."

I looked up at him, the Rob I'd known for practically my entire life, and saw a different person. I saw someone who was sweet and brave and willing to put himself out there for the sake of helping others. "Do you see a lot of this type of thing?" I asked.

He shook his head. "Not murders, not in this town at least. I see other things, though." Taking a deep breath, he seemed to collect himself before speaking again. "I see all kinds of people—kids, babies—hurt or dead in car accidents. I see women beaten and bruised because their husbands use them as a punching bag. I see kids used as a punching bag." He stopped, and I wasn't sure if it was because he didn't want to say more or didn't trust himself to speak. He looked genuinely upset.

"There are lots of bad things to be seen, even in a great little town like this, Ava. But the important thing to hold onto is all the really wonderful things here. This isn't a big city, this is a place full of people who watch out for each other. We care, and violence isn't a natural part of this community. You've got to remember that every time you close your eyes and see Ethel."

I never really thought about crime in Brewster Square, but like any other corner of the world I suppose it had to exist. People don't live side by side in harmony, despite what some might wish. And my respect for my old friend went up even more. He knew, without my telling him, what was happening when I closed my eyes. Suddenly I couldn't imagine living the life he lived.

"Thanks, Rob. I don't know what to say." My eyes filled with tears, and I worried I would become a blubbering mess.

"Don't mention it. Come on, I'll walk with you for a little bit."

"How did you know I walked?" I asked, suspicious. Did they have cameras where they saw everyone coming and going from the parking lot?

"Because I know you don't drive much, which is a good thing," he said.

I decided to leave his comment alone, since it did not dignify a response. "Don't you need your car?"

Rob's face turned a little bit red. "I'll come back and get it. I'm only going as far as the coffee shop."

It took me a minute before I realized why he was blushing about going to the coffee shop. "Rob Genova, do you have a date?"

"This early in the morning?" he asked. "What do you think?"

"I think you're going to see someone there." I don't know how I knew, but I did. "Who is she?"

"Nobody," he said. I leveled a look at him, not about to listen to his denials. "Tell me."

"No."

I smacked him on the arm, but not too hard. After all, he did have a gun. "You just admitted it, so you might as well tell me."

He shrugged. "There's a waitress I've kind of been seeing a little bit. I told her I'd stop by this morning and say hello."

I was so happy to hear this. Rob was the nicest guy I knew, and I wanted him to find someone equally nice. He deserved to have everything he wanted, especially since he had just become a sort of crime-fighting hero to me.

"So, you really ticked off the new detective last night, you know," he said in an obvious effort to change the subject.

"I won't ask you any more questions about your date, or what happened last night," I said as we walked along the sidewalk back toward the Green. "But I was wondering what you might know about Detective Rialto."

"Why do you want to know?"

"He's a little bit of a mystery, and I was curious," I said. I knew I wasn't telling the whole truth, but I didn't think it was worth it to mention Janine's theories of thin men being widowers. "So, what's his story?"

Rob shrugged. "I don't know. All I know is he's good at his job, and we're pretty lucky to have him here. I don't think he's from Connecticut, I think I heard he's from out West somewhere."

By this time we'd walked to the front of the coffee shop, Big Beans. I knew Rob was anxious to get inside. "Thanks, Rob."

"Listen, Ava, let the police handle this, okay? We know what we're doing, and I don't think it would be good for you to get involved."

I knew he meant well, but I never took that kind of advice. As soon as someone told me not to do something, it was the first thing I wanted to do. Obviously I had no experience investigating a homicide, but it wouldn't hurt anyone if I helped. Just a little.

Chapter Sixteen

I DIDN'T NOTICE ANYTHING AROUND me on the walk home because I was so focused on thinking about Ethel's murder. I didn't even count my steps. As much as I hated thinking about it, I mentally summoned an image of her at the bottom of the stairs.

Body slightly twisted, awkward. Definite head injury. Seeing the head injury convinced me. There is no way her death was from a simple fall. I tried to picture the basement steps and the railing, and remembered them both as being wooden and painted white. No sharp edges or tools were near the steps, and the railing was a typical hand rail. Heads don't cave like that on an ordinary staircase.

By the time I reached my front steps, I'd formulated half a plan of action. Half was a good start, and I decided I'd figure it out as I went along. Some things were hard to plan and needed a sense of spontaneity. I considered myself a resourceful woman.

Clearly, I needed to think like a detective. And just as clearly, I had no authority to act like one. In fact, I had a feeling I could be in big trouble with the law if I poked my nose into this situation.

But my real reason for wanting to do this had nothing to do with my brother or his wife asking me to help. Because really, what's more important, truth and justice or playing it safe? *The truth is, I have a very safe life, actually bordering on innocent. My world is made of close family, good friends, and a low-crime town. Compared to others, I live a fairy tale life.*

Maybe it was my talk with Rob earlier, but I felt an urge to step outside my circle of safety. After all, if I wanted the world to be a better place, if I wanted to keep my town secure, I had to do my part. Climbing the stairs to my apartment, I tried to think like a detective. What would Oliver do? Obviously, his first step was to interview all of the people who were there. Next, he'd probably look for someone with motive and work backwards from there.

At least, that's what I would do if I were him.

Despite my incorrect assumptions last night, it was very possible I was destined to play some sort of role in law enforcement. I had a momentary vision of getting my private investigator's license and opening my own place, working to keep Brewster Square safe. Of course I couldn't be part of the police department, since wearing a uniform and driving one of those cars didn't really appeal to me. I would take cases with merit, I would help people who were struggling, and I would charge enough money for all this to be able to support myself comfortably.

Before I got too carried away with this fantasy of mine and started googling PI license requirements, I grabbed a plastic platter and started loading it with cookies from my freezer.

My aunts had taught me well, and I always kept my freezer stocked with cookies and treats that could be taken out at a moment's notice and brought to someone who needed sustenance in their time of grief. My favorites to keep on hand were chocolate chip walnut bars, as well as the chocolate chip coconut bars. Not only did they freeze well, they also defrosted quickly enough on the drive over to someone's house.

When someone dies, people tended to gather at the house of the deceased. Although Ethel had no husband or children, I assumed there would be relatives at her house to start going through her belongings and arguing over who got what. Wrapping a layer of plastic wrap and another of foil around the platter, I grabbed my keys and headed for the door. This time I was going to have to drive.

My old Honda Civic was generally left parked in the detached garage behind the house. Our yard was fenced in, and the detached garage easily held three cars plus an assortment of lawn care junk and stuff that wouldn't fit in the attic. The building wasn't in the best of shape, and as I unlocked the garage door I made a note to check some of the boards and make sure they weren't rotting. Since my aunts were generous enough to let me live there at a significantly reduced rent, I was in charge of maintenance and repairs. I would be derelict in my duties if the garage fell down, so I should probably start caulking and repairing.

Backing out of the driveway, the car lurched onto the street and knocked over the neighbor's garbage can. *Cans go in at the end of the day on Friday. It's not my fault I knocked it over.*

Heading back down Elm and onto Church Street, I went the opposite direction from the police station and took a right onto South Main and another right onto Chartres Drive. I couldn't stop the shiver that ran through me when I drove past the house we'd been in last night, but I kept going. The new development was just past the old McAllister house. Turning left onto Sunshine Circle, I couldn't help shivering again. This time for a completely different reason.

All the houses in the new Stony River Farms development where Ethel had lived looked exactly alike. Not a little bit alike, but *exactly* alike, right down to the same trees and shrubs in the same spots in each yard. Each door was painted a Colonial blue and had matching shutters, and the houses were made with a deep taupe-colored siding. Small oak trees had been planted in each front yard, slightly right of the front door. Presumably when the trees grew taller they could provide shade for the front of the house.

I wondered if sometimes people walked into the wrong house at the end of their day, confused at the general state of sameness pervading the neighborhood.

I pulled into the driveway and was pleased to note I only had one tire on the lawn. Grabbing the plate of cookies, I marched to the front door, wondering why no other cars were in the driveway. I knew Ethel had relatives, some nieces and nephews, and wondered if maybe they were all gathered at a different house. Maybe they went to the wrong house, too.

Ringing the bell, I waited, not expecting to hear footsteps. The house felt empty. Turning from the door, I started thinking about my next step when another car pulled into the driveway.

I knew the woman who climbed out of the Lexus immediately, and had a moment's hesitation before I spoke to her. I liked Ethel's niece, Carla, and wondered how she was handling her aunt's death. "Did you ring the bell?"

Carla asked. "Aunt Ethel said she'd be here this afternoon, so I don't know if I'm too early or not."

More like too late, but I wasn't sure how to tell her. I'd never had to break the news of anyone's death before, and I wasn't sure what to do. Hugging me lightly, Carla kept talking. "Ava, how have you been? I've been meaning to come down to the store and see you and your brother, but time keeps getting away from me. The kids are getting ready for spring break in April, and we're hoping to go someplace warm."

I still didn't know what to say. "Great. You should go have fun. Someplace warm, I mean." I could probably cross grief counselor off my list of potential careers. I couldn't even say the appropriate thing, never mind telling her what happened last night. *Now what? Do I just blurt out, oh by the way Ethel's not here, she's dead?* To my relief, another car pulled in the driveway and parked behind Carla. At least now I wouldn't have to shoulder this alone, and hopefully whoever this was would be better at breaking the news to her.

Of course, of all the dead women's houses in all of Connecticut, he had to come to this one. Detective Oliver Rialto marched up the sidewalk toward us, with a scowl on his face meant only for me. "Good morning, ladies," he said. Carla looked a little confused, so I introduced them.

"Carla, this is Oliver." I tried not to glare at him. Despite what my sister-in-law said, every time I saw him the detective got under my skin. And not in a good way.

"Can I talk to you for a moment?" he asked out of the side of his mouth.

"Would you excuse us for a moment?" I said.

"Sure," Carla said. "I'm just going to go inside and see if Aunt Ethel is there."

"Wait right here ma'am, I'll be with you in a moment," Detective Rialto said. Carla looked perplexed, but she's nothing if not polite. She stood on the front steps waiting for Oliver to finish talking to me.

"Did you say anything?" he asked.

"Good morning to you, too. I thought you weren't working this morning."

"Just because I'm not at the station doesn't mean I'm not working. What the hell are you doing here?"

"I'm here to pay my respects," I said, lifting the tray of cookies. "And for your information, I said nothing. I didn't know what to say once I realized she didn't know."

Oliver nodded. "Fine. Let me handle this." Walking over to Carla, I could see him assemble his face into a mask of sincerity. Leaning toward her, he mumbled a few words while he quietly held her elbow.

Even though I was standing about six feet away from them, Carla's sigh was loud. Her eyes met mine, filled with tears, and sadness settled over me. I was powerless to make things better for her. "You probably didn't know what to say to me," she said through a watery smile. I could only nod because it was true. If Oliver hadn't come along when he did we'd still be standing out here talking about the weather or something equally mundane.

"Let's go inside so I can get the details and pass them along to the rest of the family," Carla said, turning toward the front door. "Although I have to tell you, I always figured something like this would happen."

Chapter Seventeen

I KNEW DETECTIVE RIALTO WAS annoyed with me for accepting Carla's invitation to come inside her aunt's house, but I had come to bring cookies, and I wasn't about to drop them off and leave. As Carla was unlocking the front door with her spare key, he shot me a dirty look and shook his head. I lifted my tray of cookies in answer, trying to look like I was only there to provide comfort and solace.

"It certainly is very nice of Ms. O'Dell to bring food," he said. "But I'm sure she has things she needs to do. Why don't I take that tray for you and bring it inside?"

"No, please stay," Carla said. "I haven't seen you in a while, Ava, and I'd really like it if you could be here for this." As she pushed open the front door with her forearm, she turned her head and slid her eyes over the detective. I couldn't help but wonder if he made her nervous. He was big and just a little intimidating, but I didn't think she had anything to worry about. Unless she had something to hide, of course, which I seriously doubted. Carla was more of a soccer mom than a killer mom.

But now Detective Rialto was here, and I wouldn't be able to ask the same types of questions without clueing him in to what I was doing. But at least I could listen in on whatever he asked Carla, which was almost as good.

"I may want to talk to you in private," Detective Rialto said as he followed us into the front entryway.

Carla pulled herself up straight and turned. "Whatever you want to say you can say in front of Ava. We've known each other our whole lives. I have nothing to hide from her." Pausing for effect, she added, "You're new here, aren't you?"

Detective Rialto nodded, ignoring the dig. "Fine, then we'll get started. There are some things I'd like to go over with you."

Carla led the way to the kitchen and we all sat at the round kitchen table. The house was fairly new, and everything was immaculate. There wasn't a crumb on the granite counter tops and the windows sparkled in the early morning sunlight. I noticed there were no dishes left in the sink, no shoes by the front door, and no mail lying around anywhere. Ethel's house looked like a model home, the kind that people walk through when they're deciding if they want to buy in a development.

I started taking the plastic wrap off my tray of cookies, listening as Detective Rialto filled Carla in on the details of last night. Hearing him tell the story as if it happened to someone else was strange. I couldn't help but feel a little awkward when Carla looked at me from the kitchen, coffee pot in mid-air as Detective Rialto told her I had been the person to find her aunt.

She regained her composure quickly, though, and continued making coffee as if she were just having a friendly chat with the next door neighbors. I don't know how she kept her poise in the face of this kind of news, but Carla remained calm and composed through the entire story. "We were always afraid something would happen to her," Carla said.

"Something violent?" Detective Rialto asked.

Carla was silent for a moment, and I wondered if she was trying to figure out how to explain her aunt to the detective. I'd known Ethel for a while, and I knew firsthand she had a reputation for being a pain in the neck to so many people. Describing Ethel would be complicated, since underneath the woman's prickly demeanor she had a reason for everything she did. Not everyone agreed with her reasoning, but Ethel followed her own moral code.

"My aunt was known to be difficult," Carla said. "She's always been very rigid and unwilling to listen to the opinions of others. As the president of the neighborhood association, she's had run-ins with most every homeowner in this development."

Points for discretion, I thought, remembering Ethel's screaming tirade at a town council public meeting a few months ago.

"Do you think anyone was mad enough to kill her?" Detective Rialto said.

Yes.

Carla shook her head. "No, not right now."

I looked at Carla, surprised. Everyone I knew wanted to murder Ethel at some point or other, and I was certain many still held grudges. Maybe people had trouble seeing family for what they really were. An image of Giuseppe floated through my mind.

Carla continued. "Frankly, I thought she would suffer vandalism to her house or car, maybe a few threatening notes, minor but annoying types of harassment."

Okay, she had a point. Murder was a bit extreme.

"Did anything of that nature happen?" he asked.

Carla sighed and this time tears came to her eyes. "Aunt Ethel was very independent, you know. But she was a fascinating woman, too. Most people don't know how much she travelled or the amazing things she managed to do in her lifetime. She meant well, she really did, and everything she ever did was out of a sense of misplaced morality or a skewed view of her role as a leader in this community."

"Was your aunt the victim of vandalism?" Detective Rialto asked again.

Carla hesitated, then shook her head. "She never mentioned any problems."

"Why would anyone murder your aunt?" Detective Rialto asked.

Carla's tears flowed down her face. "Why wouldn't they? She was pushy and abrasive, and she made lots of people mad."

"But, why? What did she do?" Detective Rialto pressed.

"You know she was president of the homeowners association here, right?" Without waiting for an answer, Carla kept talking. "She was big on following the rules. And the rules clearly state that a certain look has to be maintained in the neighborhood, people can only use approved colors on the exterior of the home, and permission must be obtained prior to planting anything in the yard."

I thought of the Stepford wives, but kept my mouth shut. What business was it of mine if people wanted to live in a community of uniformity? Variation is not for everyone.

"One day she got a phone call from the Tylers who live on the other side of the development. They were complaining to Aunt Ethel about their neighbors putting in one of those inflatable, above-ground pools, and wasn't it against the rules, blah blah blah."

"Was it against the rules?" Detective Rialto asked. I didn't say a word since I'd already heard the story. From many different people. Surprisingly this incident had been a hot topic for months in Brewster Square. Half the town was on the side of the folks who wanted a cheap swimming pool, because who doesn't want to be able to go swimming in the summer; the other half was on Ethel's side, because rules were rules. Seemingly everyone in town disagreed with how she handled the situation.

"Yes. Aunt Ethel got a legal injunction to force them to take down the pool. Lots of people thought she had carried it a bit too far, since it was only a pool."

"Was that the only time your aunt angered people in the neighborhood?" Detective Rialto asked. I had to stop the great big "Hah!" from escaping my mouth. Of course it wasn't the only time she'd pissed someone off, it was just the most talked about time in recent history.

"No, of course not. Where are you from?" Carla asked.

The land of know-it-alls, I thought.

Detective Rialto ignored her question. "I'll need a list of the people your aunt had any kind of feud with, as well as information on what those disagreements were about."

Carla paled. "This might take a while. Can I call my husband first? Nobody at the house knows what happened." Detective Rialto nodded, while I tried to mentally calculate how many months it would take Carla to put her list together. Many.

Taking a cell phone out of her purse, Carla didn't even glance at us as she walked to the back of the kitchen and out the French doors onto a deck. I zeroed in on her hand shaking slightly as she scrolled through her phone, probably looking for her husband's number.

"You need to mind your own business."

I pulled my mind back to the man sitting at the table with me, the one with no manners. "You're not very friendly," I said.

"It's not part of my job description to be friendly. What the hell are you doing here this morning?"

I was insulted he asked. Did he think I was heartless enough to ignore a friend's grief? "Bringing cookies, which is more than I can say for you."

"What do you mean?" he asked.

"The least you could have done was stopped and gotten some muffins or something. You don't show up empty-handed to see the relatives of someone who just died." What was with this guy, didn't he know anything? Detective Rialto opened his mouth, then closed it again. He almost looked like he didn't know what to say.

"Remember that for next time," I said. "And it doesn't have to be muffins or cookies. You can even stop and get a box of donuts or something." Reaching over and patting his hand, I hoped I'd made him feel better. Maybe it wasn't his fault he didn't know these things.

"I'm not going to bring donuts to a homicide investigation," he snarled.

I raised my eyebrows but didn't say anything. I didn't have to, because the whole cop and donut thing crossed his mind, too. I could tell by the flush creeping up his face.

"Listen, I'm only going to say this one more time. Mind your own business. This isn't like one of those books where you're going to figure out what happened. This is real life, and in real life people get hurt. Sometimes they get more than hurt. You need to stay out of our way and let us do our job or you'll be the one who gets hurt."

His reaction puzzled me. Sure, he didn't like me and probably didn't want me underfoot, but his words almost sounded like a threat. I added one more item to my mental checklist for this investigation. Could Detective Rialto know more about this murder than he was saying?

Maybe the good guy wasn't so good, after all.

Chapter Eighteen

SINCE IT WAS ALMOST LUNCH, and I was sort of halfway there anyway, I decided to drive to my parent's house for a visit. They loved it when I popped in on them, and like any good Irish-Italian-American household they always had good food. Besides, I was pretty sure I'd worn out my welcome with Detective Rialto, if I even had any sort of welcome in the first place. Sticking around to ask him more questions did not seem the prudent thing to do.

My parents lived on the very outer edge of Brewster Square in an old farmhouse that dated back to the 1800s. It was a traditional house, white with red shutters and a big wrap-around porch, with acres of land, several outbuildings full of assorted farm equipment, goats, cats and one dog. It may have had scuff marks on the hardwood floors and doors that didn't close all the way because the house was a little bit crooked on its foundation, but it was a warm home, full of sunlight, laughter, and the scent of good food.

They bought the house about five years ago, right after I got out of college. The house felt like a home, safe and comfortable. It might have been from the warm welcome they always had for anyone who visited, or maybe it was the love my parents had for their lives and each other that permeated everything around them. Whatever the reason, I loved being there.

My mother was leaning over the kitchen sink when I walked in, scrubbing with a ferocity. Dirt, smudges, and stains dared not adhere to the surface. Her glass fronted cabinets sparkled, the counters were junk-free and wiped clean, and I wondered not for the first time what my mother would do if I tried to eat off the floor. Because frankly, not only was it clean enough, but somebody ought to do it just because they could.

"Ava!" Her face lit up with a smile as she turned the faucet off and wiped her hands dry. Throwing her arms around me, she took a deep breath as if relieved I was finally home. "I heard what happened," she said, releasing me and stepping back to look me up and down. "Are you okay?"

I nodded, but my eyes filled with tears. My mother, the woman who is and always has been a constant source of comfort in my life, was the one person I could always count on to withhold judgment and let me simply be myself.

The sound of the back door slamming echoed through the kitchen. I heard my father's footsteps in the mudroom and quickly tried to dry my eyes. "This is too much for you," he announced as soon as he saw me. "Pack a bag and come stay in your room until this all blows over."

"For God's sake, Rourke, she's a grown woman, she's certainly capable of taking care of herself." My mother was right. Even if I'd felt like I needed to run home, there was no way I was going to do it now.

"She needs her parents at a time like this. My baby girl witnessed something horrific, and I want her to know she always has a place to come home to."

When my parents had moved to the farmhouse, they brought my and Giuseppe's old bedroom sets and made sure we each had a room to call our own. Everything was put in "our rooms" in the same way as it had been when we were kids so we wouldn't feel excluded from their new house. Sometimes their gesture touched me, but today, I just felt tired. Of course, I had a good reason for my exhaustion.

As I opened my mouth to ask how they knew about last night, a long, piercing wail came from the other side of the house. "I'll take care of that," my mother said. "Rourke, dear, why don't you fill Ava in on what we know. Maybe she's got more information to share with us."

As my mother bounced down the hallway toward the source of the screams, I turned to my father. "Danny's here?" I asked.

He nodded, a broad smile crossing his face. "Giuseppe dropped him off this morning. He went down for a morning nap and now it sounds like he's raring to go." The smile quickly fell from his face with his next words. "Both

Giuseppe and Janine told me what happened last night. And they've told me you're going to do some digging on your own."

I wondered if either of them had mentioned they had put me up to the digging, but I didn't ask. I didn't want to set my father off on another rant about coming home. "What did they tell you about last night?" I wondered how much my parents knew.

"They told me you were going on a ghost hunt in the old McAllister house, and you went into the basement and found Ethel dead at the bottom of the stairs." My father's gaze narrowed. "And, they told me you weren't very helpful to Oliver."

My brother is such a rat. I wondered when my parents had become friends with Detective Rialto, but before I could ask my mother came sailing into the room with baby Danny in her arms. "Would you like to hold your nephew?" She smiled at him and bounced him up and down. The child seemed to be in a better mood than he had been a minute earlier, but I knew what was going to happen.

"Um, maybe I'll hold him later," I said.

"Nonsense. Take the child so I can go get his food," my mother said, handing the kid to me and walking away. Sure enough, as soon as he was in my arms he looked up at me with adoring big brown eyes. He was a cutie, all right. Then he promptly threw up all over the front of my shirt.

"Oh dear," my mother said, coming back into the room. I wordlessly handed the child back to her and went to my brother's room where I knew there were still some old sweatshirts of his. I wasn't surprised the kid had vomited on me, I was surprised my mother hadn't seen it coming. The kid was a regular machine when it came to spewing his food.

After changing into an old, soft Yale hoodie and throwing my soiled shirt in the washer, I went back into the kitchen where my parents were talking. "I think the baby is better now," my mother said. "I don't know why he throws up so much, but at least it doesn't seem to bother him."

I didn't want to point out the obvious reasons, such as the fact that all babies threw up a lot, but baby Danny had it worse—Giuseppe insisted on feeding the kid some kind of awful organic food. Give the kid a hot dog, get rid of the rice milk, and I knew he'd be fine, but since I didn't have kids of my own I figured it was best to keep my mouth shut on this one.

Grabbing some grapes off the counter, I popped a few in my mouth and asked the question that had been nagging at me. "So, how do you guys know Detective Rialto?"

A look passed between my parents, and felt a flare of annoyance. I knew that look because I'd seen it my whole life, and it meant they knew things they were not going to discuss with me. "He's a very nice man, and I think we're lucky he decided to settle in our little town," my mother said.

"How do you know him?" I could be persistent even when I knew it wouldn't get me anywhere.

"It's a small town, Ava. We cross paths with everyone, eventually," my mother hedged. I suddenly felt like I was twelve years old again, trying to figure out what the grown-ups were talking about.

"He's a nice enough guy who is very qualified in law enforcement," my father said. "Let him do his job and everything will work out fine. Now, let's talk about someone else. Do you have anything else you want to tell us?"

It was only a matter of time before I killed my brother. Really, what was he thinking, telling my parents all about my business? I knew where this conversation was headed. But if our situations were reversed I would have done the same thing. In fact, I might have been a little bit worse when he started dating Janine.

"Your father and I like Stanley," my mother said. "It's about time you two planned a date. You've been circling each other for months now."

"Circling each other?" What did my mother think I was, a wolf?

She nodded, smiling. "He's a lovely man, and has such an interesting job as the mayor. I'm sure you'll have a good time with him."

"Take things slow," my father warned, frowning. It was such a typical father reaction that I had to laugh, and I hugged him.

"Don't worry, Dad, I'll make sure I'm home by curfew, and I won't leave my drink unattended." I reminded myself I was lucky to have a family who cared, and nosiness came with caring.

My father cleared his throat. "Now, what's all this about you doing some sort of looking into this situation with Ethel? Let the police handle things."

I shrugged. "Giuseppe and Janine are really worried, so I told them I would see what I could find out. I won't get into trouble, I'm just looking whatever the police might not have time to do." I was skating the edges of the truth with my statement, but I knew they would worry if I told them too much.

"You always used to read mysteries when you were a kid," my mother said.

She was right, but my mother didn't realize I still loved a good mystery. Some nights I stayed up until the early morning hours just to finish a book I'd started and see if I was correct in guessing whodunit.

I decided to change the direction of the conversation to see what they knew. "I'm sure this is hitting the two of you pretty hard," I said. "Haven't you known Ethel for like, forever?"

My father shook his head. "We grew up together. I still can't believe this kind of thing could happen here."

"Were you friends with her?" I asked. I knew the answer only because Ethel wasn't someone who was around much when I was growing up, and I knew who most of my parents' friends were.

"We used to be," my mother said. My surprise must have shown on my face, because my mother kept talking. "I know we weren't friends with her recently, but when we were in high school we knew her. Once upon a time she was a very different person."

I always wondered what had happened to make Ethel such an angry, bitter woman who plowed through life determined to make everyone conform to her personal set of rules and standards.

"So, what happened?" I asked.

My father shook his head and frowned. "A man."

"Who?"

"I thought you knew this," my mother said. "One day they were madly in love, then something happened and he married someone else after college."

"Who?" I repeated.

"It was Win," my father said. "I never did like that guy."

"You've always said that after the fact," my mother said. "You liked him well enough when we all went out together."

My father shook his head. "No, I never trusted him. He was a snake."

I couldn't imagine why my parents were talking as if I knew who they were talking about. I only knew one person named Win, and it couldn't possibly be him. "Who is this guy?" I asked.

My parents looked at me as if I'd grown another head.

"You know Win," my mother insisted. "Winthrop Thurgood, Fred's father. If all goes as Charlie plans, Win will be her father-in-law."

Chapter Nineteen

AS I WAS GETTING READY for my date with Stanley that night, I had trouble staying focused. My mind was buzzing with what my parents had shared. Fred's father, Win, had not only dated Ethel but allegedly carried on with her as if they had a future together.

Maybe he murdered Ethel, and he'll go to jail and leave Charlie alone, I thought, then felt bad. Negative thoughts about others never helped, but they were hard to avoid sometimes.

The thing is, I knew what had happened as soon as my parents started talking. They didn't really have to tell me, I figured it out from what I knew of Charlie's experience. Win might have loved Ethel madly, but in his heart he probably always knew they would never end up together. Ethel didn't have the money or social standing so important to Win's family, which meant he wasn't in it for the long haul with her.

I had trouble imagining Ethel as a fun, feisty girl in love. The woman I'd known was always no-nonsense, professional, and businesslike. She set her agenda for what she needed to get done and made sure it happened. Ethel was known for her pushy, abrasive manner, but honestly I think she just saw herself as a sort of champion for various causes. She was a rule follower, not a risk taker, and she lived her life within the boundaries of propriety.

I shook my head, disgusted with Win and with myself for wasting anger on him. I'd known for a while that he was not very nice by the way he treated Charlie, but this proved something beyond a shadow of a doubt: he'd always been a jerk.

And if he did have something to do with her murder, he would go to jail.

Except I suspected it would be different for a man as powerful as Winthrop Thurgood. He wouldn't have murdered Ethel, he'd have hired someone to do it, someone sleek and professional, someone who cost boatloads of money and had hidden bank accounts, someone who couldn't be traced.

But what about motive? According to my parents, after Win came home and broke Ethel's heart, they never spoke again. I hadn't heard this story before, and I always paid attention to gossip. It didn't make sense that Win would wake up one day and go crazy, having an ex-girlfriend murdered, the girl he'd been the one to dump as he climbed the social ladder of Connecticut society. Especially since it had been almost forty years since they'd dated.

I played with my hair, trying to decide if I should wear it up or down. I pinned the curls up with a barrette, then decided it looked messy and left it down. Rifling through my closet, I found a long gray skirt that went well with my short denim jacket. I liked to wear fun clothes, but, like Ethel, I followed the rules. Unlike Charlie, who laughed at me for my fashion do's and don'ts, I wore my outfits according to the season. I wouldn't be caught dead wearing white after Labor Day.

Stanley was prompt, arriving at exactly seven. He had on khakis and a button down shirt, and I had to stop myself from leaning into him to inhale his aftershave. I love the smell of aftershave on a man.

Aunt Marie and Aunt Claudia were standing outside the building, having an innocent conversation right on the front steps when I came downstairs. They didn't fool me for one second.

"What time are you going to have her home?" Aunt Claudia asked. Her question was immediately followed by Aunt Marie's comment. "Your coat won't be warm enough."

"I'll have her home at a reasonable time," Stanley said, flashing his dimple at my aunts. Spoken like a true politician, whether he meant to be or not. Offering his arm, he said, "Shall we?"

"Where are we going?" I asked.

"Where are you going?" Aunt Claudia said. "We need to know where you went in case we have to come looking for you." I kept my smile hidden at

Aunt Claudia's words. I knew she was looking out for me, and I was curious to see how Stanley handled the aunts.

"I thought we would have dinner and maybe a few drinks at the Lilac Inn. It's close enough for us to walk," Stanley said.

"All right, but be careful. There's a murderer running loose around here," Aunt Claudia said.

"Shush," Aunt Marie said. "Ava's waited a long time to go out with him, don't spoil it for her."

I ducked my head down, not sure if I was going to laugh or just be embarrassed. After reassuring the aunts we would be careful, we started walking down the street. A slight chill was in the air, but I ignored it and focused on staying close to Stanley.

The Lilac Inn Bed and Breakfast is located on the north side of the green, a quick walk around the square from where I lived. It was a gorgeous Victorian style home, painted in a variety of purple hues reminiscent of its name. The owners, John and Claire Murray, had inherited the house from John's parents. As long as anyone in Brewster Square could remember, the house had been either a boarding house or bed and breakfast. It might have a new coat of paint and a different name, but the intent was the same. Good food and a comfortable place to stay.

Saturday nights were generally crowded at the Lilac Inn restaurant. The chef had been written up in some tourist magazine as being an "undiscovered treasure", and since then people flocked from all over the state for the food. Stanley must have made reservations because John greeted us in the front entryway, grabbed some menus, and led us straight to a table. A few people were milling around or sitting on benches, obviously waiting for a table to open up.

The room had very low lighting, but each table had a candle, which had the effect of creating a soft glow in the dining area. There was a single yellow rose next to the candle, and classical music played in the background. It was the perfect setting for romance.

We had barely gotten into our seats when a rotund man whose neck seemed to be rolling out of his shirt stopped at our table. "Mr. Mayor, so good to see you tonight," he said, offering his hand to Stanley. "I have to say, that's some bit of news we've had, isn't it." He nodded a hello to me, and I tried to place him but couldn't. It didn't matter to him whether he knew me or not, though. "I voted for our fine mayor, here," he continued. "The name's Bob. Anyway, I'll let you folks get back to your dinner, I just wanted to stop over and say howdy." Nodding at me again, he started to walk away, then turned and smiled at me. "It's a good thing you have this man here to watch over you, young lady. Hopefully he'll be able to keep you safe and away from any trouble with a murderer running loose." Nodding once more, he left us in peace.

I'd barely had a minute to look over the menu when the next person came to our table. This time it was someone I knew. "Well hello, you two," said Jeanne Duchay. Jeanne and my mother had been friends for a long time, and she was one of the nicest women I knew. "Ava, dear, I heard it through the grapevine that you're asking questions about Ethel," she said. "Hopefully our steadfast mayor here can persuade you to leave it alone. This whole situation is terrible, but it's a police matter, dear."

I might have to amend my original thoughts on Jeanne. She might be nice, but she also had a pushy side to her I hadn't known about.

It went on like that all night. People stopped by our table as we were talking, ordering, and eating. I didn't dare hold Stanley's hand, knowing the whole town would be abuzz with the news and somebody would mention something about inappropriate behavior.

Sadly, although almost everyone had something to say about Ethel, most of it was not in the least complimentary. One woman went so far as to say, "It's not such a bad thing she died, is it? She was so mean, I'm sure she didn't have much in her life to be happy about." A slow simmer started inside me. I couldn't imagine where this attitude was coming from. Didn't anyone consider what would be said when they died?

As we were ending our dinner with a shared slice of cheesecake, I looked up to see Linwood and his wife walking over. Linwood's wife, Valerie, smiled down at us. "It's so lovely to see you both. I hope you're enjoying your evening."

I nodded. "The food is wonderful," I said. "Linwood, how are you tonight?"

Linwood looked at me, and I swear he looked right through me. His stare was vacant, and for a moment I wondered if he'd taken some sort of medication.

"Linwood, dear, don't you think it's lovely to see the mayor and Ava Maria out having dinner together?" Valerie said, winking at him.

He smiled at her, as if he'd suddenly woken. "Yes, yes it is dear. I think it's about time they went out on a proper date."

I sighed inwardly. *I love small town life.*

Placing a hand on her husband's arm, Valerie said, "We'll leave you to it, then. Enjoy yourselves." I stared after them as they walked away, wondering why Linwood had acted so weird. He'd been strange in the store yesterday, too. It was probably none of my business, but it sure made me curious.

"So long Mr. Mayor," Bob the ass called out in his booming voice as he walked to the door. "You've got my vote for the next election, plus you won't have to worry about any rule-following dames harassing people. Ding-dong the witch is dead, right?" With a bray of laughter, he left.

I couldn't move. Had I heard him correctly? I didn't think it was possible for someone to be so callous. "What is he talking about?" I asked.

With a sigh, Stanley pushed his glasses up. "In the election before I ran for mayor, Bob wasn't allowed to vote because he hadn't registered by the deadline. Ethel was working the voting booth and wouldn't let him in. I guess he never forgave her."

"But she was just doing her job," I said, upset that someone could have such an utter disregard for human life.

"I know, people can be harsh," Stanley said. "Let's try to ignore them for tonight."

But I couldn't. I couldn't ignore a blatant disregard for human life. And I knew, right then and there, that I would do what was right—to the best of my ability. This situation had taken on a whole new dimension. Nobody had an ounce of sympathy for Ethel, which meant the investigation into her death was going to be perfunctory at best. I couldn't let it go. This had nothing to do with Giuseppe or Janine or their concerns. Now it was about justice.

What kind of person would I be if I just let dead people stay dead without any hope of justice?

Chapter Twenty

THE SKY WAS CLEAR, AND we spent time looking up and pointing out
the constellations on our walk back. Stanley was much better at it than I was,
as the only one I recognized was Orion's Belt. It's hard to miss three stars in
a straight line.

We wandered over to the gazebo in the center of the green. I hesitated to sit
on the bench, because I knew the stone surface would be cold. Stanley took
his jacket off and laid it on the seat, gesturing toward it.

He was clearly trying to make this a romantic evening, and my stomach
did a little flip. I wasn't quite sure what a stomach-flip meant, so I ignored the
feeling and took the offered seat. "I'm having fun," Stanley said.

"Me too," I said. My mind was racing, trying to come up with something
interesting to talk about. I didn't want him to think I was boring, or tell me it
was time for him to bring me home.

"Ava, I think we should talk about us," he said. Us? I didn't realize there
was an us, but if he wanted to talk about it I should probably listen. I thought
we'd already covered this at my apartment, but I decided to listen to what he
had to say.

"We've known each other for a few years now," he began, and my mind
immediately wandered as I thought about when I'd first seen him. We were
in the grocery store, and he'd been standing in the bakery aisle, staring at

boxes of cake mix. He seemed so lost, but I wasn't sure if I should talk to him or not so I just hovered nearby in case he needed advice on the benefits of lemon cake versus red velvet (lemon every time, no contest).

"Linwood had a point," he continued. "It's about time we finally went on a date, but it's important to me that we do this right."

"Do you think we're going to do it wrong?" I asked. I wasn't really sure what we were talking about anymore.

He smiled at me. "No—sorry, I wasn't clear. I want to make sure we take our time getting to know each other, take things slow. There's no reason to rush our relationship, right?"

I was confused. Earlier, he'd been all prickly about Kenny showing up at my apartment. Now he wanted to take it slow. In my mind, when guys gave you a line like this they wanted to date other women. "Do you want to date other people at the same time?" I asked. Hadn't he just asked me about this very thing last night?

He hesitated, as if I'd caught him by surprise. "I suppose that's part of taking it slow, isn't it?"

Sitting on his jacket on the bench, I wrapped my arms around myself, wondering what came next. I liked Stanley, I thought he was sweet and funny and charming, but I was fine with taking things slow, too. I just wanted to make sure it was all spelled out and clear between us. "So, you wouldn't mind if I went on a date with someone else?" I asked.

"If you want to date other people, that's okay with me." I didn't believe him, but I wasn't about to challenge him on it. I had no intention of dating other people, but I could date Stanley and see how the relationship progressed. At some point we'd have to have another talk, but for now we could have a casual dating thing.

"Okay," I said.

"Okay?"

"Yeah, okay."

"So, you're going to date other people?" he said.

I shrugged. "Probably not, but we're taking it slow, so we could leave it as an option for either one of us."

Stanley looked solemn. "Okay, but there's one other thing." He sat next to me and moved closer. Wrapping his arms around me, he leaned in to kiss me. I had a moment of panic, hoping my breath wasn't bad from dinner and not being sure what to do with my arms and hands, but within seconds my anxiety dissipated. All I knew was Stanley was kissing me, and I really, really liked it.

When he stopped, I leaned back and looked at him. "I liked that."

"Me too," he said.

We sat in silence for a minute, a comfortable silence where we leaned against each other and he held my hand. "What are you afraid of?" I asked.

"Getting hurt."

"Isn't that the chance we take every day when we get out of bed?"

"I'm not sure I know what you mean," he said.

"Everyone's worried about getting hurt," I said. "The thing is, it's going to happen. It happens in little ways all the time. Our friends hurt us by their casual sarcasm, or someone we respect doesn't pay any attention to us. Then there's the big stuff, when someone we love gets sick or dies." Stanley's eyes had a guarded look, making me wonder what had happened to him.

"I haven't been what you'd call lucky when it comes to girlfriends," he said.

"Good," I answered.

He looked at me with surprise. "That's not very nice."

"Sure it is. If you'd been lucky with girlfriends, I wouldn't be sitting here with you right now because you'd be out shopping for new kitchen cabinets or something with her."

He laughed, the first real laugh I'd heard from him all night. "True. And it wouldn't matter what my opinion was, because we'd only end up getting what she wanted anyway."

"And she's probably going to pick something ugly and it won't match the rest of the kitchen, so you'll have to do a total remodel." I shook my head. "Looks like you dodged a serious bullet on this one."

Smiling at me, he said, "You have no idea."

We sat again in companionable silence, while my mind wandered back to the immediate problem of murder. Maybe being on a date and thinking about something as gruesome as killing was odd, but I couldn't help it. Not for the first time I wondered if I should mind my own business, but then I remembered my reasons for wanting to get at the truth. "Stanley, I've got to ask you something. I know you said you can't help me with anything to do with Ethel, but I was wondering about Detective Rialto."

He looked at me and raised one eyebrow. "So we like the detective, do we?"

I smacked him in the arm. "No, this is a serious question." I was glad the dark night hid my blush. I didn't want him to get the wrong idea. "What do you know about him?"

"I know he's a good detective, and he used to work with the DEA," he said.

"The Drug Enforcement Agency?" If that was true, and I had no reason to believe it wasn't, then Detective Rialto had made a huge change in his life. People don't usually go from big time federal agencies to small town law enforcement, not without a good reason. I had a feeling Stanley knew the reason. "Why would he come to this little town?"

Stanley sighed and ran his hand through his hair, causing it to stick up a little. I was starting to recognize this gesture as an indication of his stress. It took him a few seconds to answer. "Ava, I can't really tell you anything else. The thing is, it's not my story to tell, it's Oliver's. I'm sorry."

A deep regret was in his voice, and I had a momentary pang of conscience for putting Stanley in an awkward position. I opened my mouth to tell him not to worry about it but didn't get one word out. A sharp voice cut across the night, interrupting me and whatever remnants of a date I might have had left.

"You know what, O'Dell?" the voice said. "I am seriously thinking of arresting you. Right now."

Chapter Twenty-One

KISSING SOMEONE IN PUBLIC IS not illegal, and neither is sitting in the gazebo at night. I was furious. "What the heck are you going to arrest me for? Sitting on a bench?"

Oliver Rialto put his hands on his hips and tilted his chin at me. "I'm going to arrest you for interfering with an investigation. That's a crime."

"I have done no such thing." This man was not going to get away with making ludicrous accusations. I hadn't even gotten around to interfering yet.

"How come every time I turn around you're there? Why were you at the police station this morning? And what were you doing at Ethel's house earlier? And what are these rumors I'm hearing about you?"

"Wait a minute, how did you know I was at the police station this morning?" I asked.

Oliver rolled his eyes. "I'm a detective, it's my job to know things. Unlike some people who make assumptions based on half-baked theories of what they think they've seen, I carefully review the evidence before I can make a determination."

A couple of thoughts flew through my head. "Rob told you he'd seen me this morning," I said. I'd have to have a talk with my friend and let him know I wasn't interfering in anything before I did any more snooping.

Stanley stood, positioning himself between the two of us. "What's going on, Oliver?" he asked.

Oliver shook his head and pointed a finger at me. "I am well within my rights to arrest that woman. It is a crime in the state of Connecticut to intentionally impede an investigation."

"You know Ava means no harm, and I'm sure she'd be willing to listen to your suggestions," Stanley said.

Like hell I would. Who did this guy think he was, coming over here and ruining my date while threatening to throw me in jail? Just as I opened my mouth to yell at the fine detective, Stanley shot me a look that begged me to stay silent. Snapping my jaw shut, I crossed my arms over my chest and waited to see what would happen next.

"Oliver, why don't you tell me what's really going on?" Stanley's voice was low and soothing, and I could feel the hypnotic effect working on me, too.

Cracking his knuckles, Oliver turned around for a moment and took a breath before speaking. "I'm sorry. I'm frustrated by this case, and I don't have the kinds of resources I need. I've been getting conflicting information, but I shouldn't have taken it out on you. I'm not used to small towns."

Looking at the detective's obvious unease, I felt somewhat mollified, but my hackles weren't completely down. For all I knew this was some kind of trick to get me to trust him.

"Why don't we go somewhere we can all talk?" Stanley suggested.

My head whipped back toward Stanley. What the heck was he talking about? He wanted to interrupt our date so we could chat with this guy? The night air held a chill I hadn't felt earlier. As if reading my mind, Stanley moved closer to me. "There's obviously something going on, don't you want to know what it is?" he asked me in a low voice.

I nodded. It made sense to listen to Oliver, even if I didn't want to. "Let's go get a hot chocolate, I'm cold," I said. I turned and began walking across the green, not waiting to see if they'd follow.

Stanley hurried to catch up to me. "Where are you going?" he asked.

"Big Beans," I said. "It's the closest."

Oliver looked puzzled. "I thought that place was owned by Kenny. I heard the two of you—"

"Do you know Kenny?" I interrupted.

A ghost of a smile played across Oliver's face. "I know Kenny."

"Everyone knows Kenny. But like I said, his place is the closest, and I'm cold."

After agreeing not to mention our evening trip to my brother, we trooped over to the coffee shop. Big Beans was a funky sort of place, displaying colorful artwork and hosting acoustic musicians most nights. The walls were painted in deep blues and greens, which set off the bold art in an unexpected way.

This was my first true glimpse of Stanley as a politician. He was walking a thin line by having coffee with me and the detective, but I knew he was doing it for me.

Once we got our drinks, we found a table in the back corner and sat in silence for a moment. The usual crew of younger kids and twenty-somethings were in there with their laptops, drinking black coffee and sauntering out the back door to smoke clove cigarettes. It might look like these kids had no money from the way they dressed, but the sheer volume of electronics they carried told a different story. "Why don't you tell us what's on your mind?" Stanley said, stirring his coffee.

"And why you feel the need to arrest an innocent woman," I added. Stanley shot me another look, but I ignored him. I wasn't about to sit passively while the men around me took care of things. Plus, Stanley wasn't the one Oliver threatened to send to the big house, so he wouldn't understand my frustration.

Oliver stared at me over his cappuccino. "I'm not so convinced of your innocence."

"I had nothing to do with her death," I sputtered.

"I know," Oliver said.

"Then what are you accusing Ava of?" Stanley asked.

"I don't think Ava had anything to do with her death, but I do think she's poking her nose in where she shouldn't," Oliver said.

I sat in silence. Although I hadn't done anything wrong, yet, I knew I should keep my mouth shut. "Where are you with the investigation?" Stanley asked.

"I don't think I should talk about it," Oliver said.

"As the mayor of this town, I think the people have a right to know if there's a murderer stalking others. Should we be worried?"

Oliver sighed. "I don't think anyone is in any danger."

Stanley's demeanor was calm, but his voice held a hint of steel. "Can you tell me that with absolute certainty?"

Oliver shook his head. "Not one hundred percent, no."

"Then why don't you tell me where you and the others are in your investigation," Stanley said. This was a side of Stanley I'd never seen before, a confident, self-assured man who was used to people following his orders.

Oliver looked at me. "I'm not sure I should be talking about this in front of a civilian."

I did my best to stay calm. I knew he wanted me to react to give him an excuse not to tell Stanley anything, and I wasn't about to play into that. "Ava won't tell anyone what we talk about," Stanley said. "And this is something you need to tell me sooner or later anyway."

"Fine, but let it be known I am only talking about this with you because you're the mayor," Oliver said. "And for the record, I still don't think she should be here."

"Duly noted," Stanley said.

"So far, what we've got is a big, fat nothing."

Stanley and I waited for Oliver to say more but instead he focused on the drink in front of him. "You're positive it was murder," Stanley prompted.

"Yeah, we think she was killed from blunt force trauma to the head based on what we can see, but we don't have the final ME report, we have no murder weapon, no witnesses, and no evidence. We've got nothing but a bunch of stories about how everyone in town hated this woman, which means our suspect list is about as thick as the phone book."

I felt bad for Oliver. He was new in town, and I could see this wasn't the easiest case to start off with before really getting to know everyone. "I haven't heard anything, either," I said.

"Is that supposed to reassure me?" he asked.

"No, detective, it's supposed to let you know I'm on your side and if I knew something I would tell you." Really, what did I do to deserve that attitude?

"Would you tell me, or are you so caught up in playing Nancy Drew that you'd try to solve it yourself?" he asked.

Stanley put his hands out and said, "Okay, I don't think you're being fair to Ava. Like she said, she hasn't done anything wrong."

"Then what was she doing at the house of the deceased today?" Oliver asked.

Stanley looked at me. "I was bringing food to the family," I said.

"Perhaps you're not aware of it, but food plays a very large part of everything we do in this town," Stanley said. "We bring each other food for holidays, birthdays, weddings, births, and deaths. We take our food very seriously here."

"Then why is she the only one who showed up?" Oliver said.

"How do you know I'm the only one?" I said. This guy was really starting to get on my nerves. "Have you staked out the house to see who else brought cookies over? Maybe everyone else got there after you left today."

"True," he admitted. "I didn't stay, so more people might have shown up, but I was there for several hours."

"Didn't you have someone monitoring who visited?" I asked. "Isn't it possible the murderer came over to see what was happening?"

Oliver nodded. "It's possible, but we don't have the resources right now to post someone at the house all the time. I've arranged for increased patrols in the area, but that's the best I could do." Taking one big gulp from his coffee cup, he stood. "There is nothing else to share with you, Mr. Mayor. I've got an early morning tomorrow, so I'll be heading out."

Maybe it was my upbringing, or my inborn desire to please. "If I hear anything, I'll let you know," I offered.

Pushing in his chair, Oliver looked straight at me. "Please don't play detective."

"I'm not." My protest sounded weak even to my ears.

"And regarding your assumption about my wife," Oliver said, still looking at me. "I'm not divorced and I'm not widowed. She's missing. My wife's been missing for five years."

Chapter Twenty-Two

CRAP. MISSING FOR FIVE YEARS? How was I supposed to know? Obviously I'd missed a clue or two. A number of images flashed through my mind, none of them good. "I'm sorry," I said, not sure if there was anything else I could possibly say. But by the time "sorry" was out of my mouth, Oliver was out the door.

He didn't even finish his drink.

"Now do you know what I meant when I said it was his story?" Stanley said.

I nodded, but I still didn't really understand. What happened? Why? Did this happen in Arizona or somewhere else? I knew I wasn't going to get any more information and I'd have to settle for knowing that little bit right now. I'd dig out the truth some other way. "Maybe we should invite him over for dinner," I said. *Were they deeply in love or already on the brink of divorce?* I couldn't stop the questions in my mind.

"Maybe we should let the Detective live his life without any interference from us," Stanley said. "I know you mean well, but let's not go poking into a raw wound."

"Inviting him to dinner is not poking into a—how do you know it's a raw wound?" I said. The expression on Stanley's face spoke volumes. I'd asked enough questions, and the flow of information stopped here.

"Okay," I conceded. "I don't have to know all the details. But it's a sad story, and we should act neighborly and feed him."

"There are some things food won't solve," Stanley said. "But I like that you want to help others. The thing is, not everyone wants to be helped."

My purse started making a light, ethereal noise, almost like wind chimes. Digging through the mess of receipts and debris stored in there, I managed to find my cell phone and pull it out. "It's my brother," I told Stanley.

"You should answer, it might be important," he said.

Putting the phone to my ear, I said, "I hope this is important."

"It is," my brother reassured me. "Are you with the mayor?"

"Yes, we're on a date." I smiled at Stanley.

"Good, bring him with you."

"What? No. Now? Bring him where?" My brother's sense of drama always had poor timing.

"I've planned our next move in finding Ethel's killer," Giuseppe said. "I need to tell you both what we're going to do." It was never a good sign when Giuseppe used the word "we".

"He wants to tell us how 'we' are going to capture Ethel's killer," I said to Stanley, who was looking at me with an amused expression.

"Let's go," Stanley said. "Sounds like something we need to hear, doesn't it?"

I wasn't sure I agreed with Stanley, but I felt like I had no choice. "We'll be there soon," I said into the phone, hoping my brother realized I was annoyed with him. Couldn't this have waited at least until tomorrow? How was I supposed to have a proper date with Giuseppe interrupting?

"I don't think we should tell your brother where we were when he called," Stanley said.

Oh boy, Giuseppe's reaction would be priceless. And not in a good way. "You're right," I said. "He'll be upset, but he won't yell or anything. He'll just make me feel like dirt about being here."

Stanley laughed, surprising me. "What's so funny?" I asked.

"Families," he said. "There are so many intricacies in our relationships with our families it's hard to keep track of it all sometimes."

"Is your family drama prone also?"

Stanley nodded. "Not in the same way, though. The drama is a little different."

"In what way?" I was intrigued. I'd never heard Stanley talk about his family before. Putting our coats on, he left a tip on the table and placed his hand on the small of my back as we left. He hesitated for a long while before he answered me.

"My family has a way of being understated in their drama," he said.

"Then it's not really drama, is it?"

He shook his head. "You would think so, but in this case the understated can be deadly."

"I'm not sure I follow what you're saying."

He shrugged. "Once, my sister dated someone my parents didn't approve of. They never said it outright to her, but they made sure she knew she wasn't welcome at family events if she brought him along. It got pretty stressful."

Ouch. That sounded like downright bullying, never mind drama. I kept my mouth shut, though. After all, this was his family and I hadn't actually met them yet. Maybe they weren't all bad. Plus, my own parents had dealt with a similar sort of situation, and they had worked out fine in the end. Somehow people manage to find their way, and I hoped his sister had enough chutzpah to follow her heart.

Our walk across the town green was quick, as both of us were anxious to hear what Giuseppe had to say. Even though Stanley hadn't said it outright, I sensed Ethel's death bothered him more than he was letting on. "About Ethel," I began, then stopped. I wasn't exactly sure how to phrase my question.

"Just spit it out," Stanley said.

"Does her death bother you?"

"Of course," he said.

"Does it bother you more than other deaths have bothered you?"

Stanley nodded. "Yeah, it does. Ethel died in this town, and even though I had nothing to do with her death and I'm not a detective or anything... she was a citizen of Brewster Square who met with a bad ending. I'm in charge of this town, and it happened on my watch. I wonder if there's some sort of criminal element here, or something I could have done as leader—maybe the outcome would have been different."

We were quiet for a moment, with only the sound of our steps crunching on the half frozen grass beneath us. Stanley's hands were stuffed deep in his coat pockets and his shoulders were hunched up around his neck; I wondered if he even noticed the bitter wind now cutting through the buildings and slicing into us.

"I don't think I realized how seriously I would take this job," he continued. "Sure, I got into it for only one reason, but once I was elected I realized that people trusted me to guide the town and make sure everything ran smoothly. Town employees, citizens, all these people count on me to do it right. So yes, losing Ethel is personal to me."

"It's not your fault," I whispered, knowing the words didn't matter.

Stanley gave me a wistful look. "If only our emotions were logical," he said.

We had reached my brother's house by then. A small glow from inside Scentsations lit part of the store, and we walked around back where an outside light provided ample illumination for us and any airplane that might want to land.

"Kind of bright back here," Stanley commented.

"My brother is big on security," I said. I climbed the back staircase to the second floor with Stanley following and knocked on the door at the top of the stairs. It was old and blue and badly in need of painting, and I made a mental note as I always did that I was going to show up one day with a paintbrush and a can of paint to take care of this for him.

Clutching baby Danny in one hand, Giuseppe swung the door wide. "Come in, come in, I have to tell you what we're going to do."

I stepped inside, feeling a blast of heat. Janine hated the cold, and from September through April their home felt like south Florida. I took my coat off as quickly as possible, knowing it wouldn't be long before I started to sweat. The kitchen was old, with daisies on the yellow linoleum and a refrigerator that had seen better days, but it was sparkling clean. The smell of something baked hung in the air, and my mouth started to water when I realized Janine had probably made some sort of pie.

Janine made awesome pie. As I was draping my coat over the back of the kitchen chair Giuseppe started to speak, and I tried not to think about what Janine had baked. "I know how we're going to catch Ethel's killer." If I didn't know better, I might think my brother was excited about this.

"We're listening," Stanley said.

I silently gave thanks to whatever or whoever controlled the Universe for sending Stanley into my life. He was patient and kind, and I was falling hard for him.

Giuseppe smiled at me. "I thought about the best way to get information, then I realized we should do what we know best." So far, this was not sounding good. What the heck do we know best that could help anyone with anything? We knew how to cook pretty well, but I was fairly certain a platter of lasagna wasn't going to lure the killer out of hiding. Unless he was hungry.

Giuseppe ignored my raised eyebrows and kept talking. "We're going to do a ghost hunt at Ethel's house. Monday night, so be ready."

"But I have to work on Tuesday," I couldn't stop the whine from creeping into my voice. "Ghost hunts last all night."

"I want to get this done before the funeral," Giuseppe said.

"Why?" Stanley asked. I looked at the ceiling, knowing the response wouldn't really give us an answer.

"Once a funeral is performed, it might allow the spirit to be at rest and move on. We want to catch Ethel before she leaves so she can give us a clue about what happened." Silence hovered in the room, with the only sound coming from the clock ticking on the kitchen wall. I didn't know what to say to my brother that wouldn't sound condescending and sarcastic, so I kept my mouth shut. Stanley did the same thing.

"We don't know when the family will be able to have the funeral, so we thought we should get this done as soon as possible," Janine said. She bustled around the kitchen, wiping counters that already looked sparkling clean to me. Janine had a bit of a thing about keeping her house clean, which I guess worked out well for my brother. Plus, I suspected she was one of those women who cleaned when she got nervous. Right now the house was immaculate.

"Wait a minute," I said. "On a ghost hunt we just try to prove or disprove the existence of ghosts. You're talking about something else, aren't you?"

Giuseppe had the grace to look uncomfortable. "Does it really matter what we call it?"

Heck yes, it mattered. Because I knew exactly what my brother was talking about.

Chapter Twenty-Three

"**NO. I WANT YOU TO** think back to how we got into this mess in the first place," I said. "I hate to state the obvious, but the original ghost hunt is why we found her body." I shivered as an image of Ethel, dead, flashed through my mind.

"I got permission from Carla, she said it will be fine," Giuseppe said. "She'd like to see some closure on this, you know."

I stopped the stinging retort from leaving my mouth. I wanted to shout at my brother, demanding to know how a ghost hunt with a bunch of out-of-touch wannabe psychics was going to help anyone. But the thing is, and I knew this from experience, we can never really tell how our actions might help someone. Perhaps Carla would find some comfort in thinking about her aunt living in another form, crossing over into the great beyond after telling us what happened.

Most likely everyone would get a little hysterical and think they saw something, which would turn out to be nothing, leaving Carla and the family more confused than ever. But who was I to withhold comfort from the bereaved?

Except for one little thing. "It's not a ghost hunt, is it?" I asked. "If you think the spirit will be laid to rest soon, and you want to talk to her, it's more of a séance. And a séance summons the dead." I crossed my arms over my chest. "You want to actually see if she'll respond to your request and tell us who killed her." Did my brother think I was an idiot? I did not want to summon spirits from the dead. It was bad enough on the nights I had to go with him to check to see if they were hanging around, why would I want to converse with them?

"It's kind of a two part thing," Giuseppe said. "We'll use our equipment to hunt first, then if that doesn't work we'll summon."

"I'm not really getting what the difference is," Stanley said.

"Oh, it's quite a difference," I told him. "Ghost hunting is just sort of poking around, seeing what's in the kitchen. A séance wakes them all up, rouses them from wherever they are."

"Sounds... interesting," Stanley said. "Sorry I'll miss it." Was he serious? Stanley wasn't going to be by my side for this harebrained adventure my brother was dragging me into? "I have a town council meeting, and I have to be there," he explained. I suppose he had a viable excuse, but I didn't like it. I kind of wanted him around for protection, but I wasn't sure what I needed to be protected from.

"Maybe you can come to the house when the meeting is over," I said, hopeful he could make it.

"Nope, sorry, can't allow that," Giuseppe said.

"Why?" Stanley and I spoke at the same time.

"If we're in the middle of contacting someone from the spirit world I can't have the doorbell ringing," Giuseppe said.

"So he'll just come in. He won't make any noise," I said.

"No, Ava, that won't work. We must create an atmosphere where Ethel feels safe enough to communicate with us. She's been through a trauma, it won't be easy to get her to talk."

I held back a snort, but only because Stanley was there and it wouldn't be ladylike. My brother kept talking, oblivious to the death daggers shooting from my eyes. Have I mentioned I hate séances?

"If he walks into the middle of what we're trying to accomplish he might inadvertently chase her away." He shrugged. "Sorry, sis, but we can't take the chance."

"Why do I have to be there?" I asked.

Giuseppe stared at me as if I'd grown another nose. "You found her, you're the key to all this. Besides, as lead investigator in this whole thing, you're going to want to know if we collect any evidence."

"I think the police would see it differently," Stanley offered.

Giuseppe waved a hand at us. "They're not really getting anywhere, are they? She's my only hope."

Great, me and a séance. I was fairly certain they didn't offer Communicating with the Dead classes at the police academy, so now I had to shoulder that burden. Janine, still furiously scrubbing the stove, hadn't said a word. "Janine, what do you think?" I asked. Maybe my sister-in-law could talk some sense into my brother, because I sure as hell wasn't having any luck.

Janine jumped a little, but didn't let go of her hold on the paper towel and spray bottle. "I don't want to get involved in this. I hate séances," she said.

"Janine isn't going, she doesn't like this kind of thing," Giuseppe added, just in case I didn't understand what his wife just said.

Some things weren't fair. "I don't like them either," I said.

"But you're the lead investigator," Giuseppe said, as if saying it changed everything. I suppose love really does conquer all, because I was the one stuck having to do some dopey, scary-as-all-heck event, while the woman he loved got to stay home. Of course, odds were she'd stay home and clean, but still.

"I'm only trying to do what's right for my family," Giuseppe said. If he meant to be reassuring, he failed. I was not reassured. I tried to rationalize my feelings, knowing they were ridiculous. What could really happen? It's not like I expected some demonic force to be unleashed upon me and swallow me into the bowels of hell. I shivered. That's exactly what I expected to happen.

I took a breath. It was time to get a grip. The worst thing that could happen would be I got tired and ended up cranky the next day. Giuseppe was still talking. "This is an important night, and I'd like to get it done before the killer figures out what we know."

Chapter Twenty-Four

WAIT A MINUTE, WHAT THE *heck do we know?* I wasn't aware of any special knowledge we had about this murder, and if we had it why weren't we telling the police? Seeing my confusion, Giuseppe answered my question before I could ask. "Remember, everyone knows I'm in touch with the spirit world. Sooner or later the killer is going to realize our methodology."

"That doesn't make any sense," I said. Stanley quietly moved to the kitchen table and sat down. He must have figured it would be a long night, and not in the way he had planned.

Even though it probably didn't matter, I wasn't going to let my brother get away with this twisted logic. "According to your logic, the murderer would be after Kenny, too." You'd think I'd said something nice about Pol Pot. Giuseppe's face twisted into a sneer, and even Janine paused in her cleaning to shoot me a look of disbelief.

"Maybe Kenny doesn't have the talent your brother has," Stanley suggested.

"Kenny doesn't have any talent," Giuseppe said. "Everyone knows that. He's a fraud." I wasn't sure how you could tell who was a fraud and who wasn't when you couldn't even tell what was real and what wasn't, but maybe it was better to keep my mouth shut.

"Stanley, would you like some pie?" Janine asked. I knew he was getting the goods because he'd just complimented her husband. Recognition of my brother's talents went a long way with Janine.

"No, thanks, we just had dinner," Stanley said.

"Well, here, have some soda instead," Janine said. "I got these littly bitty bottles because they're so cute, and because sometimes you just want a little bit of soda." It was better to just go with what Janine said, even if it didn't make sense. I also knew my sister-in-law wouldn't allow Stanley to get out of there without eating or drinking something.

I looked at my brother and waited. I knew that look he had on his face: he was considering something big. It was the same look he always got right before he had an idea I would try to talk him out of. "Everyone knows I don't like Kenny much," Giuseppe said. "Never have, never will." A true statement, but I waited. There was more.

"But putting my distaste for the man aside, I think we should consider the possibility that Kenny may be the murderer."

Wait—what? "G, are you serious? What makes you think Kenny either has the strength or the motivation to actually kill someone?"

Giuseppe counted on his fingers. "First, Kenny didn't like Ethel."

"Nobody liked Ethel," I said. Those words were starting to sound old even to my own ears.

The second finger came up. "Second, why did he come to the store the day of the murder and try to get in on the ghost hunt?"

"Because for some odd reason he wants to do what you're doing," I said.

"And third, it would be perfect PR for him to solve this murder based on receiving messages from the dead. His business would explode from all the calls he'd get."

My head was about to explode from what I was hearing. "You are out of your mind. Do you really think Kenny would murder someone just to drum up business?"

My brother had the grace to at least squirm a little. "I'm sure he didn't think it through," Giuseppe said. "But this is something we're going to have to consider. I believe he's capable of all sorts of things, he just hasn't been caught yet."

I hated having to defend Kenny, of all people, but I had to say something. "No, on this you are wrong, completely wrong. Kenny did not kill Ethel, period. Your reasoning is flawed, and frankly, if he hears you running around town saying stuff like that Kenny's likely to sue you."

"That's true, sweetie," Janine said. "A lawsuit is right up Kenny's alley."

"But he asked to join us –"

"I'm going to have to agree with Ava on this one," Stanley said. "It doesn't make sense for him to start killing. He never exhibited any violent behavior before, right?"

Giuseppe and I looked at each other, and I knew what he was thinking. He was remembering all those childhood incidents where Kenny's cruelties ripped the fabric of our young existence. He was a typical schoolyard bully, always taunting, always getting others to join in making fun of whoever his target was for the day. Or in my brothers case, for Giuseppe's entire education at public school. Or most of it.

But could a childhood bully progress to murder? How does someone go from playground insults to taking a life? I shuddered, knowing full well it was possible. I just didn't think it was possible in Kenny's case.

"And you need to be careful of that detective, too," Giuseppe said.

I didn't even have to ask who he was talking about. "Please don't tell me you think he's a suspect," I said.

"No, I don't think he's a suspect, but I do think he has a dark and tortured past. And you, my sister, like to heal the wounded, so you need to stay away from him. He can heal just fine all by himself."

"What do you mean I like to heal the wounded?" I wasn't sure if that was an insult or not.

"I mean you are a kind and giving person, and every time you meet someone who is struggling with loss or getting bullied or anything along those lines you respond by becoming emotionally available to them," he said. "Then you confuse your feelings of wanting to help with feelings of attraction."

Thanks, G, I thought. *My date is going just fine, thanks for helping with your lame-brained ideas.* "No worries, he is truly not my type," I said, glancing at Stanley.

"I don't want to see you get hurt, emotionally or physically. Investigations can be dangerous. What are you doing to protect yourself?" my brother asked.

"What do you mean?" I said.

"He's right." Stanley said. "If Kenny is the killer," seeing the look on my face, he was quick to add, "I'm not saying he is, but if there's even a remote possibility, you need to take steps to protect yourself more than ever. He knows where you live and he knows where you work."

I didn't even try to suppress the big dramatic sigh I'd been holding back since this conversation started. At least Stanley had the common sense not to comment on what my brother had said about the detective. "Okay, for the sake of argument, let's pretend Kenny is the killer. Can anyone enlighten us as to why he would bother to come after me, too?"

"Maybe he's escalating," Giuseppe said.

"For cryin' out loud, he's not escalating. Never mind, can we drop this conversation?" I said.

"We need to find out how she died, so we can start to put together a better profile of the killer," Giuseppe said.

"First of all, you need to stop watching so much television. Nobody here knows how to do a profile or figure out if a push down the stairs indicates the killer is a forty year old schoolteacher because who else could it be. Second of all..." I stopped because I realized I had no second of all. Giuseppe was right, we didn't really know how Ethel was killed.

An image of the body and the blood rose in my mind. I pulled my cell phone out and started digging through my purse. "What are you doing?" Giuseppe asked.

"Shut up," I said, but nicely. Siblings can do that. I found the card I was looking for, and dialed the number. The voice that answered sounded suspicious, and rightly so.

"It's me, Ava. Ava Maria Sophia Cecilia O'Dell." Just in case he knew anyone else with a name like mine. And probably because I was a little bit nervous. I wanted to sound confident, but I wasn't sure he'd answer my question. "I wanted to ask you something."

There was a silence on the other end, so I waited, wondering if he was going to hang up. "Spit it out, girl, I don't have all night. I have an investigation to run," Detective Rialto said.

I swallowed past a lump in my throat, and tried to project a sense of poise and self-assurance. "I was wondering when you'll have the results of Ethel's cause of death," I said, hoping I wasn't speaking too quickly.

"As a matter of fact, I received them tonight right after I left you." There was another brief silence, followed by the sound of shuffling papers and coughing. "Okay, Ava Maria Sophia Cecilia, I suppose you want to know the details."

I held my breath and considered it a good omen that he remembered my entire name. No easy feat for some in this town. "I think it might make us all feel better if we knew." It was the best I could come up with to steer him away from my private investigation.

There was another pause before he spoke. "Okay Miss Nosey Pants, I might as well tell you. You'll probably read about it in the paper tomorrow, anyway. But I have one stipulation."

Uh-oh. Stipulations were never good.

"I want to tell you face-to-face. There's something else I want to talk to you about."

Chapter Twenty-Five

OLIVER WAS WAITING FOR ME inside the front foyer of my apartment building, happily munching a chocolate biscotti my aunt must have given him. My aunt makes the best biscotti, so even though I wasn't really hungry my stomach sort of flipped. I was sure it had to do with the biscotti and not the fact that I was worried about why he wanted to see me.

His name is Detective Rialto. Do not call him Oliver, he's not your friend. He's law enforcement, and he's here to do a job.

Stanley had not been happy about leaving me to meet with the detective alone, but I could tell he didn't want to come across as overbearing. We parted at the front of Scentsations, with him giving me one more kiss. "Call me if you need anything," he said, pushing his glasses up his nose. "I'm here for you."

Stanley was sweet, and his kiss left me slightly breathless. But right now I had to put his kiss out of my mind and focus on business. I was going to hear what the detective wanted to talk to me about and hope it was something along the lines of, "We've caught the killer, your insights were so helpful." I knew better, but I could still hope. I was still learning how to investigate this type of situation. Maybe later I'd see what I could find online about becoming a private investigator.

"So, you found the place," I said. I wondered if he'd checked to see if I had a record or not, or if he ran a background report on me.

Detective Rialto gestured to the staircase. "Lead the way."

I hesitated, wondering at the wisdom of allowing this man into my personal space. Was he going to yell at me again? "Can't we talk here?" I asked, pointing to the ground.

"On the floor?"

"No, here in the foyer." Letting him come up to my apartment felt personal, almost too personal.

"What I have to discuss with you is private," he said. "It would be better if we spoke where there was no possibility of being overheard." His eyes wandered to the door of my aunt's apartment, and I knew, as I'm sure he knew, that she was listening. "I'm not a bad person, you know," he said in a quiet voice.

"I know," I scoffed. Despite my initial disdain of the man, I was sure he must have some redeeming qualities. And even though he could arrest me whenever he wanted, I wasn't afraid of him. "I'm upstairs. C'mon."

As we walked upstairs I tried to refrain from counting the steps out loud. It was important to remain professional in these situations. Once inside my place, I threw my keys on the counter and turned to him. "So, tell me about Ethel." The direct approach was always best.

"Like I said, you're going to read this in the newspaper tomorrow, since those jackals got hold of the information too." He paused, lost in thought. "It was a strange death, Ava. A large number of people didn't like Ethel, but the way she died... I've never quite seen this before."

I didn't want to interrupt him, but I was dying to know how she was killed. Poor choice of words, but he was dragging this thing out longer than it needed to be. *Get to the point.*

"I'll get to the point," he said. "Someone twisted her neck, which is what caused her death."

I sort of stopped breathing. I had not expected something so... odd. "But, her head, it was..." I didn't know how to finish my statement.

"The wound on her head, which is what you're probably referring to, was caused postmortem."

"So, someone twisted her neck then bashed her on the head after killing her?" I was no expert, but it didn't sound right to me. Murder is never right, but this was weird. A crime of passion? A mistake? This was not a typical killing.

"Forgive the pun, but that sounds like overkill to me," I told him. Something occurred to me. "Can you tell if she was killed from the front or the back?" I asked. Not that I believed her ghost might have seen anything or could really tell us something useful, but it was worth asking.

Detective Rialto shook his head. "No, whoever did this came up behind her and killed her."

"And pushed her down the stairs? Or did it all happen in the basement?" None of this made sense. Why would someone do this? Could it have been a crime of retaliation? Maybe the police knew more and he was still holding out on me, not giving me all the information. "Do you know anything else?" I asked.

"No, we're not finished working the crime scene," he said. "We think she was killed upstairs, but nothing is conclusive. We still have some tests to run."

I was silent, thinking about Ethel's last moments. She must have been terrified. Nobody should have to go through that—I don't care how many homeowners she pissed off.

Oliver walked through my living room and over to the window, seeming to take everything in at one glance. I couldn't tell what he was thinking, but it didn't matter, right? Who cared what he thought of my apartment? We were not going to best friends or start hanging out together. He hated me.

"The other thing I wanted to talk to you about," he began. I waited, patient. I had a feeling he was going to ask for something, just because he was fidgeting a little. In the short amount of time I'd known him, Oliver didn't fidget. This could only mean one thing. I had something he wanted.

"I know I've told you to stay out of this investigation, but I also know you won't," he said. "You strike me as an interfering sort of woman."

I didn't bother being nice. "What the heck kind of idiot do you think I am? I have no intention of being found dead in a basement."

"Nobody has any intention of getting killed, but it happens. I don't want to argue with you, but it's clear to me you can be a bit... inquisitive. Here's what I want you to do."

I tried to put my annoyance aside so I could pay attention to what he was saying, but this guy was seriously pushing my buttons. Maybe sometimes I was a little curious about things, but that was none of his business. "What do you want from me?" I didn't bother to keep the sarcasm from my voice.

"I want you to keep your ears open. If you hear anything about this case, if you hear anyone saying weird or suspicious things, call me right way."

Silence spread throughout the room. I couldn't believe what he'd just asked me to do. "So, I'd be sort of working with you."

"No, you'd be telling me things you heard," he said, cracking his knuckles.

"Things I heard related to the case, then reporting it to you, and helping you solve the case. Which is kind of like working with you," I insisted.

"Fine, call it what you want," he relented. "The thing is, I'm relatively new in town and the people who have lived here their whole lives have a different type of insight. I'm simply asking you to tell me what you hear or know. That's it. I don't want you doing anything. I don't want you questioning people. I don't want you putting yourself in any danger."

This request would make my work so much easier. But first, I had to tell him the one thing guaranteed to annoy the heck out of him. "I have to tell you something, but you have to promise not to be mad," I said.

He looked up at the ceiling. *He's either looking for cracks or praying for guidance.* "Why don't you tell me, then we can talk about it," he said.

"My brother has been very upset by this whole situation," I began. "He believes that Ethel's murder is going to hurt his business."

"His ghost hunting business?" Oliver asked.

"Yes, and his store business, too. So, I sort of promised him, Itoldhim I'dhelphimsolvethis." I finished the last part of my sentence quickly, hoping Oliver wouldn't get mad and take me off the case. Not that I was officially on the case, but I didn't want him to tell me to mind my own business. Again.

"Can't you just tell him no?" Oliver asked, crossing his arms over his chest.

"Not really. He's my brother, and he needs my help," I explained. Did the detective have any remaining family, or was his wife his only family? Did he have children? There was so much I still didn't know about him.

"I know exactly how to handle him," Oliver said.

Chapter Twenty-Six

"**YOU'RE NOT GOING TO PUT** him in jail, are you? Because he's got a wife and a baby. Plus, I'd lose my job, and it would be bad for the Brewster Square economy if his store closed." I knew I was babbling, but I couldn't stop. I had to make sure Oliver didn't arrest my brother.

"I'm not going to arrest him," Oliver said.

"Then what are you going to do?" I asked. His words hadn't filled me with confidence, and I had to protect my brother.

"I'm not going to do anything. You are," Oliver said.

"I'm not going to arrest him or bring him to the jail. I won't." I shook my head. Was he smiling at me or did he have stomach issues?

"No, but you are going to tell him that any interference from either you or him will result in both of you being arrested and having to appear in court on charges of interfering with an investigation." He looked smug, and I knew he wasn't going to like what I had to say.

"That won't work," I said. Before he could tell me all about the law, which I knew from the look on his face he was about to do, I rushed to explain myself. "The thing is, my brother won't care. I know him, especially when he gets an idea in his head. He'll think the law only applies to other people, or outsiders, and we know enough people in town to get around it. I have a better idea."

"I don't like the sound of this," Oliver said. "And I don't see why you can't just warn your brother off. Tell him I said so, and tell him I mean business." Instead of looking like he meant business, Oliver looked a little lost. Lord knew I could identify—it wasn't always easy dealing with my family. But it was definitely worth it, because my family was awesome, and that's what I needed him to understand. A little eccentric sometimes, but awesome.

"Listen, I get your point, and don't worry, we aren't going to interfere. But why don't I tell Giuseppe a variation of the truth?" I asked.

Oliver's eyebrows drew together and his eyes flashed. "I'm not so sure I like the sound of this. I'm already pushing it by asking you to share information with me, I don't think I can compromise anything else. When the murderer gets caught and this goes to court I need to have an airtight case."

"I know, but just listen. Since you've asked me to tell you anything I hear about, it's sort of like I'm working with you, right?"

"No," he said.

"So, if I'm sort of working with you, I can tell my brother I'm undercover," I said. The pieces of the plan were coming together in my mind as I talked, and I was confident this was a great idea.

"You can't say that," he said.

"And then every now and then you can give me something I can pass along to him, and I can tell him everything else is confidential," I said. It was brilliant, really, since we wouldn't be giving Giuseppe anything he wasn't supposed to know.

Oliver rubbed his forehead and stood in silence for what felt like forever. "I knew you were going to be trouble in my world." His voice was low, but I heard every word, and I think he meant for me to hear him.

"I'm not going to apologize for who I am," I said.

Looking up at me, he smiled. "You're right, you shouldn't ever apologize for that. Let's say I go along with this harebrained scheme of yours, what sorts of things are you envisioning sharing with your brother?"

"Only things I'm allowed to repeat," I said. "Like what you told me tonight, since it's going to be in the newspaper tomorrow anyway."

Oliver nodded. "Handle your brother however you want. But here's the thing: if I think you're giving him information you either haven't shared with me or telling him something that could potentially harm the case, there will be hell to pay. You will go to jail. Are we clear?"

I nodded. "Absolutely." I knew we weren't done yet, but Oliver didn't know that because he was walking toward the door. "Um, Detective Oliver—" I flushed, confused. In my head he'd become Oliver, but he was the detective, and instead of saying his last name it all got jumbled up before it came out of my mouth. The blush spread across my face, a rare occurrence for me, and I could only hope the light was low enough to hide it.

"How about you just call me Detective Rialto?" he said. His face had no emotion, and his voice was not unkind. I didn't know how to take that.

"Sure. Detective Rialto, just to keep you updated, I want you to know we have access to Ethel's house Monday night," I said.

His entire body grew still, which scared me. I wasn't sure why it scared me, but it did. He was so... official. "Why are you going to Ethel's house?"

Sometimes telling people things was like ripping off a Band Aid, you just had to do it quick and get it over with. "We're doing a séance to see if Ethel's ghost can tell us anything about her murder," I said.

"You're doing a séance," he repeated.

I nodded.

"To talk to a ghost," he said.

I nodded again.

"And you'll probably call me and tell me what the ghost said."

I hesitated. "Do you want me to?" I knew the question would drive him nuts, so I couldn't help myself. I was trying not to laugh.

"I am going to assume that you have permission to be there," he said. When I nodded, he added, "I want you to call me as soon as you're done with this thing and let me know you're safe. I'm not interested in hearing about a ghost, but I am concerned for your and your brother's personal safety. How many people know about this plan?"

"I'm not sure," I said. "Honestly, Giuseppe put it together, so anyone who'd listen to him has probably heard about it."

"You know this is not a good idea," he said.

"I know."

"But you're going to do it anyway, aren't you?"

The good detective was starting to understand me. "Yes," I said.

"Fine, go ahead."

I couldn't believe what I'd heard. Did he just give me permission to do something? "So, you're okay with us going in there and doing this?" I asked.

I needed to hear it again.

"I'm okay with that," he said. "But on one condition only. We're going shopping. I don't want you living alone without protection."

Chapter Twenty-Seven

THE NEXT MORNING I STOOD clutching my box of bakery muffins in the express line at the local grocery, twelve items or less. I couldn't stop myself and began counting the items in the cart in front of me. I think the woman had eleven items, but it was hard to tell because she kept positioning her body in front of the food.

When Oliver left last night, he had told me to be ready for him at nine o'clock this morning. His tone made it clear there would be no arguing the point. At least I could fortify him with food before he took me to wherever it was he was going to take me.

Intellectually, I had no real objection to guns. I'd grown up in a house with guns, and my dad had shown Giuseppe how to shoot. Charlie's father used to hunt pheasant, which her mom cooked in one of the most delicious stews I'd ever tasted. I still believe the only reason Charlie's dad stopped hunting was because both Charlie and Giuseppe used to kick up such a fuss about killing that neither of her parents wanted to listen to it anymore. Of course I took every opportunity I could to harass my brother about the bacon cheeseburgers he loved to eat.

But I wasn't sure a gun was a good idea for me. Did I really want the responsibility of owning a firearm? What if something went horribly wrong? What if someone broke into my house and used it against me, or even worse, against my aunts? Could I shoot to kill or would I make everything worse?

There were ninety-two steps from the cash register to my car. I threw the grocery bag on the front seat, got in, and lurched out of my parking space. I was home in three minutes and counted 159 steps from my car to the inside of my apartment. Like I said, I count things when I'm nervous.

At exactly nine o'clock, the knock sounded on my door. *I can always say no, I don't have to do what he says.* Ushering Oliver into my apartment for the second time in less than twenty-four hours, I opened my mouth to tell him what I thought of his plan. "Detective, I appreciate your help, I really do. But the thing is, even though I'm pretty sure I can handle a gun just fine—"

"I'm not," he said, glaring down at me.

"What?"

"This isn't about a gun, this is about getting you protection."

"I'm confused," I said. To prove the point, my left eye started twitching. Just a little bit, but geez this guy knew how to throw me off. "If we're not talking about a gun, what exactly are we talking about? Bow and arrow? Baseball bat?"

"Weapons will not protect you unless you know how to use them. No, I'm talking about something else, something that will change your life for the better, something that will help you and someone else," he said.

I did not like the sound of this. Suddenly there was talk of a "someone else", and that did not sound like something I wanted to deal with at the moment. Did he want me to be a foster parent or something to some teenage thug? I had enough trouble, I couldn't be responsible for another person. Besides, what kind of self-respecting thug wants to live with a woman who has a degree in English Literature and sells aromatherapy products?

"Did you know that every year approximately five to seven million companion animals enter shelters in the United States?" Oliver asked. Without waiting for an answer, he kept talking. "Of those animals, around four million are euthanized. Killed. Slaughtered."

I blinked, not liking where this conversation was headed. I had to change the subject, quick. "How... sad. Do you need a license to carry in Connecticut?"

"And did you know only ten percent of those animals received by the ˙ ͻlters have been spayed or neutered?" There was no stopping him, the ˙ ͻs on a mission to educate me. Who knew the hard-boiled detective ͻft spot for animals?

"Do you have a pet?" I asked, hoping again to derail the conversation. Maybe if I could get him to talk about his German shepherd or something he wouldn't say what I thought he was going to say.

"Did you ever see the loyalty a dog has for its owner? Did you ever watch a police dog and a handler work together? Dogs were bred to co-exist with humans and help support our species."

I tried to lighten the conversation. "Dogs, huh? I guess that would explain why I've never heard of an attack cat."

"Cats are wonderful, too," Oliver said, a little too enthusiastically for my liking.

"I don't do the whole litter box thing," I said. I had my limits, and he'd just reached one.

"No, a cat won't do you any good right now," he said.

"I'm not so sure a dog would, either."

"A dog will stay with you, be your alert system. A dog will be your friend and protector for as long as he lives."

Oh, boy. "Listen, Detective, I have trouble committing to what I want to eat for lunch. I'm not sure bringing a dog into my home is such a good idea."

"Ava, you're putting yourself in the middle of a murder investigation. You're putting yourself in danger. Frankly, your other choice is to either have someone move in with you or get a gun, neither of which I see happening," he said.

I wasn't sure what to think of his statement. Did he mean I wasn't a responsible citizen or did he mean no one in their right mind would want to live with me? "I don't think I like what you just said," I told him. "I know you mean well, but this is my life and my business, and as much as I adore dogs I'm not sure I'm ready to commit to having one right now."

Oliver looked at the floor, quiet. After a moment, he looked back at me, and I swear it looked like he was ready to cry. "I understand," he said.

"Good, because I don't mean for you to take this personally, but a dog is a huge responsibility. You can't just go get a dog on a whim, you've got to be ready to take care of it and pay for it and walk it and clean up after it... " He didn't say anything, and I couldn't read his face. "What?" I asked.

He shook his head. "It's nothing, really."

I waited a moment, giving him a chance to explain. Clearly something was wrong. "Tell me," I said. "Something's bothering you, and I can't imagine it's the fact that I don't want a dog. That would be kind of weird, you know."

"Fine. I'll share this with you, but I don't talk about it often," he said. He took a deep breath, waiting a moment before he spoke again. "I can't help but wonder sometimes if my wife... if she'd had a dog... maybe she never would have been..."

This was so unfair. I didn't even know the whole story, but I knew it was bad.

"Anyway," he continued, "I used the same arguments with Jennie, my wife. We didn't have the time, it was a big commitment, everything you just said. After she was kidnapped, I couldn't help but wonder, what if we had a dog? Would a dog have helped her?" Looking me in the eye, I could see he was trying to force a smile. "Sorry," he said. "I guess I get a little passionate about protecting people after what happened. I go over and over it in my head, and wonder how I could have saved her."

It was a low blow, but he had a point. *I've wanted a pet, I just never got around to it. But I need to make sure I'm doing this for me, not for some crusading detective trying to save his past.* It's difficult to make a life changing decision on the spot, but sometimes there are no other options. "Give me a minute to make a phone call," I said.

"Who do you need to call?"

"The aunts," I said. "I want to make sure it's okay with them if I have a dog."

Chapter Twenty-Eight

THE AUNTS WERE THRILLED WITH the idea of a dog in the building. "It's been a long time since we've had one," Aunt Maria said. "When we were growing up we always had a dog. We'll help you take care of him."

"Make sure he's got a good temperament," Aunt Estelle said. "Not too dominant, you know? I can't wait to take him for walks."

"Stay away from those purebreds," Aunt Claudia said. "Nothing but trouble with that kind of inbreeding, just like the royals. I'll go get some dog food."

Suddenly I lived with the dog whisperers. Who knew they'd like the idea so much?

Oliver drove, and on the way he told me about the shelter. "It's not really a dog shelter, it's a rehab facility, and they have dogs, too," he said.

"Rehab facility? Are the animals are in physical therapy, with walkers and wheelchairs and stuff?" I'd never heard of a place like that in Brewster Square.

Oliver smiled, his first real smile of the day. His dark good looks were accentuated by his smile, and it was hard to remember why I'd been annoyed with him. My brother's words from last night floated through my head, making me question myself. Did I really try to heal people who'd been wounded? Maybe that was the root of the confusion I was feeling toward Oliver; I didn't want a relationship with him, but I hated seeing the extraordinary level of pain he had shown when talking about his wife.

I felt sorry for him, but I could never let him know. First of all, nobody wants people to feel sorry for them. Second, there was no doubt in my mind he'd take full advantage of it.

"Animal rehabbers are trained professionals who step in to help heal wounded animals brought to their facility," Oliver said. "They're supposed to be licensed by the state, and once the animal has recovered the rehabber releases them back into the wild. So, birds with broken wings, fox with broken legs, that's the sort of thing you're going to see at this place."

Looks like I wasn't the only one around who liked to heal things. "So, are the dogs we're going to look at injured?" I didn't think I wanted a dog who needed special care. I'd finally adjusted to the fact that I was going to have a roommate, I didn't want to have to deal with medicines and therapy and whatever.

"No, apparently this woman just happens to have dogs who need a home. Nothing wrong with them as far as I know."

There was something just a little bit evasive about his answer. "Have you been here before?" I asked.

"No," he said. I waited, knowing there was more. Sure enough, after a solid three minutes of silence, Oliver spoke again. "I have a friend who works with the state regulatory agency, he told me about this place."

"There's more to this story, isn't there? What aren't you telling me?" I asked.

He smiled again. "Maybe, but it won't make a difference with you getting a dog. Remember, you're doing a good thing for yourself and another living creature."

Great, I was stuck in the car with James Herriot.

The place he was taking me to was located on the northeast side of town, completely opposite where my parents lived. There were some very steep hills over there, and a big old granite quarry that generations of local kids had snuck into at night to drink beer and make out.

As we turned into a rutted, unpaved driveway, I couldn't help but notice the junk scattered around the yard. Rusted wheelbarrows, rolled up chicken wire, and a school bus with flat tires dotted the landscape. Soon, an old house came into view, with a front porch that had a sagging roof overhang.

The roof looks like it's about to fall down any second now. The house was in desperate need of a paint job, and I was willing to bet a month's salary those single paned windows were useless at keeping the winter cold out. *This is almost as scary as the old McAlister house.* I sincerely hoped the dogs weren't kept in the basement.

Someone walked out from behind the house into the driveway as we pulled to a stop. I recognized the bright colors and the big gray hair immediately. "Hi there," Oliver said, climbing out of the car. "I called earlier. I'm Oliver and this is Ava. We're here to see the dogs."

She wasn't a big woman, but she gave the appearance of being big simply because of her clothing. Shapeless and brightly colored, the clothes masked her body completely. Her hair, as big and as gray as ever, stood out in a halo effect around her head. "I know you," she said, pointing at me. "You found that body—the dead woman."

Looks like I had a new reputation. "Yes, I remember seeing you at the house," I answered.

"Great," Oliver muttered. "She remembers you, but I'm invisible." Speaking louder, he said, "So, you mentioned you have dogs for sale?"

She nodded at us, arms crossed. "Name's Debbee, two b's and three e's."

Two b's and three e's, what the heck is she talking about? As I scrambled to figure out what she meant, she kept talking.

"D – E – B – B – E – E. Debbee, except I changed the spelling to look like a honeybee. I love 'em."

Uh-oh, weirdo alert. I tried not to be judgmental, but some people, like Debbee-two-b's-three-e's, made that task difficult. Oliver and I exchanged a look, and I was relieved to see his anxiety ratchet up a notch. *Good, he's the one who dragged me out here in the first place*, I thought. *Didn't he interview her at the scene of the crime? He should've known better.*

"You want some food, too?" Debbee asked.

I shook my head. "No, thanks, I ate breakfast already." Based on what I'd seen of the outside of her house, I already knew there was no way I was eating anything here.

Exasperated, Debbee said, "Okay then, did you want to buy some food? People love my bread, especially the rye bread I make. Homemade, organic. Good for ya."

"No thank you, we're fine," Oliver answered.

"You sell food?" I asked. Oliver shot me a look that told me to shut up, but I couldn't help it. What kind of food did she sell, and who would buy something from a place like this?

Nodding, Debbee straightened. "Yep, it's all organic, no chemicals. Breads, cakes, vegetables, all sorts of stuff. Usually I make my deliveries to locals, kind of old-timey like. You know, just like the milkman used to do."

I smiled, hoping it masked the sick feeling settling in the pit of my stomach. *She'd probably lose a whole lot of business if her customers came and picked up their food. One look at this place is all it'd take.*

Oliver cleared his throat. "Where do you keep the dogs?"

"In the basement, usually," Debbee said.

Oh Lord, no, this can't be happening.

"But I brought them outside for you to look at."

Thank you, God. I'll try to go to church again.

Turning, Debbee started walking around the back of her house. We followed, with me shooting burning dagger looks at Oliver in between watching where I stepped. Oliver carefully avoided looking at me. "Did you interview her at the crime scene?" I hissed, trying not to let Debbee hear me.

"No, I somehow missed that pleasure," he hissed back.

When we circled around the house I could see an enormous red barn and what looked like a huge chain link fence dog run to the side of the barn. The dog run was divided, and I counted a total of twelve small sections, with fencing on the top as well. The smell of feces and God knew what else was overpowering. I tried to breathe through my mouth and not think about it.

She keeps dogs in there? "Those cages look a little small for dogs," I said, wondering if maybe she kept toy poodles or Chihuahuas or something.

Debbee shot me a withering look. "Those cages are for the care and rehabilitation of raccoon and fox. It's important to have metal instead of wood so they can't chew through their cage."

As she said it, I looked more closely. Sure enough, it looked like a pile of gray fur was sleeping in one of the cages.

"Don't go near it," Oliver mumbled to me. "You can get all sorts of nasty diseases from those animals."

"Don't worry, you don't have to tell me twice," I said. I had no desire to get near a wild animal with sharp teeth. Especially an animal who might be angry at having to be here, in this hovel of a yard. Really, weren't there supposed to be inspectors or something to make sure home businesses like this were clean? The whole place made me want to go home and take a shower.

As we neared the barn, I could hear yips and yelps coming from the side. Craning my neck, I could see a small, fenced in circle filled with a wiggling mass of puppies.

Puppies. Not dogs, but little, baby dogs.

"I thought they were full grown," Oliver said.

Debbee didn't even bother looking at him when she answered. "I do have full grown dogs. They're not for sale. The puppies are."

One of the puppies stopped playing and came to the fence, wagging his butt as we approached. He was all white, with a black patch over his eye and two black spots on his back. I thought maybe he'd been waiting for me.

"I don't think a puppy is really what we're looking for," Oliver said. "We wanted a full grown dog."

I leaned over and picked him up, feeling warm puppy burrowing into the crook of my arm. Next thing I knew, he was sniffing my head and neck, and gave me one little, tiny kiss on my cheek. Just one. "It's a boy! We'll take this one," I told Debbee.

"A puppy isn't going to help you," Oliver said. "I was thinking more along the lines of a full grown dog, one who can protect you, or at least bark. Puppies yip, dogs bark. This one is only going to chew your furniture, and that won't do you any good."

The puppy was staring into my eyes, and I swear I knew exactly what he was thinking. "He can't wait to go home," I said. "He's going to love living with us."

"Us?" Oliver asked.

"Me and the aunts," I said. "Let's go, we've got toys to buy."

"Not so fast," Debbee said. "Do you know how to care for an animal? Are you ready to make a commitment? Do you have any idea what a puppy needs? Do you have a vet?"

"Yes to all your questions," I said. "How much for the puppy?"

"He's some kind of hound dog, right?" Oliver asked.

"Yep, he's a walker hound," Debbee said. "Known for being stubborn. Sure you can handle him?"

There was no way I was leaving without my dog. "How much?" I said.

"Three fifty," Debbee answered.

"No," Oliver said. "You told me on the phone all your dogs were strays and mutts. Nobody pays that much for a dog of indeterminate origin."

I looked around the yard, littered with debris and the sagging barn with peeling paint. The whole place was not only messy, but dirty. I couldn't leave this puppy to whatever fate this bizarre woman had in store for him. "I'm not leaving without my puppy."

Oliver took his wallet out, starting to count cash. In the process, his badge could be clearly seen. "How about one hundred?" he asked.

For the first time, Debbee looked nervous. "Sure, that'll work. Don't tell anyone I gave you a discount, though. I've got bills to pay in order to feed and house these animals, and they don't come cheap."

As Oliver counted out the bills to her, I couldn't help peeking into the barn. After all, the door was open, so it wasn't like I was snooping or anything.

I could see rows and rows of barrels. Each had a label, identifying things like regular, rye, and wheat. *Must be flour. Although from the looks of it, she's got enough barrels in there to get her through Armageddon.*

Debbee saw me looking into her barn. "You sure you don't want some bread? I can give it to you at cost."

I tried to keep my face neutral and not reflect the repulsion I felt. "No, thank you, we're fine."

Once we got in the car, I wrote Oliver a check to cover the cost of the dog. He wouldn't stop complaining. "You've made a big mistake. This is not the dog I had in mind for you," he said.

"Sometimes that's how life works," I told him. "Besides, what you had in mind and what was supposed to happen are obviously two very different things. What happened to your big speech about stray animals and puppies dying in the street?"

"I never said anything about puppies dying in the street," he said. "I was trying to—"

"Relax, I'm kidding," I said. "Let's stop at the pet store, I want to get some chew toys for Sparky. I have a feeling this little boy is going to need lots of toys to keep him out of trouble."

"His name is Sparky?"

"What else would it be?" I said. I couldn't hear what Oliver muttered, but maybe that was for the best.

The fun part about the big box pet store is taking your dog inside with you. While Sparky and I shopped, Oliver told me he had something to take care of. "I'll be right back, I'll meet you out front," he said. We didn't care, Sparky and

I were having fun looking at leashes and collars and chew toys. Front paws on the edge of the cart, we steered our way through what was essentially a toy store for dogs.

After paying for our purchases, I waited outside the front of the store. Clipping his new collar and leash on him, I picked Sparky out of the shopping cart and put him on the ground in case he had to do his business.

The next thing I knew, someone attacked me from behind.

Chapter Twenty-Nine

MY DOG BOWED, BUTT IN the air, tail wagging, and barked at my attacker.

Oliver's voice was disgusted. "That's dog-speak for 'let's play'. He's not going to help you when you need it."

"Great," I said. "Can you let go of me now?"

His grip around my neck loosened, and his arms released me. Oliver had come up and grabbed me from behind, putting one arm around my neck and the other around my body, pinning me to him. An old woman stopped in her tracks, assessing Oliver, and said to me, "Are you all right, dear? Do you need help?"

I shook my head. "No, thank you ma'am, we were just playing. I'm fine."

The woman, probably somewhere in her eighties, sniffed at Oliver before walking away. I could hear her muttering something about boys not acting like gentlemen anymore.

"What the hell are you doing?" I asked.

"Trying to prove a point," he said. "This is why you need a different kind of dog. I walked up and grabbed you from behind, and your goofy puppy wanted to play instead of defend you. How is that going to help?"

"You're right, I'm going to have to train him to bite you. C'mon, let's get in the car," I said, walking away. I might have to rethink my original opinion of Oliver. I'd thought he was a buttoned up, by-the-book kind of guy, but apparently not so much when it came to animals. Or maybe something about me brought out the craziness in him.

We got in the car. "Anything new on Ethel?" I asked.

"You're not going to distract me," he said. "And no, there's nothing new, other than the fact that anyone in this town could be a suspect."

"What do you mean?" I knew what he meant, but I wanted to keep him talking about something other than Sparky.

"Nobody liked her," he said. "I've never seen one person have such a negative effect on so many people."

"That's not necessarily true," I said. I wanted him to understand the strange relationship most people had with Ethel. Most of us had had some sort of run-in with her in the past, but only because she was passionate about what she believed in. But she was just as passionate about defending others, too, she just didn't let everyone know.

I remembered running into her at the post office several years ago. Literally. I was in a hurry and wasn't watching where I was going, and the next thing I knew I'd bumped into someone and knocked them and their stuff onto the floor.

When I looked down to see who it was, Ethel sat surrounded by hundreds of envelopes. I apologized profusely, and bent to help her retrieve her mail. As I was gathering the envelopes, I couldn't help but notice the return address on each one of them.

The North Pole.

Each year, Ethel took the time to answer children's letters to Santa, put a stamp on it, and mail it back. At the time, she brushed off my questions and wouldn't look me in the eye. I'd like to believe it was because she didn't want to make a big deal out of it, but now I'll never know. The thing is, if we don't grab an opportunity to talk with people in the moment it happens, that chance might disappear—forever. You never know when you'll lose someone, and you never know when your own time is up. I didn't share those morose thoughts with Oliver, but I did tell him about Ethel and the Santa letters.

"She had a lot of good in her, she just didn't let everyone know what she was up to," I explained.

Oliver didn't say anything for almost two whole minutes. Finally, he spoke. "Do you think she could have been up to something nobody knew about and gotten someone mad?"

"I think anything is possible with her," I said. And it was true. If there was one thing I'd learned, it was not to make assumptions about anything anyone did, said, or thought. You just never knew with some people.

Oliver cleared his throat, glancing over at me sitting in the passenger seat with my arms wrapped around Sparky. "Are you sure you know what you're getting into with a puppy? Have you ever trained a dog, or dealt with puppy messes? It's not too late to take him back, you know."

My eyes narrowed at him. "Take him back? You don't take a living creature back like it's some kind of unwanted birthday sweater your old uncle who can't see two feet in front of him bought you for your seventeenth birthday."

"That's not at all specific," he commented drily.

"Yeah, I've got quite a family. Anyway, you don't have to worry. We always had a dog when I was growing up, and the aunts are really excited to have this little guy around. Besides, my parents live on a farm."

The silence in the car had a weight to it, something I'd never experienced before. "What does your parents' farm have to do with anything?" he said.

I knew I had to be patient with him. "I visit my parents all the time, you know. So, it's like having animal experience by osmosis, because I'm around the animals." Seriously, did I have to explain everything to this guy?

I could see Oliver grinding his teeth. "That's the most ridiculous thing I've ever heard."

"No, it's not, and you shouldn't grind your teeth like that, it's not good for you. You'll need a lot of dental work later in life. Or maybe soon, I don't know how old you are. The point is, I've got people I can rely on when something comes up and I'm a responsible person. So don't worry. Besides, this was your idea in the first place."

"What happens when he chews your favorite pair of shoes? Or destroys the new comforter you got on sale at the mall? Are you going to dump him at the nearest shelter?"

I was horrified he would even ask that question. "No, I'll go shopping and replace it all. And probably buy him some new toys, because if he's causing that much trouble he's obviously bored."

We pulled in front of my apartment building. Oliver put the car in park. "I don't understand much of what you just said about the farm thing, but I suppose it doesn't matter. Good luck, and remember our deal. Call me if you hear anything, and I mean anything at all."

I started to get out of the car, but Oliver's voice stopped me as I was closing the door. "And do not, under any circumstances, do anything foolish. Your job is to listen, period." We'd been over this already, and he didn't deserve an answer. I started to close the door again, and stopped when he leaned across the seat. "And for the record, I'm not old."

As I watched my new puppy sleep in his bed later that night, I realized Oliver had never said exactly how old 'not old' was, but it didn't matter. I had a feeling I'd be learning a lot more about the detective in the near future, since I was now part of his team. Unofficially, of course.

Chapter Thirty

SUNDAYS WERE MADE FOR SLEEPING in, and I had the excuse of a new puppy to stay away from morning Mass at the Catholic Church on the corner. I hadn't been to church in about ten years, but I still tried to come up with fairly reasonable excuses for the aunts. I knew they were probably worried about my soul, and I tried to ease their minds a bit every now and then to let them know I wasn't going to hell when I died.

The Catholic Church and I didn't exactly see eye-to-eye. I might have wanted to have a spiritual community to connect with every week, but that wasn't going to happen at our local church. About ten years ago I'd been asked by the church elders to stop attending, another small fact I kept from my family. I was the only person I knew who'd been uninvited to church.

The reason they asked me to stay away was because I'd started getting really vocal about accusing the priest of being a thief. Back then, I had a habit of sitting in the church, quietly meditating and sorting through the mysteries of the universe in my mind. During one of those mediations I saw the priest doing a couple of things. He was swigging the communion wine like a dehydrated soldier while putting the candlestick holders in a jacket pocket. The wine part was expected, everyone knew the priests drank wine whenever they could. How the heck else could they do their job without a little extra help? It was the candlestick holders that made me angry. Sure, he could have been taking them home to polish them or something, but since he gave the congregation a big lecture on stealing the following Sunday and accused someone in the congregation (not a specific someone, mind you) of stealing them, I couldn't keep my mouth shut. I saw it as my duty, morally and spiritually, to tell everyone what I knew.

The next week the candlestick holders were back on the altar, the priest thanked the thief for bringing them back, and the elders called me into a room in the basement to have their little talk with me. Basements have never been a good place for me to be.

Although my family knew about my accusations, they never knew I'd been asked to leave, and I never told them. I knew it would stir up trouble, and I wasn't interested in ruining Sunday mornings for everyone. Besides, sooner or later that priest would leave, they always did. I just had to wait it out.

But I got used to sleeping in on Sunday mornings and having a huge cup of coffee while I watched the news shows. Later, I might make myself a brunch or have dinner with my parents or aunts. Not going to church sort of made my schedule easier, and I saw no reason to change now.

On this particular Sunday, getting my laundry done had gotten interesting. Like most puppies, Sparky had a real love of socks, and he kept taking them out of the laundry basket and trotting through the house with them. I patiently replaced each sock he took with a chew toy, but apparently the toys were not nearly as interesting.

With the laundry done and the house cleaned I decided to focus on the case. I sat at my desk and turned on the computer, pulling out a new file folder and a pen. Since this was the first time I was attempting to investigate, I knew I had to be organized. I would start by making a list, then I would have a clear vision of where I was going. I thought for a moment before writing:

1. Ethel's recent fights (ask family and neighbors, check minutes of Homeowner's Association Board meetings... public?)

2. New owners of house. Background?

3. Other area crimes

At least it was a start. Although number one might take a while, given Ethel's ability to piss people off, numbers two and three should be easy enough. I made my first phone call to my friend Jackie, who was a Realtor. Jackie put me in touch with the Vice President of Ethel's homeowner association. Our conversation was a bit awkward, but it got me what I wanted, which was the minutes to the last few board meetings.

"Why are you so interested in our association?" she had asked, her voice tinged with suspicion.

"I'm thinking about buying a home there," I said, keeping my fingers crossed, "and my father told me the best way to get a sense of a neighborhood is to get involved in the association."

I waited a moment, wondering if she would buy my story. I could hear her hesitation on the phone, so I hurried to add, "I'm the sort of person who likes to get involved, you know, help out with neighborhood events and stuff like that. I just wanted to get a sense of how you all functioned." *This should do it*, I thought. Organizations loved it when you told them you wanted to get involved.

Sure enough, ten minutes later the last three months of meeting minutes were sitting in my email inbox. As I read through them my frustration grew. Nothing in the minutes pointed to a motive or a killer in Ethel's death. *Of course it's not going to be easy*, I chided myself. If it was, the police would have figured it out by now.

Finding out who Ethel had been fighting with would take more time, and I made a note to talk to people in the store and in the neighborhood when I had the chance. Next on the list: the new owners of the McAllister house. A quick internet search turned up nothing interesting, so I forked over the twenty-five dollars for an online background check website. I reasoned that I might need to do this again, so it was a good investment, even though I still hadn't learned anything new.

A check of the crimes activity on the local police department website showed me the various crimes committed throughout Brewster Square on the week Ethel was killed, but there was nothing that could have been in any way related to her death.

A long shot, but worth looking into, I thought.

As I sat looking out my third floor window onto the town green, I remembered my conversation with my parents. Could Winthrop Thurgood, her old flame, have had anything to do with killing Ethel? *No, that doesn't make sense*, I realized. Too much time had passed, and he had too much to lose now. There's no way a guy like him would do this. He might crush her spirit and destroy her financially, but as much as I didn't like Win I couldn't see him being involved in any way.

I had one more thing to look into. I wanted to know who I was working with. I wasn't being nosy, but I wanted to know Oliver's story if I was going to continue a working relationship with him.

An hour later I called Charlie. "Charlie, it's me. You are not going to believe how sad this is," I said.

"Have you noticed we never actually say hello to each other?" she said.

"I'm sorry, hello." I was horrified for a moment, wondering if I'd insulted my friend. Sometimes I open my mouth and speak before I think about what's going to come out.

"What's sad?" she asked.

"Oliver. His story. All of it. I wonder how he got here? Of all the places he could have chosen to move to, he ended up in Connecticut. Why do you think he came here?"

The brief pause in the conversation should have clued me in to her next question. "Who is Oliver?"

"Detective Rialto, sorry."

"How did we get to be on first name terms?" I could hear voices in the background, and realized I was probably interrupting her.

"Charlie, I'm sorry, are you in the middle of something?"

"No, I'm with Fred's parents at a thing they're having today at the country club. I was already hiding out in the bathroom because I needed a break."

That girl had to learn to stand up for herself with Fred's family. "Are they giving you a hard time?"

"Never mind," she said, which meant yes, they were giving her a hard time. "Tell me about the detective. What's so sad?"

The details were displayed on my computer screen, right from the beginning. The newspapers covered Oliver's story every day for almost two weeks. I tried to get the facts straight in my head so I could start at the beginning. "Oliver was married. I saw pictures of her, she was beautiful. Long, blonde hair, tall, size two with curves... I'm talking model-like stunning."

"Was? Sounds like she's dead."

"Nobody knows," I said. "Oliver worked for a federal agency when this happened—"

"CIA? FBI? Which one?" Charlie interrupted.

"Drug Enforcement Agency," I said. "DEA. Anyway, he was undercover, working to bring down some big drug lord from Mexico."

"Mexico?"

"This was while he was living in Arizona. There's a huge drug problem in Mexico, and a lot of their product finds its way across the border. And, as you know, it's a brutal, all out war down there, with people getting killed all the time. Those guys are not nice."

"They're drug dealers, what did you expect? It's not like they sell Avon for a living."

"This went way beyond the typical drug dealer not nice thing," I told her. "From what I've read, the head guy in charge of operations, the one that Oliver was up against, is described as having no soul. He is driven by power and violence, and will do whatever is necessary to maintain control over the people. His particular specialty is beheading those who go against him."

"Now you're using the present tense. Do you mean this drug guy is still around?"

I nodded even though she couldn't see me. "Yes, but he's gone kind of underground. Nobody knows exactly where he is, but rumor has it he's still in charge."

"So, I don't get the sad part. Is the sad part because our detective friend, who I didn't realize was actually our friend until now, failed to put a bad guy in jail?" I wondered how much longer Charlie had until someone came looking for her. For her sake, I hoped talking to me helped her gain her sense of confidence back so she wouldn't take any crap from Fred's family.

"No, the sad part of the story is when somehow Oliver's cover was blown, and he was beaten pretty badly and left tied up in a warehouse. Someone called the DEA office headquarters in Phoenix and let them know where Oliver had been left."

"This story is starting to sound familiar," Charlie said.

"You'll remember it when I tell you the rest," I said. "I'd read about it, but not in-depth until today. Anyway, while Oliver was being held captive someone broke into his home and kidnapped his wife. They left behind a note, and nothing else. To this day she has not been located."

"They never found her?"

"No, but the assumption is that she's dead," I said.

"That doesn't make sense," she said. "I remember seeing this on the national news a while back. But, for a big, bad drug lord guy not to do his thing and leave her alive instead of sending her head back in a box or something—"

"Wasn't that a movie?" I said.

"I think so," Charlie said. "Anyway, you'd think this criminal would want the credit for the murder."

"Maybe not. After all, in some ways not knowing is way worse. Oliver's life just sort of moves on, but not really. He's not a widower, he's not divorced, he's a married guy with no wife."

"Why are you looking into his background?" Charlie asked. "Do you have a thing for him?"

"No." The man fascinated me, but in a way I didn't understand. I was interrupted by a beeping on the line, meaning someone else was trying to get through. I usually hate call waiting. It is incredibly rude to answer a call from someone else during a different phone conversation, but that's exactly what I was going to do.

"Charlie, I've got a call coming in, hold on," I said, then clicked over.

"I'm calling to check on the baby," the voice said on the other end, not bothering to identify herself. "Is she okay?"

"I think you have the wrong number," I said.

"I should have known you wouldn't take this seriously," the voice muttered.

"Who is this?"

"It's Debbee," she said. "Remember, you took a dog from me?"

Her tone annoyed me. "I didn't take anything from you, you were paid for the dog and agreed to the purchase."

"Are you taking care of him?" she said before giving a loud sniff, as if her sinuses were all congested. Wow, this woman hit my last nerve and grossed me out at the same time.

"No, I locked him in the basement and haven't bothered to feed him. Of course I'm taking care of him, why would you ask me such a stupid question?"

"You'd better be taking good care of him," she growled.

"Thanks for calling, have a nice day," I said, and hung up, switching back to Charlie. "What a freak," I said.

"I presume you think you're speaking to someone else," the nasal voice answered. Oh, crap, it was still Debbee. Well, I wasn't about to let her push me around.

"No, I knew it was you. And it is kind of freaky, you calling like this. Do you check on everyone who buys a dog from you?"

"I make sure the animals are taken care of. I'm calling to make sure you're feeding him properly. You should come back out to the house and buy my food. It's organic, and it's good for the dog."

This time I got it right when I hung up on her.

"Charlie, you still there?"

"Yes, but I've got to go," she said. "Who was it?"

"The organic lady, the one who had the puppy."

"Puppy?"

Oops. I'd forgotten to tell Charlie about Sparky. "He's adorable, you'll love him," I said.

"You got a puppy? What do the aunts think?"

"They think he's great," I said. "Call me later."

No sooner had I gotten off the phone with Charlie than it rang again. Reaching for the phone, a knock sounded at the door. Too many people trying to reach me couldn't be good.

Chapter Thirty-One

"HOLD ON," I CALLED OUT as I reached for the phone.

"Kenny is on his way up, just letting you know."

"Thanks, I'll take care of him," I told Estelle. It was sweet that they warned me whenever he came around.

The door wasn't even open all the way when the smell assaulted my nostrils. That man needed to cut way back on the cologne. As much as he used, it was a weapon all on its own. I blocked the doorway, not letting him in. "What's up, Kenny?"

"I want to talk to you," he said.

"So, talk."

He sighed, shifting his weight from foot to foot. "Ava, can I come in?"

"I don't think that's such a good idea."

"We missed you in church today."

"No, you didn't. Get to the point."

Kenny looked wounded, but I knew better. His look—probably practiced in front of a mirror—was for the sole purpose of getting what he wanted. I raised my eyebrows, waiting.

"The thing is, I want to talk to you about your brother's group. Please. It's important."

I knew better, but he had said the magic 'please', so I stepped aside to let him in.

Once inside, he started pacing. No doubt about it, he was agitated. He didn't even notice Sparky sniffing around him, wagging his cute little tail. This was a change for Kenny. He always projected confidence, whether it was warranted or not. "Ava, I want you to give some thought to leaving your brother's group and joining mine instead."

I tried to arrange my face in a neutral expression, since getting upset with Kenny was generally a big waste of time. He never noticed or cared how others felt about a situation. "Are you insane?" I asked. This was weird, even for him. He must have some sort of ulterior motive.

"For one thing, it would keep you out of trouble," Kenny said.

"What do you mean?"

"Ava, you cannot be part of something where you found a dead body, then start poking around trying to figure it out and expect to stay safe."

Okay, maybe this time he did care. But Giuseppe's accusations about Kenny being the murderer sounded in my head. I still didn't believe it, since this was Kenny we were talking about, but maybe anything was possible. "What do you know about the murder?" I asked.

Kenny locked both his hands behind his head, a gesture I knew meant he was frustrated. "Ava, please, leave it alone. I don't want to see you get hurt."

"Is that a threat?" I asked.

"No!" he said. I swear I saw tears in his eyes. "Ava, you're in over your head, and you know it. I'm trying to help you here."

"I'm fine."

"You're stubborn, is what you are. What're you gonna do if this guy comes after you next?'

"What makes you think someone is going to come after me? It's not like I know who murdered Ethel." I gave Kenny my most piercing stare. "Do *you* know who killed her?"

"Why are you lookin' at me like that? I hate when you do that." His pacing was starting to get to me, but I was afraid to invite him to sit down. He'd never leave if I did.

Sparky ran and got a chew toy, dropping it at Kenny's feet. Honestly, how anyone could ignore such cuteness was beyond me.

"No, I do not know who killed her, but it's not like she wasn't asking for it."

"Nobody asks to get killed, Kenny."

"You know what I mean. She was full of sour prunes, that lady."

"Kenny, what do you know about Linwood?" The question stopped him in his tracks. I should have asked him as soon as he came into my apartment.

"Seems like a nice enough guy, for an old guy," he said. "Why? What's he got to do with anything?"

"I read something weird in the newspaper, something he wrote."

Kenny waved a hand in the air. "You can't pay attention to anything they print in that thing. It's full of garbage."

"What about the article praising your coffee shop as a one-of-a-kind town treasure, providing a much-needed cultural outlet?" The comment was rhetorical since I could easily predict his reaction.

"That was different. It was opinion, not news. And it was a good opinion, too."

He was so easy to lead in a conversation. "Linwood wrote an editorial piece, and I can't believe they printed it."

"Why, is he some sort of right-wing nutbucket?"

"No, but the letter was... odd."

Kenny looked up at the ceiling. "Honest, Ava, you drive me nuts. I never know what the heck you're talking about. Get to the point already, will you?"

Maybe he had a point. I did tend to add more information for dramatic effect sometimes, but it only made the story better. "It's not like this is some sort of book or something," Kenny said.

"Fine," I huffed. "The writing was a bit stilted, but basically the editorial stated all citizens in Brewster Square needed to be vigilant about our security because there are threats here, and we need to be on the lookout for all of these... threats."

"What kind of threats?"

I shrugged. "He never came out and said any specifics, which is what made the piece so odd, but he sort of hinted at foreign threats, terrorists or something. His letter said that if we were not careful about our safety it could lead to serious security issues."

"What the heck does he mean?"

"I don't know," I said. "I wanted to get an idea of what you thought of Linwood, whether you thought something might be wrong with him."

"You think he's crazy?" Kenny asked. "He has a point. Isn't that what the feds are always telling us, to report suspicious behavior?"

I shook my head. "True, but his letter rambled and didn't make much sense. It's sort of stream-of-consciousness. I just read it this morning, I hadn't seen it before."

"Was it in today's paper?" Kenny looked around, probably wondering where I'd stashed the Sunday paper.

"No, it was online. This was printed a few months ago."

"What the heck are you doing reading the newspaper from a few months ago? Forget about yesterday's news, you gotta stay up to date."

I couldn't tell Kenny that I'd been looking for clues about the murder and snooping into Detective Rialto's past. It was none of his business, and I didn't want to listen to him yell at me again. "I was doing some research and came across the letter," I said. The phone rang, interrupting Kenny before he could ask more questions. It was my aunt.

"Incoming. Again," she said, hanging up.

Before I'd replaced the receiver, a sharp knock sounded at the door.

Chapter Thirty-Two

STANLEY STOOD AT MY DOOR, flowers in hand and a smile on his face. "I've got a basket of food and a bottle of wine. Let's have a Sunday picnic," he said.

"Don't you think it's a little cold for a picnic?" Kenny asked.

I didn't take my eyes off Stanley. "No, I don't."

To his credit, Kenny knew it was time to leave. With a soft grunt he buttoned his jacket and squeezed out the door, shaking his head as he angled around Stanley and me.

Grabbing my coat and keys, I looked around for Sparky's leash. "Where do you want to have a picnic?" I asked. The day was sunny, but Kenny was right when he mentioned it was still a little cold outside.

Offering me his arm, he said, "I've set up a space heater for you."

I stared at him for a moment. "A space heater?"

"In the gazebo. It has electricity, you know, for the bands that play in the summer. So I took the liberty of setting up a space heater because I know you don't like the cold weather."

I narrowed my eyes, assessing the situation. "What made you think I'd be home or not busy?"

He laughed. "Busted. Your aunt called, told me Kenny was here harassing you, and I should get some food and wine and take you out for the whole town to see. I thought it was a great idea, and the whole town can see us in the gazebo, right?"

I smiled. "Sounds like a plan. Let's stop downstairs to drop off Sparky. I don't want to leave him alone yet, and I'm sure my aunts will be happy to watch him, especially since this was their idea in the first place." We looked down at the puppy, who wagged his entire body at us. A stuffed chicken was hanging out of his mouth.

"He's cute," Stanley said. "He won't be much protection, but he's adorable."

"I know, but I couldn't leave him in that hellhole."

"I don't blame you. I haven't been out there, but from what you've said it sounds like the place wasn't fit for the little guy." He leaned down to pet Sparky for a moment, tugging at the toy to play and rubbing his belly when the puppy rolled over. Stanley looked up at me and smiled, then stood. "These are for you," he said, shoving a bouquet of daisies at me. "They reminded me of spring, so I thought you might like them."

"They're beautiful, thanks." I took the flowers and put them in the one crystal vase I owned and placed the arrangement on the coffee table where I could see them as soon as I walked in the door.

Within minutes Sparky was tucked safely away with Aunt Maria and we had retrieved a picnic basket from Stanley's car, parked outside. Soon we were walking hand in hand across the green to the gazebo. "Thanks, this is nice. I'm glad to be out of the house," I said.

"What have you been up to today?"

I decided not to tell him about my snooping. I had a feeling Stanley would not like my Oliver-related snooping, and I knew how he felt about me looking into the Ethel thing. But he was the mayor, and perhaps Stanley knew more than he realized he knew. Maybe I could get him to talk without him knowing why I was asking questions.

"Do you go to St. Olaf or Trinity Church?" I asked.

"What makes you think I go to church?" Stanley replied, spreading a blanket on the bench for us.

"I assume, since you are a politician, it would be in your best interests to spend time and be seen in one of the churches," I answered.

"How terribly cynical of you," he said. "But to answer your question, if I go to church it's usually at Trinity."

I had hoped he went there. That was the church Ethel attended, a big old

Episcopalian structure that had been built when the town was first formed. Ethel had always been organizing something for the church, whether it was a dinner or craft show or mission trip.

Stanley leaned over and flipped a switch on the space heater positioned under the bench. Sure enough, warm air started to blow around us, and I was thrilled about the heat. "Have you gone to Trinity recently?" I asked.

"Why all the questions about church?" Stanley said. "Don't you go to the Catholic church here?"

I nodded. "Yes, but I've been thinking about switching." That statement caught me by surprise, even though it had come out of my own mouth. Maybe I missed going to church, maybe it was time to find a new church home. I thought about it for a moment, then remembered why I was asking. It had nothing to do with me going to church, and I sure could not see myself hauling my butt out of bed early on Sunday morning.

"Is it crowded?" I asked.

Stanley shook his head. "No, but I guess that depends on whether you go to the early morning service or the ten-thirty service. It got a lot more crowded after Ethel died."

Perfect. Since he brought the subject up I could just go ahead and ask. "Why would Ethel's death make the church more crowded? Do you think people felt guilty for saying mean things about her?"

"No. I think people are worried a killer is loose in our town."

"So they're going to church to pray about it? Or are they hoping there will be safety in numbers?" Either reason didn't sound like it would stop a killer.

Stanley smiled. "I have a different theory. I think they're going to church to check each other out, network a little, see if they can figure out who the killer is."

Now that did make sense, and I said so. "Besides, it's always someone everyone's surprised about, isn't it? Like a church deacon or something."

"Exactly," Stanley said. "Remember BTK? People were shocked about him. Wasn't he some sort of church guy?"

"Yeah, kind of like Son of Sam, who became a born again Christian," I said.

"Don't forget Ted Bundy, who volunteered on the suicide prevention hotline."

It was true. Killers were often people we didn't expect, people with hidden selves who never let the world see who they really were. I wondered who that could be in our nice little town.

"Hard to believe it's happening here in Brewster Square," Stanley said, echoing my thoughts. "But I wanted to talk to you about Ethel's murder."

"I know it's not something you can get involved in, and I completely understand," I said. "I wouldn't want you to jeopardize your job as mayor, and I won't ask for your help again."

Stanley shook his head. "I've been thinking about what you said. I've decided I want to help you."

This was a surprise, and maybe even slightly suspicious. Was he trying to get me to stop looking into the murder by inserting himself into my investigation?

"I know I said I couldn't help you, but that's not exactly true," he said. "Remember, I do lots of computer work. There may be something I can dig up for you, some sort of detail I can track down online. People don't always know how to utilize online resources."

"Why did you change your mind?" I asked.

Stanley's eyes hardened a bit. "I know it's not a surprise that I like you, Ava. You should know that I'm loyal to a fault. I'll stand by you no matter what."

Hmmm. This was a nice piece of information, but it wasn't really telling me why he had changed his mind. "That's great, Stanley, but why do you want to help me now? Of course I appreciate it, but it's a complete change from what you said to me earlier."

With a grim look on his face, Stanley answered, "Because of this." Reaching into his coat pocket, he pulled out a plain white envelope and handed it to me.

I looked at it carefully. Printed on the front it read 'copy'. "What's this?" I asked, feeling the first stirring of unease.

"You can open it. It's not the original, it's a copy. The original had my name printed on the front."

I pulled out a white sheet of paper and read the typewritten note.

Tell your girlfriend to forget about Ethel. It's none of her business.

Chapter Thirty-Three

I WAS SPITTING MAD. WHAT kind of a dweeb tries to threaten me by sending my boyfriend a lame note like that? I couldn't help it, the note reeked of someone trying to be a bully, and I hated bullies.

Did this person really think they could boss me around? The only person in my world who could tell me what to do was my brother, and even he had limits. Clearly, this was some kind of coward who was trying to warn me off. "Thanks for telling me," I said through clenched teeth.

"Are you mad at me?" Stanley asked.

I shook my head. "No, I'm mad at whoever wrote this note. How dare they tell me what to do? Do I look like someone who takes direction from anonymous letter writers?" Then the obvious occurred to me. "I'll bet whoever wrote the note is the person who killed Ethel."

Stanley nodded. "I thought the same thing. I turned the original over to the police this morning."

Crap. Even as I was thinking of what that meant, my cell phone rang. I looked at the little window, and sure enough, there was Oliver's name on my screen. I'd programmed his number into my phone so I could call him with updates, but I had a feeling I knew why he was calling me now. "It's the police," I said to Stanley.

"You'd better talk to them," he said.

With a frustrated sigh, I answered my phone. "Hi, Oliver," I said in a cheerful voice. "What's up?"

Stanley raised his eyebrows at me, but didn't say a word. He didn't have to, as I'm sure he could hear Oliver's baritone voice booming through the phone.

"Forget everything I suggested to you," Oliver said. "I want you to stay as far away from Ethel's murder as possible. If you even hear a whisper of anyone talking about it, turn around and run in the opposite direction."

"Okay," I said.

There was a silence on the other end of the phone. "I mean it, Ava. I don't want you talking to anyone about it."

"You can't arrest me for listening to what others are saying," I told him. Stanley's eyebrows went up even further, and I could tell he was dying to hear the entire conversation.

Oliver's voice turned to a low growl. "Ava..."

"I'll see what I can do," I said. It was the most noncommittal thing I could think of to say. I knew Oliver was telling me this because of the note Stanley had received, but I couldn't let my brother or my family down. I'd promised to help, and I had every intention of keeping my promise. Even if I was being threatened.

"You are officially off the case. If I find out you are in any way involved, I will arrest you and hold you for obstruction of justice."

Seriously? Not even a please or thanks for the help anyway, Ava, it's been great? Mr. Personality strikes again. "I'm going to the ghost hunt," I said. "You can't tell me not to."

"There are always consequences to our actions. Be sure your actions do not provoke anyone," Oliver said, and hung up.

I put my phone back in my bag, wondering what to do now that I'd been officially warned away.

"What was that about?" Stanley asked.

"I'm off the case," I said without thinking.

"When, exactly, were you on the case?" Stanley's tone alerted me to the fact that there might be a problem.

"I don't think I was really on the case," I said. "I was just supposed to pay attention and let Oliver know if I heard anything around town."

"Was this a formal arrangement?"

Oh boy. Stanley's tone had definitely changed. "It wasn't in writing," I said with a defensive note in my voice.

"Did he approach you about helping him or did you offer?"

I have to admit, Stanley was making me a little nervous. He might have run for mayor so he could have health insurance, but he sure did have that "official and important" tone of voice people in positions of power used. He was using it on me, whether he realized it or not.

"Stanley, did I do something wrong? Are you mad at me? Because I would have done everything I'm going to do anyway. I'm trying to help my brother, remember?"

Stanley shook his head. "I know you want to help your family, an admirable quality, but Detective Rialto should know better than to involve you in an active investigation."

I was confused. "But you just offered to help me, too. You said you wanted to help. How is that different?"

"It's different because I was going to help you by seeing what we could discover online, by digging through computer records and trying to find information. The good Detective was asking you to be physically involved in something where you could get hurt. I'm not even sure what he asked of you is legal."

There was a silence between us as I thought about what Stanley said. I don't think he realized what he had just communicated to me. "You're jealous of him, aren't you?"

Stanley looked up at me, a blush creeping up his face. "No, there's nothing to be jealous of. What makes you think that?"

"Because you're getting all protective of me, and I've never seen you this upset at anyone else before," I said. "But let me tell you, it's not Oliver's fault I'm involved. I told him I was good at detective work, and I told him —"

"I don't care what you told him," Stanley interrupted. "The fact is, he's a professional who should know better. And this isn't the first time, either."

Stanley stopped talking, but I wasn't sure what he had been referring to. "What do you mean?" I asked. "First time for what?"

Stanley looked me directly in the eyes, focused and passionate. "You know you could get hurt, right? Whoever murdered Ethel probably wouldn't think twice about killing you, too. The people in this town are acting like a bunch of lunatics, and you're out there trying to catch a murderer, like it's the easiest thing in the world."

I nodded. "It's not like anyone would know what I was doing."

Stanley shook his head. "What makes you so sure? Did you hear about what happened to Oliver's wife?" I nodded, not liking where this conversation was going. I think I knew what Stanley was going to say before he even said it.

"I heard it through the grapevine that he did the same thing with his wife, used her to help him close his cases. Except it backfired on him, and she ended up dead. I think her death was because of him."

Chapter Thirty-Four

I'D NEVER SEEN STANLEY MAD like that before, and I didn't know what to make of it. His accusation that Oliver was somehow responsible for his wife's disappearance struck me as a little harsh, but then I wondered if he knew something I didn't. As the mayor, maybe he had access to information the rest of us couldn't get. Or maybe he just didn't like Oliver.

Of course we fought about it, with me insisting Oliver never made me do anything I wasn't already going to do and trying to make Stanley understand it was better to do things—I didn't come right out and say "snoop around— with the full knowledge of the police. Stanley, however, insisted Oliver was in the wrong, and stomped off muttering something about jobs.

I hoped Oliver wasn't going to get in trouble because of me. In fact, in the showdown of Oliver versus Stanley I wasn't entirely sure who would win. They were both incredibly stubborn.

I was sort of at loose ends with myself after my picnic with Stanley and decided to go see Charlie. I knew it would be good for me to be with a friend instead of locked in my apartment, alone and isolated. Besides, Sunday nights were always times when I never knew what to do with myself. Time slowed, nothing happened, and I wondered if there were things I was supposed to be doing instead of sitting around looking at the scenery.

Visiting Charlie made my day worse. As soon as I got to her apartment I could tell something was wrong.

Charlie lived in the really nice section of town, down by the beach. Her house was always quiet and peaceful, a pond of serenity in our sometimes busy little town. Knocking on the door, I waited a moment, listening for Charlie's footsteps. Instead, all I could hear was a thudding noise.

What the hell is that noise? I don't like this...

I reached for the pewter-colored door handle on her glossy red door, hoping she'd left it unlocked. Sure enough, the handle turned easily, and I let myself into her house.

I could hear the thudding noise more clearly now, and knew it was coming from the living room. Walking toward the sound, I realized I could hear something else. The sound of Charlie.

"Such — *thud* — an — idiot — *thud* —"

"What are you doing?" I asked, stepping into her living room. Charlie was poised over her couch with what looked like a foam baseball bat in her hand. "What the heck is that?"

She looked up at me, her face flushed and her eyes moist. "It's my stress reliever. I needed to hit something. Fred and I broke up." As soon as she said it, Charlie sank onto the couch and began to cry.

Uh-oh. What did his father do now?

I sat next to her and put my arms around her. "I'm so sorry," I said, patting her back and not sure what else to say. I really believed she and Fred were going to be together forever, so maybe this was temporary. Hopefully they could work it out.

"I hate him," she said between hiccups.

I wasn't sure exactly what Fred had done, but it couldn't be good. Charlie loved everyone. "Hate's a strong word," I said. "Maybe you just really don't like him right now."

Charlie looked at me, eyes reddened and mascara running. "He's cheating on me."

"I hate him too," I said. "What happened? Are you sure?" I'd like to think I was a good judge of character, but I think everyone wants to think that of themselves. After knowing Fred for the past few years, though, I was sure I had him pegged as one of the good guys. Could both Charlie and I be blind to his deception? Could he possibly be a cold and calculating man who was bent on hurting people?

"When I went to the house earlier, I heard his father on the phone, making plans. He said Fred would meet his date at the country club later tonight, and hopefully he would be all finished with me by then."

And there it is. Nice work, Win. "So, all you heard was Win talking on the phone? Are you sure you know what he was talking about?" I asked.

"I know when I'm being cheated on." She started crying again. "When Win saw me he gave me that self-satisfied little smirk he gets, then he told me how lovely it had been to know me. He made it very clear he was saying good-bye."

"But we both know Win has been trying to break you and Fred up for a long time," I said. "Listen, maybe you heard whatever he was saying on the phone, but I think you should talk to Fred about what his father said. Win's a big jerk, maybe he's pulling some kind of underhanded villain thing."

That got a weak smile out of my friend, so I pushed a little harder. "I wouldn't be surprised if Win had planned this whole thing, and he wasn't even talking to anyone on the phone. He probably just put on a big act for you. He can't help it, it's part of his evil persona."

I could tell I was making Charlie feel a little bit better, and after a half gallon of moose tracks ice cream we were both happier with the world. "How did we ever live without this flavor?" Charlie said.

"I don't know, but it's got all the essentials for a good meal. Peanut butter for protein, chunks of chocolate for anti-cancer, and, um..."

"And ice cream is part of the dairy group, which we need for our bones," Charlie finished for me.

When I left her house a while later, my friend was in better spirits but looked tired. "Get a good night's rest tonight, you're going to need it for tomorrow," I said.

"I'll make it through the work day somehow," she said, standing at the front door with me.

"Don't forget, we're going to Ethel's house tomorrow night," I said. "I need your support for this ghost hunt that's actually a séance."

I wasn't sure about leaving Charlie alone, but she insisted she needed the time to herself. "I have to decide what I'm going to say to Fred so I don't look needy and insecure," she said. "I'll meet you at Ethel's tomorrow, though. I wouldn't miss this for anything."

***

Monday dragged, and Stanley did not call me all day. When I spoke to Charlie at lunchtime she said that Fred hadn't called her, either. I was not in a good mood, so I might have been a little hard on my brother when he asked me if I wanted a big lunch.

"Is there a problem with the amount of food I eat?" I said.

"No," he answered. I could tell he was confused by my question because of the little wrinkle on his forehead, which irritated me even more.

"Why would you ask me if I wanted a big lunch? Clearly you're trying to tell me something."

"No, I was wondering if you wanted to take extra time during your lunch break. I thought— "

"You thought it was time to tell me I need to go on a diet? Well, let me explain to you the average, healthy American woman is a size fourteen, not a zero. Since I'm a little below that number, I think I am at a perfectly acceptable weight."

"—since you're doing all this extra work with the Ethel thing you might need some time for yourself," he finished.

After that touching moment of fun, we avoided each other for the rest of the day. I admit I may have been a little harsh on him, but in my defense I was feeling a large amount of pressure. I had not found anything in my investigation, I had no idea what to do now that Oliver warned me away, and Stanley was mad at me, too. But I was going to be at Ethel's house tonight.

Inside, with access to the whole house. Would anyone think it was strange if I went into her room or her office and took a quick look around?

Yes, I'm sure they would, so I'd have to be careful not to let anyone see me. This could be my chance to find something important; something that would give me insight into what Ethel had been involved in before her death.

As I thought about the murder I became more convinced that Ethel had to have been killed because somebody wanted her to stop doing something. She must have been either preventing something from happening or telling someone she would prevent something from happening. In other words, she was probably doing what she'd always done, only this time it got her killed.

By the time my brother and I arrived at Ethel's house, I had a plan. If I let my brother think I was seriously involved in this ghost hunt thing, I stood a better chance of snooping. I'd been preparing him since we got in the car, saying things like "I hope we'll at least be able to feel Ethel's energy tonight," or, my personal favorite because it was so brilliant, "Hopefully we can help her spirit be at peace, allowing her to evolve into the next level of her creation." Words to live by, right? I figured my brother would just set me loose in the house as soon as we got there.

As my brother finally maneuvered the car onto Ethel's street, he swore. "How the freak am I supposed to park? Why are all these cars here?"

I shrugged. "I dunno, maybe someone decided to have a party because they're attracted to all the positive energy we're bringing in tonight."

"Cut it out, okay?" he said. "I know you're up to something, but I don't know what it is. Just try to behave tonight."

Looking down the street, I pointed. "I think there's a spot over there, in front of that house."

Finally, he parked, and we started trudging back toward Ethel's house. I could see Carla walking toward us, and dozens of people milling about in the yard. "What the heck is going on?" I said. "This is way more people than we've ever had at one of these things."

"Maybe she double booked," Giuseppe said. "Carla probably forgot we were coming, and scheduled a Pampered Chef party for tonight too."

"Yeah, that's exactly what I'd do if I were busy planning a funeral," I said.

Carla was walking toward us with a worried look on her face. We met her on the front lawn of Ethel's house. "I'm sorry, you guys," she said, pulling at her sweater. "I'm not so sure this is a good idea."

Chapter Thirty-Five

"CARLA, DEAR," MY BROTHER SAID, hugging the woman. I hated to admit it, but she really didn't look well. Her skin was a pasty-gray color, and she kept alternating between twisting her hands around her sweater and wrapping her arms around her body. Both gestures looked compulsive. "Everything will be fine," my brother continued. "When did all these people arrive?"

"They've been showing up all day," she said. "I mean, people have been showing up, and some animals, I think, and there was food. Lots of food, which is good because otherwise I wouldn't have eaten, but, gosh, isn't it hot out here? I'm kind of hot..." Her voice trailed off as she looked out at the street, a vacant stare in her eyes. "What?"

"Carla, are you all right?" I asked. From where I was standing the answer was an emphatic "no", but she nodded like a bobble-head doll.

"Everything's great," she said. "But there are just so many people. Maybe we shouldn't do this, maybe it's a sign."

"Of course it's a sign," my brother said. "It's a sign that we're on the right track and we have the support of the community."

Of course he thought we were on the right track. I loved my brother, but I viewed this whole ghost-business thing as a crutch for him. He never could stand the thought of people he loved dying, like our cousin Victor. Giuseppe and Victor had been close, more like best friends, and after Victor died I noticed Giuseppe took an even bigger interest in anything to do with ghosts, hauntings, and psychic phenomenon. I understood completely, since there was nothing I would like better than to be able to sit around and chat with those who had crossed to the other side, but I felt more practical about the whole thing. I thought that believing in the existence of ghosts was a crutch used by many people to help them through their grief. Yet, here I was, helping my brother. *The things I'll do for my family*, I thought, shaking my head.

I shot a look at my brother and said to Carla, "Can you excuse us for a moment? I need to ask my brother a question about the equipment." Grabbing Giuseppe's arm I pulled him closer to the curb. "Can't you see she's sick?" I hissed. "We shouldn't make her do this in her condition." Besides, there were way too many people here, which meant I had less of a chance to look through Ethel's stuff without being discovered. I didn't think I should mention my brilliant plan to anyone, though. Some people might not understand the difference between investigating and being nosy.

"If she's not feeling well this will take her mind off things," he said. "Besides, it's now or never. Since I'm in charge, I say we go ahead and do this. We'll be in and out of here in no time."

Walking away from me, Giuseppe went to Carla and put his arm around her, leading her up the sidewalk toward the house. I followed, muttering the entire time about ungrateful brothers who didn't realize the consequences of their actions.

A large number of people were milling about on the front lawn, as if this were some kind of neighborhood cookout. Some had drinks in their hands, others were munching on snacks. "Who brought the food?" I asked.

"Some of my friends dropped off a few casseroles, and one of the local vendors came by with a whole crate of organic breads. It was really very kind of her," Carla said.

I tried not to shudder, but it happened anyway. Organic breads probably meant Debbee, which meant I wouldn't be eating anything at this house tonight. I'd been to her house, and I knew the condition it was in, but I couldn't say anything to Carla. Besides, I wasn't so sure she should be up and walking around right now, much less worrying about what her guests were eating.

I watched as a woman I didn't recognize pushed her way past the others to stand in front of us. "Why are we here?"

My brother turned his full smile on her. I knew he did it more to disarm than anything else, and sure enough, it worked. I watched her melt at his attention, and return the smile. She then batted her eyelashes at him. *Who does that?* I thought.

"I mean, why are we at this house instead of the haunted house?" she asked. *Uh-oh, I do not like the way she is looking at my brother.*

"Who are you?" I said.

Without taking his eyes off her, Giuseppe said, "This is Sara, our newest member of the group. Sara, this is my sister."

I offered my hand for a handshake. "Nice to meet you, welcome to the group. Have you met Janine yet?" I said. Mentioning Giuseppe's wife was definitely in order.

"She's the reason I'm here," Sara said. "Janine told me that with my kind of high-level gift I'd be a great match for the group. So, G, why aren't we at the house where the murder took place?"

She called him G? I couldn't wait for him to yell at her, as I knew how much he hated that. And frankly, I didn't like this woman and the way she looked at my brother one bit.

"The house where Ethel was murdered is still a crime scene," Giuseppe said. "Shall we get started?"

Wait, what? No yelling, no telling her not to call him G, no anything?

"Wait for me, G," I said.

"Don't call me that," he said.

"How come she can but I can't?" I asked, not even trying to keep the whine out of my voice. "I'm only your sister, who happens to be good friends with your wife."

"Who can do what?" he said.

I shook my head. Men are really dense sometimes, and my brother was no exception. "How come Sara can call you G, and you don't get all upset?"

"Oh, her... she was one of Janine's roommates from a long time ago. They're like sisters."

Mmmhmmm.

"We've got everything set up already," he said, not really bothering to answer my question. That was fine with me, I'd find out everything I needed to know about our newest member anyway. Especially if she was someone

Janine knew.

Something wasn't right in the house, but it took me a moment to figure out what it was. "Giuseppe, where's all our equipment?" I asked. "You've only got the cameras set up in one spot, and there's no EMFs, no sensors—is it still in the car?"

"We don't need anything beyond the cameras set up in the dining room area," he said, avoiding my eyes.

"Why not?"

"Because all we'll really be doing tonight is focusing on the séance portion."

Chapter Thirty-Six

FINE. IT WASN'T A BIG surprise to me that my brother had this planned all along, or that he wasn't honest with me from the beginning. He knew I knew from the second he'd told me his plan for tonight, so I'd just as well get over it. *I can handle this. I'm a big girl. I'm not afraid.*

"What are you going to do if a ghost really appears?" a niggling little voice whispered in my head. *I'm going to go home, that's what. Where I'll be safe with my dog and my aunts and everything comfortable and familiar.*

But right now I had bigger concerns. Lots of people were milling around, and from the looks of things Giuseppe wanted to get this party started. I only had a little bit of time to snoop—um, investigate. I had to hurry.

I hightailed it up the stairs. I'd never been in Ethel's bedroom, but I was confident I'd know it when I saw it. If I was lucky, she kept her office up here, too. That was one the place sure to be full of information about what she was doing before she died. I'd take any kind of clue at this point.

Giuseppe said he'd set up a camera in her room, so I'd have to be on the lookout for it. The last thing I wanted was the ghostbusting team watching me paw through Ethel's things.

I went up the stairs as stealth-like as possible, trying not to draw attention to myself. All the doors in the hallway were closed. The first few doors I opened were so sparsely furnished that I assumed they were guest rooms.

Finally, I noticed the last door at the end of the hall was slightly ajar. Of course it would be the last one.

G—Giuseppe—must have left it open when he went in to set up his camera. I pushed the door and it swung in silently. The voices downstairs were loud, and as the sounds drifted up I was reminded that I did not have the luxury of time. Hearing snippets of some of the conversations, I hesitated, listening.

"The mist is incredible..."

"I swear the dead are all around this place. We must be over a burial ground."

"Is that a dragon?"

I shook my head, wondering how my brother managed to attract these people.

Slipping through the doorway, I entered Ethel's room. I knew it was her room because Giuseppe had set up the camera in here. I also knew he wouldn't mind if I was in here, but there was no need for the weirdos downstairs to watch me. That would be creepy. I grabbed the folded blanket off the foot of the bed and threw it over the camera. Perfect, now nobody knew what was going on in here.

I wanted to be methodical, and decided to start with the night stand next to the bed. The dresser probably held mostly clothes, but I would save that for last. Pawing through a dead person's pockets was not high on my list of fun activities.

I had to yank pretty hard to get the drawer open because so many papers were jammed in there. Bingo! Her drawer was a direct contradiction to the neat and ordered home downstairs, so I figured there had to be some kind of evidence shoved in here. I didn't know what I was looking for, but I knew I'd know it when I saw it.

I sorted through the papers, which consisted mostly of unopened envelopes. From the looks of things, they were all bills. Unpaid bills?

With so many of us doing our banking and bill-paying online, I knew this bunch of bills told me exactly nothing. If Ethel did everything on her computer, she didn't need the paper copies. But why would she save them?

Maybe they were unpaid, and maybe that had something to do with her murder. I looked more carefully at the return addresses, wondering if debt could lead to murder. Usually it just led to a collection agency.

I didn't see anything unusual, just the typical electric, water, and gas bills. I was hoping for a cell phone or credit card bill which would have given me information on Ethel's private life. Clearly I knew how to snoop.

I also saw lots of bills from a medical lab, and after a moment's hesitation tore one open. I needed some kind of information and this was all I could find.

The first bill contained charges for a routine pap smear. The next bill had charges for an influenza test. The third bill was charges for strep throat. All I could figure out from this was that Ethel didn't have very good health insurance.

I was starting to wonder if I should go through the other drawers, too, when I heard a sound behind me. Turning, I saw Linwood. Something about him didn't look quite right, and I stood, not sure why alarm bells were going off in my head.

"Linwood, I didn't hear you come in," I said.

"She's not here, you know." He wasn't looking at me but had crossed to the dresser and picked up a framed picture of Ethel and her niece that was sitting on top. He was a little too close for comfort, and now my only means of escape was to scramble across the bed to get out the door.

"She's not here," he repeated. Linwood's stare was vacant as his hands took the frame apart, removing the backing and taking the picture and glass from the frame.

"I know, Linwood, but Giuseppe insists on going through with trying to contact her spirit. He thinks we might get some sort of answer."

I was regretting having thrown the blanket over the camera, since it meant that nobody knew what was going on in here. Right now, my idea of privacy was not such a good one. Especially with what I was thinking. Linwood's hands shook and his face was slack. *Maybe he's having a stroke or something. Maybe it's all in his head, and he didn't do it, and I'm not really trapped with a killer.*

Killer? Did I really think this sweet man was capable of that? "Linwood, are you okay? What are you doing up here?" There's no way he could have hurt Ethel. He barely knew her, so it wouldn't make sense. Besides, he was nice. Nice people don't go around killing their neighbors.

"I killed her, you know. She needed killing."

Chapter Thirty-Seven

SO MUCH FOR MY NICE people theory. I didn't know what to do. Was this a true confession? Could it be so easy? There was a definite downside, though: if Linwood had really killed Ethel, I was stuck in her bedroom with a killer.

"I saw you find her, but you couldn't see me. I watched you."

Chills ran up and down my body as I remembered the noise I'd heard in the basement that night. The killer had been down there with me, just as I'd thought. I reached into my pocket and pulled out my cell phone. Linwood wasn't even looking at me. I scrolled to my recently received calls, and pushed the button to connect me with Oliver.

Slowly, I put the phone to my ear, but Linwood wasn't paying attention. Instead, he was picking at the bedspread with one hand as if there were lint or something on it. I looked him over, wondering if he could overpower me, and decided that yes, he could. After all, he'd taken the picture frame apart and now stood there with a piece of glass in one hand, glass that could cut me. I gripped the phone, hands trembling, and willed Oliver to answer.

"Detective Rialto," the voice came over the line. I'd never been so happy to hear someone.

"Hi, Linwood said Ethel isn't here," I said in a rush. I didn't know how much time I had, or whether or not I could make it over the bed and escape.

"He's in Ethel's bedroom with me, and he told me she's not here."

Something in my voice must have alerted him to the fact that all was not well. "Are you okay?"

"No," I said.

"Are you at Ethel's house?"

"Yes."

"Are you safe?"

"No."

"I'm on my way."

I started to edge my way around the bed, then stopped. How was I going to get by Linwood? Would he just let me waltz out of the room? *I wonder if today is the day I'm going to die.* I couldn't stop the thought, but I could do my best not to get killed.

"Come here," he said.

I froze, not sure what to do. He was standing only about five feet away from me, and my back was to the wall. I had nowhere to go, but there was no way I was going to make this easy for him. *I don't want to die, I'm not ready. Not yet.* I thought of my mother and father, my brother and Sparky. I thought of Stanley and everything that might have been. I started counting the items on the dresser. Perfume bottles: one, two, three...

Linwood took a step toward me and my breath caught in my throat. I had to do something. As I started to tense my muscles to leap onto the bed, a cloud of gray appeared between us.

What the—

The gray mist began to take a form, and I stood stock-still for a moment, trying to process what I was seeing. *Ethel?* But Ethel was dead, and I didn't believe in ghosts. *Run,* a voice in my head commanded. I didn't need to hear it twice.

I threw myself onto Ethel's bed, rolled over and off the other side and landed on the floor with a solid thump. I didn't stop to assess whether or not I'd been hurt, instead lunging for the door and flinging myself into the hallway. Without looking behind me, I raced down the hall and practically fell down the staircase.

"Giuseppe!" I shouted. "Help!" Things were not normal. Like a bad dream, nobody paid any attention to me.

A man wearing a hideous Hawaiian print shirt called out to me. "Can you see her? She's here, you know." I didn't know this guy, but I had a moment's confusion. Was he talking about the shape I'd just seen?

"I need help," I said, grabbing his arm.

"It's amazing, she's here, right over there," he pointed to the far corner of the room, completely ignoring my distressed plea.

I started to get nervous, wondering if everyone had gone crazy. "What are you talking about?"

I heard the voice I knew all too well, the voice from the phone and the previous ghost hunt. "Ethel is here. She has come with a message from beyond."

Crap-a-roni, just who I needed. Debbee was nuts. I glanced over to the bottom of the staircase, wondering when Linwood was going to come thundering down to try and kill us all.

"Can I have your attention, please? We have a situation—"

Giuseppe ran into the room, interrupting me. "They see her, they really see her, can you believe it?"

"G, thank God you're here." I grabbed onto him, relieved. "I found—"

"This is so much better than anything Kenny's group could come up with," he interrupted. "Think of the press we can get out of this. Think of our reputation... we might even get our own show out of this..."

Clearly my brother was having trouble focusing. "Listen to me, Linwood is upstairs, we need to—" The voices of everyone around us grew louder, drowning me out, and my brother began walking away from me.

"She hasn't crossed over."

"She wants to speak with us, she has something to say."

"There are others with her, we must pay attention..."

Finally, I saw a police cruiser pull up outside, lights flashing and parking right in the middle of the street. I watched as Rob ran from the car to the front of the house.

"Police, everyone freeze!"

You would think that people would stop what they were doing when an armed officer burst through the door, but it was as if they couldn't hear him.

"I said, freeze! Everyone stop what they're doing right now!"

I caught Rob's eye and shook my head. By now I was more than a little panicked, and made my way over to him.

"What is wrong with these people?" he asked me. "It's as if they can't hear me."

I counted thirty-six people, and not one of them was acting normal. To my utter horror, tears welled in my eyes. I did not want to cry, but it was all too much. "I don't know, Rob, all I know is that Linwood is upstairs in Ethel's bedroom, and he told me he killed her, and when I came downstairs nobody would listen to me. It's like they've all become zombies or something."

Other police officers had come in behind Rob, including Oliver, and they heard my last statement. "Has anyone taken any drugs tonight?" Oliver asked me.

I shook my head. "No, not that I'm aware of. Giuseppe would not approve of substance abuse, and I've never seen drugs or alcohol during a ghost hunt before."

"I'm calling for back-up, and I'm requesting medical personnel, just in case," Oliver said to Rob. "Take Ava outside and keep her safe. She's our only witness right now."

My stomach dropped and my legs felt weak. I thought I was going to throw up, but the thought of how embarrassing that would be stopped me from losing my lunch. This was real. A killer was upstairs, and for the first time I wondered if Linwood had done something to everyone here. Could he have poisoned them all somehow?

I went outside with an officer I didn't know, grabbing hold of Giuseppe's sleeve on the way out and dragging him with me. "What's going on?" he demanded as I pulled him along. "Why are the police here, and why are you pulling on me?"

"You're coming outside where it's safe. I don't want to have to explain how you died a weird death at the hands of ghost-hunting crazies to your son when he gets older." Holding onto my brother calmed me somewhat, but I had to ask him to see if he'd been affected. "G, can you see Ethel?"

"Stop calling me that. Does it really matter if I can see her?"

"Yes, it matters. Just tell me the truth and stop worrying about what others will think."

My brother pouted for a moment, then leaned in and spoke in a low voice. "No, I can't see her, but—whatever—everyone else can. Clearly we've found something, right?"

I was so relieved the tears that I'd been holding back spilled over. I couldn't help but hug him. "I'm just glad you're okay."

"What are you talking about?"

By this time we were standing on the front lawn of Ethel's house, and the police had started ushering people out, keeping them sorted in groups. I wondered if they were sorted according to levels of craziness, but suddenly found myself too tired to even ask anyone. The adrenaline rush I'd had upstairs must have worn me out.

I looked around, hoping Oliver and Rob had found Linwood and that neither of them were hurt, then I froze. Again. Linwood walked toward me, coming from the back of the house. He was moving at a fast pace, striding with purpose, headed straight for me.

Where was Oliver? Where was Rob? Even Giuseppe had moved away from me and was talking to other people in his group.

Linwood stood in front of me, taller than I remembered, shaking his head. "You must be a spy, just like her. I have reason to believe you've gone over to enemy territory, and for reasons of national security you must be eliminated." In his right hand he still held the piece of glass from the picture frame, and his arm raised. Everything slowed as my mind screamed *Run*. Before I could move, though, a big blur crashed into Linwood from the left side, knocking him to the ground.

I stared at the two men on the ground, watching as the weapon was pried from his hands and cuffs were put on Linwood.

Oliver had saved my life.

Chapter Thirty-Eight

"YOU HAVE THAT LET-DOWN feeling," Charlie said, pulling a bottle of pinot noir from the refrigerator. "You gathered all this evidence and tried to solve the case and it turns out to be the old guy with Alzheimer's disease who did it."

"We assume he did it, but we don't know for sure," I said, watching her pour the wine into two glasses. I hadn't told her everything that had happened in Ethel's bedroom. Part of me wondered if I'd made up the gray mist in order to save myself, but mostly I knew what I'd seen. I wasn't sure how I felt about my vision, so I decided not to think about it at all. Ever.

"Of course we know he did it," she said. "The doctor all but told you that. It's one of those things you didn't see coming, so you're bound to feel confused."

"Confused?" A tail thump from the corner echoed my question. Sparky must have thought I'd said, "Let's go for a walk and get some treats," because he was suddenly on his feet and chasing his tail.

"He is a cutie," Charlie said. "Sure—bewilderment, confusion, all that. For what it's worth, I think you'd make a great detective. You were asking all the right questions."

"I'm not sure I did enough," I said, handing Sparky a chew toy. "I'm not sure I'd be good at that kind of work. When the you-know-what started hitting the fan at Ethel's house I froze. I was useless."

"You were not useless," Charlie said. "You called it in and got out of the room. What else were you supposed to do? Handcuff him yourself?"

I smiled, basking in the knowledge that my friend Charlie was always my champion. I was a lucky woman; I had the unwavering support of my family and I had a super-amazing friend who believed in me. What more could I want?

Before I could answer her, a sharp knock sounded at the door. Eyebrows raised, I looked at her. "Have you patched things up with Fred?"

She shook her head. "Nope. No way. Not after what he said to me. He's going to have to come crawling back and offer up a big old heaping portion of 'sorry' because, because..." She stopped to take a swallow of her wine, and the knock sounded again.

"Want me to get it?" I asked, wondering if it was Fred with a bouquet of "sorry" flowers. I would be happy for her if it was him at the door; it was easy to see that those two belonged together.

Banging her glass down onto the side table she answered. "No, I've got this." I was surprised she didn't break the glass, but didn't say anything as she strode to answer the insistent knock.

Before I could say, "Make sure you check to see who it is," Charlie had thrown the door open and started yelling before she realized who was standing in front of her.

"What the hell do—oh, sorry. Hi, Detective, can I help you?"

Oliver looked around Charlie. "When she didn't answer her house phone, I suspected that Ava might be here, so I took a chance and came over. Can we talk for a minute?"

I nodded, watching him as he came in. He was a very handsome man who had just saved my life. I was beyond grateful to him. But there was more. His good looks, his obvious intelligence, it all added up to one heck of a package.

One very mysterious package.

It was all so simple, I realized. I really liked Oliver; I thought he was an interesting and vibrant person. I knew we were destined to become friends. I don't know if he knew that, but he'd figure it out eventually. I didn't actually hate him, which was sort of a surprise to me after all the nasty thoughts I'd had during the case.

He looked a bit surprised at my wide smile, but given the fact that someone had tried to kill me earlier that night I didn't blame him. He was probably wondering how much wine Charlie and I had been drinking.

"I'm sorry to do this, but I have a few questions I have to ask. It won't take long, and I thought you might be more comfortable here instead of at the station."

I nodded and put down my wine glass. "No problem, I'll tell you anything you need to know. Just let me use the restroom first."

As I went to use the bathroom, I could hear Charlie playing hostess. "Can I get you something to drink? Maybe you'd like a cup of coffee?"

"No, thank you ma'am, I'm fine."

I sighed as I shut the door to Charlie's bathroom, mostly out of a sense of awe. Every time I went in there I was happy-envious. Charlie has a wonderful decorating style and she's turned her bathroom into a spa-like oasis. I relaxed into the mint green and sky blue luxury, admiring the fluffy towels (where did she get them, they reminded me of cotton candy), and was marveling at the cobalt-blue vessel sink (I loved that bowl-look in a bathroom sink) when I heard a loud crash.

I turned off the water and wondered what to do. If someone had broken in, surely Charlie would be fine because Oliver was out there with her. After all, he was armed and trained for dangerous situations. But I couldn't hear anything else, and that was not a good sign. What if this was some type of home invasion, and Oliver was taken by surprise, unable to help Charlie? I couldn't leave my friend at the hands of criminals.

Something's wrong. I'd hear Charlie and Oliver talking if they'd knocked something off the counter. It's too quiet out there. I slowly opened the bathroom door, sending out a prayer of thanks that the hinges didn't squeak and I could be stealthy. Silence coated the house. I made my way down the hallway in a half-crouch position, wondering what the heck I could use as a weapon.

When I reached the end of the hall, I dared to look around the corner into the living room on the right.

Oliver was flat on the floor, arms out to his side, eyes closed.

Chapter Thirty-Nine

"IT'S NOT WHAT YOU THINK," Charlie said, looking over at me. "He'll be fine, I'm sure. We've just got to get him up."

"What did you do?"

"Charlie didn't do anything," a voice to my left said.

I recognized the voice, but I still jumped. "Geez, you scared me. What the heck is going on?" I said. Oliver's eyes were open, but I wondered if I needed to get him to a hospital or something. "Someone better start talking, and quick."

"It was my fault," Fred said. Charlie's boyfriend stood in the kitchen looking like a scared five-year-old. "I thought he... I thought they... I didn't..."

"Spit it out," I said, kneeling next to Oliver and putting my hands on his face. Oh, God, what were we going to do if something really bad happened to Oliver? His skin felt warm to the touch, but I didn't know how to check for brain damage or anything serious. I looked at his chest to see if it was moving, if he was breathing.

"I'm fine," Oliver said, closing his eyes. "I'll probably have a black eye and my hip is a little sore from falling down, and right now I don't think I want to move." He cracked one eye open to look at me. "And you can take your hands off my face. Body temperature takes a while to decrease after death, so you'd have no way of knowing right now by touching me if I were alive or dead."

How the heck did he know what I was thinking? I sat back on the floor, relieved Oliver was alive and annoyed he could read me so well.

"Ohmygod, am I going to jail? Because I didn't know. I didn't mean to assault an officer, I thought that—it looked like—when I came in there were these wine glasses and Charlie looked so sexy and—"

"You thought I looked sexy?" Charlie asked.

"Of course I thought that, I always think that," Fred said, gazing at her with anguish. "You're the most beautiful woman I've ever known, the most amazing—"

"Sorry to interrupt, but can we get to the part where Oliver ended up on the floor?" I said. At this point I didn't care if I was being rude, I needed answers. The man who'd saved my life earlier today was lying on the floor, and I wanted to know why.

"I came to see Charlie so we could talk things through. I've missed her so much." Fred's words were rushed. "I wasn't really thinking, I just let myself in. I usually do, we both—when I came in here and saw two glasses of wine and heard the soft music and saw the detective, I thought... I thought..."

"You thought I was having a romantic evening with your girlfriend and decided to punch me in the face," Oliver finished.

"I'm so sorry," Fred stammered. "I shouldn't have done that. Even if you were here on a date or something, that was a stupid thing to do. I let my emotions get away with me, and I am so sorry. If I've caused any injury I'll pay the bill, I am—"

"So sorry, I know," Oliver said. Finally, he opened both eyes and pushed himself to a sitting position. He looked at Fred and Charlie for a long moment before he answered. "Don't worry about it. I'm sure I've done something somewhere along the line that caused me to get smacked tonight. Let's just consider it karma and forget about it."

A brief image of the newspaper article flashed through my mind. What did he mean? What had really happened to Oliver's wife? Was she still alive somewhere?

The sound of Charlie's voice interrupted my thoughts. "How about I get you a glass of that wine? You might need it now."

"No, thank you, I'm still on duty," Oliver said, standing. I stood as well, not wanting to be the only person sitting on the floor. "Ava, let's go get some pizza and talk."

"Thanks, but I'm not hungry."

"I don't care. Let's go get some pizza and talk," Oliver said. "Get your purse and let's go." He nodded at Charlie and Fred, who were standing with their arms around each other. I wasn't sure why the heck either of them needed comfort when it was Oliver who had gotten punched in the face, but clearly the two of them weren't paying any attention to Oliver and me.

"Sparky can stay with Charlie for now. You and I have things we need to discuss," Oliver said, holding the door open for me.

Chapter Forty

THE PIZZA RESTAURANT AROUND THE corner from Charlie's house has amazing food. Their pizza is great—the crust is perfect—and it always smells like garlic when you walk in. But they have great sandwiches, too, and they make a sub sandwich with chicken cutlets, eggplant, and melted cheese. It makes me happy just to think about it.

We got a table pretty quickly, and after ordering two Dr. Peppers Oliver began to study my face. I waited a full second before squirming. "What?" I asked. "Is something wrong?"

"How are you holding up?"

"I'm fine," I said, mostly because that's what you said no matter what was happening in the world.

"Mmmhmm. Now, tell me how you're feeling."

"Hungry."

"Stop it with the jokes, Ava. Someone tried to kill you today, and I know that can be an unsettling experience."

I laughed. I couldn't help it. The term "unsettling experience" sort of got to me in a way that made something distinctly un-funny suddenly seem funny. And I kept laughing.

There is no doubt about it, Oliver is a patient man. When I finally started to get a grip on my emotions, he leaned across the table and took my hand in both of his hands. "You're going to go through this period of feeling unstable, and you're not going to know when the emotions will hit you. It might be like this, uncontrolled laughter, or next time you might cry. Just go with it and let it out."

"I think I'll be fine, now," I said, taking a steadying breath. "I don't know why that struck me as funny."

"Because you went through a life-or-death situation today, and your world tilted a little. And you'll have an episode or two like this again. Feel free to call me if you have trouble dealing with any of this."

If anyone knew about life-or-death stuff, it was Oliver, but I didn't want to discuss that right now. We had other matters we needed to talk about. "So, what do you know about Linwood?" I asked. "Does he really have Alzheimer's?"

Oliver leaned back in his seat and ran a hand through his hair. "I don't know. Alzheimer's diagnoses are difficult, and there are lots of different types of dementias he might have. But yes, his wife told us he'd been acting strange for the past six months or so, and she knew he killed Ethel."

I sat up straight. "She knew? She didn't say anything?"

"Did you want her to tell everyone her husband did it?"

"Yes," I said. "What if he'd killed someone else? Doesn't that make her some sort of accessory?"

Oliver nodded. "It does, but I'm going to let the lawyers untangle this whole mess. This will probably never reach court, you know."

I'd surmised as much, but hearing Oliver say it made me sad. "But Ethel didn't deserve to die like that. She didn't deserve to be murdered for no reason and not have someone pay for doing something so heinous."

"I know, but I think you have made up for her ignoble death."

"What do you mean?"

"You took the time to try to help, to try to find her killer. You cared enough to do something," Oliver said.

He was right, but only sort of. I'd cared because of my family, and because I didn't want to see my brother get hurt. And a little bit because I wanted a new career.

Oliver reached across the table and grabbed hold of my hands again. "I know you're telling yourself you only did this for your brother, but give yourself some credit. You stepped in when nobody else wanted to, and you did something for a woman who most people claimed not to like."

"Why did someone try to stop me?"

"Do you mean the letter?" he asked. When I nodded, he took a breath before speaking. "Apparently Linwood's wife was concerned about you discovering the truth. She admitted to us that she sent you the letter."

A moment later I realized what that meant. It meant she thought I was smart enough to figure out the case. It meant I might have the makings of a detective after all.

"This doesn't mean you're a good detective," Oliver said.

"How do you do that?"

Oliver shrugged. "I can read you. You have a very expressive face."

"Great. Anyway, why are we here? Did you need to talk to me about something?"

"Yes, I just need you to go over your statement one more time and sign it."

"Why?"

Oliver sighed and put his fingers in the bridge of his nose. "Because it's what I need you to do. Review your statement. Sign it."

"Okay, fine, I was just asking." Yeesh, you'd think I asked him something difficult.

We reviewed what happened, with him asking me the same questions he'd asked earlier. This time he gave me a funny look when I told him what had happened in the bedroom, but my lips were sealed. No way was I telling him I saw a ghost. He pulled a written copy of my statement out of a folder and I signed it, happy to be finished with this whole thing. By that time our food had arrived, and I was grateful for some good pizza to focus on, despite my earlier claim of not being hungry. There's nothing like a veggie combination to make the world better.

"I don't know how you can eat that," Oliver said, biting into his pizza.

"That stuff you're eating is going to give you a heart attack. Cram much meat on your pizza?" He had ordered the meat lovers special, with pepperoni, sausage, meatballs, and God knew what else.

"Should I start eating that organic stuff your friend makes?" he asked, winking at me.

It took me a moment to realize he was talking about Debbee and her organic yuck. I shuddered. "I know it's mean of me to say this, but her food has got to be gross."

"Why is it mean?" Oliver asked around a mouthful of pizza.

"Because my mother taught me if I didn't have anything nice to say, don't say anything at all. And I really don't have anything nice to say about that place. If people saw how she lived, I'm sure her sales would plummet."

Oliver stared into space for a moment. "I'm sure the health department has inspected the premises."

"Mmm," I said, more because my mouth was full than out of anything useful to add. I was sure they had as well, but she was probably one of those people who made everything perfect before the inspection so they never really knew that she lived in a pit.

We finished our pizza and talked a bit, mostly about the differences between living in the northeast and the southwest. Oliver was funny and interesting to talk to, and he was good company. But I missed Stanley.

On the sidewalk outside, Oliver looked down at me and smiled. "Miss your boyfriend, don't you?"

I laughed. "I guess I am easy to read."

Oliver gave me a hug. "Go home, call Stanley, get some rest. It's over now, and you don't have to worry about a murderer loose in your town."

I shook my head. "I know you're right, but I'm not sure it's over."

"What do you mean?"

"I think there's something still going on. Remember earlier, all those people at the house claimed to see things. I have to tell you, that was weird."

"I wouldn't worry about it too much," Oliver said. "Sometimes people see what they want to see, or they get carried away with a crowd mentality. These things fade with time."

I knew he was probably right, but I couldn't shake the feeling that there was more to it than his simple explanation.

Chapter Forty-One

I DROVE HOME WITH SPARKY, happy for Charlie and Fred but still uncertain about where I stood with Stanley. As if I had conjured him simply by thinking about him, there he was on my front porch, surrounded by the aunts. He stood when he saw me approaching. "They interrupted the town council meeting to tell me what had happened. Are you okay?" Without waiting for an answer, he came down the porch steps and wrapped me in his embrace. "I was worried."

With my face pressed against his chest I wrapped my arms around him. I could hear Sparky's tail thumping against the ground as he wagged it, sniffing around our feet. This was where I needed to be.

"I'm fine," I said. "It was a little scary, but I'm not hurt or anything." By this time my aunts had gathered around me as well, and I was enveloped in family love. "Come inside, we'll get you something to eat," Aunt Maria said.

"I'm fine, I just had pizza," I told them. Looking up at Stanley, I added, "With Oliver." If there was going to be anything of real substance between Stanley and I, we needed to communicate and agree on things.

Stanley hung his head. "I'm sorry. I shouldn't have said the things I said. I was so worried about your safety that I got a little carried away, especially since I didn't have the whole background on Oliver." He leaned over and gave Sparky a scratch behind the ears.

The whole background? This sounded like Stanley had some information to share. *I wonder if he's going to tell me what he knows or if he's going to stay quiet.* Stanley was discreet, which meant I wouldn't always know everything that was going on in our town.

"We're going to leave you kids alone to talk things out," Aunt Estelle said. Maria, Claudia, and Estelle turned and walked back up the steps, taking seats on the chairs scattered across the front porch. They were far enough away to give us privacy, yet close enough to keep an eye on me in case I needed help.

I stood quiet for a moment, listening to the birdsong around me, feeling warm and savoring the support and love of my family and boyfriend.

Yes, my boyfriend. At that moment I knew Stanley and I could have something special if we chose to work on it. I had no doubt, though, that it would take some work for both of us. Both of us had a tendency to be a little, um, hardheaded.

"Listen, I wanted to ask you something," he said, leaning his forehead against mine. "My family is having an anniversary dinner for my parents in May, and I was wondering if you'd come with me. You can meet everyone—my family."

This was big. Stanley's family lived in Stonington, a small town about an hour's drive up the Connecticut coast. It was a gorgeous little town and one I loved visiting, but I wouldn't normally jump in my car and drive up there. Meeting Stanley's family was a significant step forward in our relationship.

"I'd love to," I said. "Why don't you go inside with my aunts, I've got to get my phone out of my car. I left it on the seat." The only reason I remembered this was because I couldn't wait to call Charlie and tell her. Maybe we were both finally getting lucky in the boyfriend department.

Stanley kissed the top of my head, and went up the stairs to sit with my aunts. I smiled and waved, giving them the 'one second' signal to let them know I'd be right back. A flash of gray appeared in my side vision, and before I could turn my head the voice next to me hissed, "I'm here to take him back."

For the second time in a twenty-four hour period, everything slowed. Sidewalk pebbles crunched beneath my feet as I turned to face my nemesis. Who else could it be but the one person I'd already decided was crazy: Debbee.

"What the heck are you talking about? Why are you sneaking up on me like that?" I demanded.

"You are not worthy of caring for an animal. You have put this young one's life in jeopardy today, and you must give him back. I won't have him mistreated."

"You've got to be kidding me. I don't know what you're talking about." Except I did know what she was talking about. This fool woman thought she was going to take Sparky back home with her. A rage built inside me that I had never experienced before. This woman, this insane excuse for an animal lover, thought she was better equipped to raise my dog than me, sent me into a cold fury.

Who the hell does she think she is?

Before I could say anything, Debbee saw Sparky on my porch and tried to move around me. I stepped in front of her, blocking her way, and before I realized it I had reached out and shoved her backwards. "That is my dog, and you are seriously close to trespassing. You can get the hell out of here or I'll call the police." I'd had a rough day already, and this bitch didn't intimidate me in the least.

"Mine," she growled, and moved to go around me again. When I tried to block her way, she darted back in the other direction. Grabbing her by the arm, I spun her around so she was facing me again. She stepped closer to me, her face turning a deep red and her voice an angry timbre.

"Puppies are not property, they're children. The law is on my side with this," she snarled, spittle flying in my face.

"You're insane," I said. "I don't know what you've heard, but I have not in any way mistreated my dog."

She lunged for me, and I tried to step out of the way, but something blocked me and I tripped. Trying to stop myself from falling, I reached out and grabbed hold of Debbee, pulling her down with me. We landed on the sidewalk, and I realized it was Sparky who had been in the way. Apparently he wanted to join in the fun and games.

As soon as she saw Sparky, Debbee's eyes lit up. "Come here, baby, come home with mommy," she crooned. Sparky's ears were flat against his head, and he lay down on the sidewalk, quivering.

"Stop that, you're scaring him with your evil voice," I snapped. "What is wrong with you?"

A shadow loomed above us, and hands reached down to help me up. "I'm going to have to ask you to leave, and I will be notifying the authorities of this incident," Stanley said.

Debbee got up and brushed herself off, looking Stanley up and down as if he were a fly on her fudge brownie. "And who the hell are you? The geek police?"

"No, I'm the mayor of this town, and while I am very familiar with you and your recent business of selling baked goods I was not aware that you also had a license to sell animals. I do hope you are up to date on all of your business permits."

Go, Stanley. The horrified look on Debbee's face was priceless. "I don't need a permit to sell a puppy," she said.

"According to our new code laws, passed just last month, indeed you do," Stanley said. "And by the way, when was the last time the health department paid you a visit?"

With a snort and a stomp that made me wonder if she had some sort of equine blood in her, Debbee gave us one last venomous look and marched away. I expected her to turn at any moment and yell, "Watch out, I'll get you, and your little dog, too!"

Evil witch. I was shaking, fury pounding through my body. Stanley draped an arm over my shoulder. "You okay?" he asked.

I nodded, not certain I could speak. Mixed in with my anger was the overwhelming urge to cry. I didn't understand what was happening to me.

"I think you've had a rough day, let's go inside," he said with a kindness that almost undid me.

Climbing the steps to the porch, my aunts reached out to pat my back or squeeze my hand, showing me they loved me in any way they could. "Come on, I don't care how much pizza you've had, I think it's time for dessert," Aunt Maria said.

"That's right, Estelle made a nice apple pie before we went out tonight, you come have some," Aunt Claudia said.

"Where did you go?" I sniffed.

"To the new funeral home," Maria said.

"What? Why? Who's dead?" I asked, worried that I'd missed something important.

"Nobody's dead," Claudia answered. "We went to the open house to check things out. I heard they were going to have food and everything."

I couldn't think of what to say, so I kept my mouth shut. When did funeral homes start having open houses? I shook my head. It really had been a long day.

"Food will make you feel better," Maria said, draping an arm across my shoulder. "Let's go inside."

Chapter Forty-Two

IT HAD ONLY BEEN ONE day, but it felt like weeks. Nothing had changed, but everything was different. I was in a constant state of thankfulness for the gift of being alive, alternating with a relentless vigilance should Linwood escape the confines of his hospital prison and hunt me down. I was scared, and once in a while I even got mad.

It was such a short period of time, really, compared to my entire life, only minutes that I spent with Linwood up in Ethel's bedroom. How could it have affected me in such a lasting and profound way?

Oliver told me he had seen this kind of thing before; people go through these life-or-death circumstances and come out the other side with a minimized version of PTSD. Maybe he's right, but I hoped the up and down feeling wouldn't last. I had things to do.

Plus, I was trying hard not to think of that mist of gray. Really hard.

The temperature was rising, as it was the first day of April, but the rain had been relentless all night, creating a dark, dreary day. I must have been thinking about it all night, or maybe even dreaming about it, because when I woke up that morning I knew what I had to do. I called Giuseppe at home. "Hey, I might be a little bit late today," I said.

"You okay?" I'll give him credit, he had been overly protective in the past twenty-four hours, constantly checking on me and making sure I was fine.

Between my brother and Stanley I should have felt safer than a cow at a vegan convention.

"I'm going to visit Valerie," I said.

"Do you want me to come with you?" Giuseppe asked.

"No, but thank you. This is just something I've got to do." I hoped that by visiting Valerie I could not only get some answers about this whole bizarre situation, but maybe I could find some peace, too.

"Why don't you take one of the aunts with you?" he asked, interrupting my thoughts.

"Are you kidding? Which one of them would let us visit in peace without clocking that woman upside the head?" I knew my aunts were mad at Valerie, because I heard them calling her "that woman" and saw the scowls on their faces whenever they referred to her. I couldn't blame them; after all, I harbored a bit of my own resentment toward her. But I knew that seeing her face-to-face would help me understand why she did what she did. If she would see me.

Frankly, I didn't have the energy to have a door slammed in my face, so for once in my life I was practical. I called and asked if I could come over and visit. She sounded nonchalant on the phone, as if it was every day that the woman she wrote a threatening note to and who her husband tried to kill called her. I took extra precautions and let everyone know where I was going and made sure my cell phone was fully charged. Just in case she tried to do the same thing as her husband.

"Take your time," my brother said. "Do you want me to sit outside in the car and wait for you?"

I could feel a small smile playing on my face. This was the protective brother I loved, the one who paid attention when I needed help and really wanted to be there for me.

"Are you gonna make me a sandwich!" he yelled. "Jesus, Janine told me she was gonna make me something to eat. What's a guy gotta do around here to get a little food?"

Well, okay, maybe he was hungry, but his attitude toward his domestic situation had nothing to do with how much he cared about me. Janine, on the other hand, had probably already clocked him upside the head. "I'm good," I said. "Go eat your sandwich. I'll talk to you later."

Since it was raining, and her house was a short distance away, I decided to drive. I got there sooner than I wanted and sat in the car for a moment, taking deep breaths. When Valerie appeared in the doorway, I decided it was time to get out of the car.

She ushered me into her home in silence, and I couldn't help but wonder again what I was doing there. She might be mad at me, and I might be walking into a trap. But if that was the case I was prepared. I'd loaded up with large amethyst crystals from the store, knowing they turned my purse into a weapon. If I knocked her on the head with the purse, I had a good chance of getting away.

Valerie led me into her kitchen, and finally said, "Have a seat. I made some coffee, or I can boil water for tea if you prefer." She looked at me, perfectly coiffed, patiently waiting for an answer.

I decided to get straight to the point. I'd known the conversation would be uncomfortable, but I hoped to avoid as much of the awkwardness as possible. "I wanted to tell you how sorry I am about Linwood. I'm sure this isn't easy for you."

Valerie sighed and sat at the table. "I'm the one who should be apologizing to you." She looked up at me, and to my horror big, fat tears started leaking from her eyes. "I love him so much that I didn't stop to consider the consequences of my actions. I just wanted to protect him."

I pulled out a chair and sat across from her. "I can relate to that. I do things all the time to help my family, and I'm sure if I ever get married I'd feel the same way about my husband." Well, not really, I couldn't see myself covering up a murder, but I was trying to be polite. "How long has he been..." I wasn't sure how to say the words. How long has he been sick? Ill? Crazy?

"I've known for almost a year that something is wrong," Valerie said. "At first I thought it was just age creeping up on us, and maybe if we worked hard to keep our minds active and our bodies healthy we would be fine." She took a deep breath and looked down. "But doing the daily Sudoku puzzles were not going to help him."

"Did he receive a diagnosis before all this... happened?"

Valerie shook her head. Her words were so soft I had to strain to hear what she said. "A wife knows. One day he came home visibly upset, his hands shaking. He told me we were under attack, and soon they were going to start drafting kids and a bunch of stuff that didn't make any sense. But his hands really told me everything I needed to know."

"What do you mean?" I asked.

"His hands didn't stop shaking." She finally looked up at me. "I know it sounds too simple, that I knew something was wrong because he had a tremor, but it's true. I knew in my heart that my Linwood was leaving me, a little at a time." Her voice broke on the last sentence, and I couldn't help but feel her pain.

"I'm sorry," I murmured, not sure what to say. How do you express condolences to someone who has lost their life partner already, lost him to a disease that robbed him of who he was? "Did you try to get him on medication?"

Valerie stared out the window. "I made sure he ate healthy all the time. Even before this happened, I was careful about the foods I served him. I've been reading about food additives for years now, and I always bought organic."

Organic. The image that popped into my mind was not one of health, but of filth. "Did you buy your food from a health food store? I don't know of any around here," I said, hoping to sound nonchalant.

Valerie shook her head. "No, I bought it from a woman who lives out on the edge of town, Debbee. I liked the idea of buying local and organic, as it supported the community. All the books I read said to buy local."

Hmmm. Something was off, but I couldn't quite put my finger on it. My internal radar was buzzing, but I couldn't quite pinpoint the problem. "Did you like her food?" I knew my question was lame, but I couldn't think of anything else to ask.

Valerie sat up straighter. "No, dear, I didn't eat anything I bought from her."

I stared at her. "But—didn't you want to eat healthy, too?"

"Of course I did, but I have a food allergy. I don't eat wheat or gluten. I find it's easier for me to buy wheat and gluten free food for myself so I don't have to think about what might be in the other stuff. I never ate her food."

Chapter Forty-Three

SINCE MY CONVERSATION WITH VALERIE had gone so well, I thought about going to see Debbee next. *Am I crazy? What the heck would I say to her?*

But the truth was that I didn't like the way things were between us. For some reason Debbee thought I was a bad person, not deserving of a dog. I knew she wasn't quite right in the head either, so I should just ignore her. *But there's more to Debbee, I know there's something going on. I need to finish this investigation.* Clearly she had nothing to do with Linwood's attack. If that were the case, other people would be acting just as strange as Linwood. *They have been. At the house, the day Linwood attacked me. Everyone was wacky.*

What would I gain by going to see her? Nothing. In fact, I'd probably end up in a fight or, at the very least, getting kicked off her property. But I had my handy purse full of rocks, so what was there to lose?

I dug my cell phone out of my purse and pulled over to the side of the road. Dialing Aunt Claudia's number, I thought about what to tell her. When she answered, I said, "Hey, it's me. I just wanted to let you know everything went fine with Valerie, and I'm leaving her house now."

"I'm glad to hear that, dear. At least I know she didn't do anything else to hurt you."

"No, I'm fine. I'm just going to go take care of one more thing before I come home."

A grim silence travelled through the cell phone airwaves. "Where are you going, dear?" Claudia's tone was casual, but I could feel her intent.

"I'm going to see Debbee," I said, cringing as I waited for her reaction.

After a moment, she answered, "Are you sure that is a wise choice?"

Maybe Claudia would have some insight into what was bothering me. "Something's going on there. I don't know why I feel compelled to go see her, but I do. I think she's up to something, or something weird is going on, I'm just not sure what it is."

Claudia's response was immediate. "Do what you have to, dear. Call me when you leave."

O-kay. That was easy. A little too easy, but maybe Claudia was busy. Wasn't she going to lecture me or tell me not to go? "So, I'll see you when I get home," I said.

"Bye." And just like that, she hung up. Odd. Usually Claudia took the time to talk with me, to go through everything and figure out the best course of action. She and Estelle both said things like, "Haste makes waste," and a bunch of other sayings that would stay in my head forever.

Maybe she had a cake in the oven or something.

I remembered how to get to Debbee's place, but drove past her driveway before I realized I was there. I stopped the car, reversed and pulled into the driveway, bouncing my way over the muddy ruts, past the rusty equipment and junk littering the side of the path. At least the rain had stopped for the moment.

I sat in the car and stared at the house. I was glad I had Sparky. Now he didn't have to spend any time living here. Frankly, I was surprised the place hadn't been condemned. Trying to focus, I thought about what I was going to say. Maybe I'd go for a let's-all-try-to-get-along approach.

Nobody answered my knock at the door, so I wandered away from the house and started walking back toward the dog runs where I'd first seen Sparky. The silence was heavy, and I felt a strange tingling at the base of my spine.

This place is definitely creepy, I thought. My imagination had taken over, understandable after everything that happened to me. But in the stillness of the yard, I couldn't bring myself to call out for Debbee.

The barn door was partially open. Debbee was probably working in there, doing whatever it was she did to her food before she sold it. I put my hand on the door, hoping I didn't get splinters from the cracked wood. The door gave a loud squeak as I pushed it open wide. The scene in front of me was shocking, to say the least.

Barrels were stacked in the front corner as if they were no longer used. Lined up against the back wall was row after row of clear, plastic containers with lids, the kind that were usually in health food stores with bulk food items. The dozens of containers were filled with what looked like different types of grains. On either side of the barn were long, gleaming white tables with a variety of knives laid out along one of the tables. A large sink with a gooseneck-spout faucet jutted from the wall in the back corner. But most surprising of all was the cleanliness of the place. I could see the shine of the knives on the table, glinting from the sunlight pouring through the windows up high.

"Debbee?" My voice sounded hesitant, and I wasn't sure if I should be walking around in there. I took a couple of steps inside, walking toward the back wall. The bins were labeled, which was a good thing because some of them looked very similar to each other. I recognized some of the names, but others I had never heard before. Wheat, Teff, Quinoa, Einkorn, Barley, Rye...

The rye bin caught my attention, and I wandered closer. Peering in, I could see that the grain was actually very colorful, with what looked like little purple flowers. *Wait, I don't think that's supposed to be there. I wonder where she gets this stuff from—*

Thwap. The noise startled me, and I spun around. Debbee stood behind me, hands outstretched. But they weren't empty. In her right hand she held one of those gleaming knives I'd just seen on her table.

I swallowed and took a step backward. Unfortunately, there was no place to back up to. This scenario felt way too familiar. "Hey, I was looking for you, and I knocked at your house but I couldn't find you. I came out here to talk."

To my relief, she walked over to the table and put the knife down. "Okay," I said, trying not to sound too relieved. "How about we go outside and, um, we can talk about things?"

Facing me, she reached into her voluminous dress and pulled out a gun, pointing the thing right at me. "I don't talk to witches," she said.

Chapter Forty-Four

I HAD EXPECTED OUR TALK to go a little differently. Clearly my purse full of rocks was not going to help. I put my hands out in front of me, as if by doing so I could stop a bullet. "Listen, Debbee, I'm sorry we got off to a bad start, but—"

"Be quiet," she said. Her voice was low and soft, sounding only slightly insane. "I know what you are, and you shall be silenced for your sins. You shall not harm us again, nor will you bring ruin and chaos as I know is your plan."

Someone got up on the wrong side of crazy this morning, I thought. *What the hell is she talking about?*

"Debbee, I'm thinking that if we can just talk to each other, you might see we have more in common—"

"I don't consort with the devil," she said. "I can see the demon forces at work around you, and I will not succumb to the lure of your siren call."

Siren call?

"They are here," she said, looking at an area behind me. "I can see they have begun to gather."

I flashed back to the moment at Ethel's house, when everyone was wandering around the place talking like this. They all sounded slightly off, and I thought I knew why.

"Debbee? What's in these grains?" I gestured to the bins behind me. "Is everything in here safe for human consumption?" *I must really like living on the edge*, I thought. *I need to figure out a plan to get out of here, not worry about whether her grains are good or not.*

"That is my life's work, it is part of my job to properly feed the people with food not tainted by chemicals."

"Yeah, I don't like the chemical thing either," I said, hoping to show her I was an ally. The sound of sirens started up in the distance. I wondered if there was some way I could get my cell phone out of my purse and call 911 without Debbee noticing.

"Then why have you not eaten of the pure food? Why do you put impurities in your body, food like pizza?"

"I didn't know pizza was impure," I said, trying to play along, hoping that was what she needed to hear.

"When I saw you eating with him, I knew you had him in your sights. You are doing the devil's work, acting as his whore, and you must be stopped."

Whoa. Had she been watching me and Oliver? Besides, crazy or not, nobody called me names like that. "Who do you think you are calling me a whore, when you are clearly out of your mind?"

She waved the gun at me. "You need to come with me now, so I can do this right."

I crossed my hands over my chest. "No." She might be the one with the gun, but I wasn't going to do what she asked. She'd have to shoot me first. The sound of sirens was growing closer, and I could only hope they were headed our way.

"I can see this isn't a good time for us to have a talk, so I'm going to leave now," I said, starting to inch my way to the left. I had no last minute plan, no way of knowing if I could outsmart her. She was clearly a few bulbs short of a chandelier, but I figured I was better off just trying to walk away than trick her. Plus, I'd read somewhere that eighty-seven percent of people survive gunshot wounds. *Just don't think about the other thirteen percent.*

As I started to skirt around her, she waved the gun in my face again. "You're not going anywhere, witch."

"I need to go home. Really, let's set up a time when we can have lunch or something and talk about this more." Maybe if I acted like nothing was wrong, she'd take the cue and let me go. "How about if you bring some of your food over to my place and we can sit down and talk about everything?"

Her face twisted, and she looked at me with sheer hatred, the force of which made me step back a little. But I'd had enough and stood a little taller. I wasn't going to be pushed around by some aging hippie with poor hygiene.

She raised her gun higher, pointing at my chest. "You cannot consort with—" I jumped forward, shoving the gun toward the ground.

Crack.

Debbee looked at me for a moment, our eyes connecting before she dropped to the ground.

Chapter Forty-Five

"WEREWOLVES ARE FINE," I SAID. "Maybe even a vampire."

"I think she's delirious," Giuseppe whispered to my mother. "She doesn't know what she's saying."

"She's not delirious, she's just had a rough time lately," my mother said, laying her hand on my forehead.

I was in a hospital bed, staring up at the ceiling. After rescuing me, the police had insisted on loading me into an ambulance to get checked out. Machines beeped in other rooms and the bustle of nurses' activity went on around me.

I cleared my throat. "As I was saying, werewolves and vampires might be fine, but I am not—I repeat, not—having anything to do with ghost hunters again."

Both my mother and brother were silent, probably knowing better than to say anything. I looked up at the doorway to see Stanley hovering, a weary-looking Oliver behind him. "Come in," I said. "I think it's safe here." I wasn't sure anyplace was safe anymore, but what the heck.

The men came and stood beside me, Stanley taking hold of my hand. "Are you hurt?" he asked, pushing his glasses up.

"The doctor said I'm fine, no injuries. I should be able to go home soon."

"I know your aunts are waiting for you in the reception area," Stanley said.

"They wouldn't let everyone in at the same time to see you."

I half-smiled. "I'm sure they had something to say about that."

Oliver shook his head while Stanley grinned at me. "I believe Estelle said something nasty in Italian to the lady behind the desk," Stanley said. "And I'm pretty sure I know enough Italian to figure out what the word means."

"Never mind what Estelle said," my mother interjected. "We're just thankful that woman didn't kill you."

"Plus we're thankful for Claudia," Oliver said.

"Claudia?" I must have missed something.

"Yes, she's the one who called the police," Oliver said. "She called 911 right after she spoke with you and told them your life was in danger and they needed to get out to Debbee's farm immediately. I believe it took her a few minutes to get them to believe her, but Claudia can be quite persuasive when she needs to be."

I exchanged a look with my brother. Persuasive was a good word for Claudia. Normally soft-spoken, with more good manners than Emily Post herself, Aunt Claudia was not someone to mess with, especially when someone in her family was in danger.

"I got cupcakes," my father said, striding into the room.

"Rourke, I don't know if she can eat cupcakes," my mother said.

"Lillian, I don't care. My baby almost got herself killed twice this week. She's always liked chocolate cupcakes, so I'm giving her chocolate cupcakes."

I smiled and blinked my tears away. "Thanks, Daddy."

"You go right ahead and eat as many as you want," he said, putting a brown bakery box in front of me. "And if you just want to eat the frosting, feel free. Whatever you want, pumpkin." My father must have been fairly shook up about recent circumstances to allow something like that. Usually he told me the same things my aunts did: waste not, want not.

I struggled to sit in a more comfortable position. Hospital beds were not designed for optimum comfort. "I have a question," I said. As I looked at the anxious faces peering at me, my heart rate accelerated. I hated to ask this, but I had to know. "Did I accidentally shoot Debbee?"

Everyone around me exchanged a look, but nobody said anything. "Did I?" I asked, worried that I'd killed someone. "Did I kill her?"

"Debbee's not dead," my mother said, placing her hand on my arm. "And no, you didn't shoot her."

Oliver cleared his throat. "The shooting at Debbee's farm is only one piece of this investigation. This whole situation has gotten quite complicated. But to answer your question, Officer Genova shot Debbee."

"Rob?" I looked at Giuseppe, who nodded. "Is Rob all right?"

"You've got some good friends, Ava," Oliver said. "When Officer Genova responded to the scene, he saw that Debbee had her weapon trained on you and was worried for your life. He acted quickly and de-escalated the situation."

"By shooting her," I said. "Is he in trouble?"

"There's going to be an investigation," Stanley said. "It's required anytime a police officer shoots someone, but clearly he saved your life. The only thing he might get in trouble for is not following protocol and announcing himself, telling her to drop her weapon, that sort of thing, but I don't think he's going to get in trouble."

Oliver shook his head in disgust. "What?" I asked. "Why does that upset you?"

"He should have followed proper procedure, instead of reacting without thinking."

"Maybe if he had followed procedure I wouldn't be here talking to you," I said.

"Maybe," Oliver acknowledged. "There's something else, though. We need to talk."

I knew what was coming. I'd known it since I saw those purple flower things in Debbee's grain. "She was poisoning people, wasn't she?"

"I don't think she meant to do it," Oliver said. "In fact, she's her own victim since she consumed the food too. But yes, anyone who ate her breads recently ingested something called ergot, which causes fairly severe problems. The good news is that this hasn't been going on for very long, so hopefully not too many people have been affected."

"Remember the Salem witch trials?" Giuseppe said. "Ergot poisoning is one of the theories about why everyone acted crazy and started making outlandish accusations."

This sounded familiar, but I couldn't quite remember how ergot could cause that level of problem. "Wouldn't food poisoning cause you to throw up? How could it have caused the Salem witch trials?"

A nurse walked in at the tail end of my question. "Time to take our vitals," she said. I made a face. I hated it when medical professionals used words like "our" and "we". There is no "we" in "hospital", there's only "spit". She must have noticed the look on my face, as she hurried to say, "Lucky for you, I can answer your question, too, as most of us have been reading up on this very issue since our new admissions. Initially ergot poisoning causes gastrointestinal problems, then if left untreated it leads to things like headaches and itchy skin. After that it leads to hallucinations, which is when it gets really interesting."

I flashed back to the bizarre behavior of the crowd at Ethel's house. "Holy canoli, all those people were eating Debbee's bread. Is the whole town sick?"

"I only eat Janine's food," Giuseppe said. "And thankfully we belong to an organic co-op so baby Danny didn't eat any of that... stuff." He made a face when he said it, looking upset and mad at the same time.

The nurse unwrapped the thermometer attached to a rolling machine, stuck it in my mouth, and nodded. "Lots of people are here right now. Police department's been going through town looking for folks who bought Debbee's food. It's a mess, I'll tell you."

Since I had a thermometer stuck in my mouth, all I could do was nod. When the machine beeped, she took the thermometer out of my mouth and nodded. "Your temp is normal. I'm going to take your blood pressure now."

"Will everyone be okay? Has anyone died?" I asked, looking at my family. I hated to think people had been hurt by one woman's carelessness. The nurse wrapped the blood pressure cuff around my arm and started pumping.

"It might take a while, but we think we've got this contained," Oliver said. "People are in the hospital now and are being monitored. I don't think the poisoning has gone on long enough to cause anyone's death."

"How did this happen?" I asked. I wanted to place the blame entirely on Debbee, but I knew there was a chance this wasn't her fault.

"She got careless," Oliver said. "She imported some grains from a grower in the tropics, and they were infected with ergot. She never realized those dark flowers were deadly. She's also..." Oliver stopped talking, looking a bit flustered.

"What? Mentally ill? Unstable? In need of serious medication?" I asked.

Oliver had the grace to look uncomfortable. "Due to privacy laws, I can't tell you too much about her situation, but your assessment might be correct. She is currently resting comfortably while waiting for an evaluation."

Good, then maybe she would get the help she needed. I'd known for a while that Debbee was not all there, but I hoped that with the proper medical attention she would find her way back to some type of normalcy. Mental illness was not fun for anyone, and hopefully she had family or someone to help her through.

"Is it possible..." I began, then stopped. I didn't know if I wanted to get started on this, but once it crossed my mind I had to ask. "Is it possible that Linwood ingested her... food and doesn't have Alzheimer's?"

Stanley squeezed my hand. "His wife wondered the same thing," he said. "She brought him here for testing. We won't know right away, but it's possible."

"What's he doing out of jail?" Giuseppe asked.

"He was out on bail," Oliver said. "I think the judge was lenient because of his condition, and the doctors testified that being in prison could exacerbate his symptoms. He is being monitored, though, with an ankle bracelet because of his violent tendencies, and he is restricted to staying at home."

The Velcro made a scratchy noise as the nurse ripped the cuff from my arm. "Looks like everything's normal."

"Good, then I'm leaving," I said.

"You have to wait for the doctor," she said. "He should be doing his rounds in a few hours."

I swung my legs off the bed and stood, looking for my purse. "Mom, Dad, can you give me a ride?"

"Whatever you need, sweetheart," my father said. I smiled. I could always count on my parents to help me.

"You cannot leave until you get the doctor's signature," the nurse reiterated.

"Mmm," I answered, opening the closet door to get my shoes. "Tell the good doc I said thanks, I'm checking out."

"You can't just leave," she insisted, her face turning red.

I'd like to think I had enough influence from my parents and my aunts to know how to gracefully handle the situation. I just wanted to go home, see Sparky, and take a long, hot bath.

"She's pretty stubborn," Oliver said.

"In a good way," Stanley added.

"You might as well put those papers together, because she's leaving," Oliver said.

I reached for my coat. I figured the doctor could call and yell at me later.

"So, sis, I was wondering, if you're up to it, there's a house over on—"

"No," I said.

"We were going to—"

"I don't want to do any more ghost hunts, G. No, okay? Just no." Clearly my brother did not understand me, so I was going to have to explain this once and for all. "I'm not helping anymore. This is it. I'm done. Over. Goodbye."

"It's an open house," my mother said. "Giuseppe and Janine are thinking about buying it."

Oh.

Stanley stepped forward and put his arm around me. "We'll figure out a time that works for Ava, and we'd love to take a look at it."

Giuseppe's face lit up as if we'd given him an extra birthday present. "Thanks, guys, I really appreciate it. This is the perfect place for us, with more space and a big backyard for Danny. The neighborhood's great, too."

I felt bad for being so short with my brother. After all, he was only asking for advice on something. "I'd love to see it."

As we walked down the hallway toward the elevators, Giuseppe kept talking about the house. "It's a little older, might need some work done, you know, update the kitchen and bathrooms and all that, but I think we can get it at a really good price."

"I hope there's not too much work to be done," my father said. "You should get an inspection before you make an offer, make sure this is something you can handle."

My brother pushed the down button for the elevator and waved his hand in the air. "Don't worry, Dad, the price isn't low because of the condition of the house."

As the elevator dinged and the doors opened, my heart sank. I knew what was coming even before Giuseppe said it.

"The house is cheap because it's haunted."

**Turn the page for an exciting preview of the next book
in the Brewster Square series...**

Birding in Brewster Square

Ava Maria Sophia Cecilia is excited to meet Stanley's parents, but that weekend was not at all what she expected. The man she thought she knew has been hiding something big, her detective friend Oliver is acting strange, and weird things are happening with a group of... birders?

Ava is soon busy with family mysteries, missing persons investigations, and trying to avoid Debbee, who is determined to befriend her. In addition, she has a powerful vision the night her brother insists she host a shamanic workshop. Immersed in shaman chasing, wedding reception food, and wildlife viewing, the stakes are high for both Ava and the person she is desperately trying to save.

Birding in Brewster Square
Chapter One

BABY DANNY DIDN'T MEAN TO ruin things for me, it just worked out that way. His contribution to my weekend was only the start of something bigger. Much bigger and much worse. And I couldn't blame a baby.

This particular Friday was important, my plans had been in place for weeks, and of course I was running late. Before I left work, my brother had asked me to shelve the new merchandise for the store at the last minute. Apparently that job had to be done *right this second.*

Maybe I should blame my brother for how it all started. Not because of the work he asked me to do—yes, it had been last minute, and yes, it could have waited—but because of his bizarre food issues. Baby Danny's parents—my brother and sister-in-law—always give that poor sweet baby some type of foul-smelling, organic food that any normal human being wouldn't feed to their fish.

I loved my nephew, I really did. He was adorable and sweet, but I made certain to never, ever pick him up right after he'd eaten. The child was incapable of keeping a meal down, and who could blame him. After every meal it was only a matter of time before his all-natural, organic, GMO-free, antibiotic-free, taste-free, super food was regurgitated.

I stopped by my brother's house after finishing at the store. It was only going to be for a minute. I had to drop something off. Without thinking, I picked up baby Danny.

And just like that, my new, beautiful, aqua-blue silk blouse, meant to complement my red hair and make me look sophisticated, was toast. My hair wasn't looking so good, either.

I shoved the baby back at my brother Giuseppe and grabbed a towel. After trying to get most of the organic cement off of me, and failing miserably, I gave up. I'd have to fix myself once I got to Stanley's house. I said a quick goodbye and hustled down the street and around the corner to where Stanley was packing the car.

"Ready?" he asked, slamming the hatch closed.

"Almost. I need my suitcase for a minute."

Stanley shook his head. "You'll have to wait until we get to my parent's house. I've arranged the china on top of our luggage and strapped it down so nothing moves or breaks. Everything is perfectly packed."

Stanley's mother had insisted that Stanley bring his grandmother's fine china with him when he visited. The china had been sitting in storage at Stanley's house for years, but for some reason she needed it *right this second*. Said china was now boxed up and resting on top of my suitcase in the hatchback of the car. The suitcase that contained clean clothes.

"But—I need a shirt." And a mirror. Or maybe it was better not to know.

Stanley looked at his watch. "We have to leave now so we don't hit rush hour traffic." He glanced over at me. "Besides, you already have a shirt on."

He squinted a little, and I knew he had seen the stain. He was just too polite to say anything.

"But I... I have something in my suitcase that I need. Can't live without. Really." I gave him what I thought was my sweetest smile, but it must have been more of a grimace because he just shook his head.

"If I unpack now, it will put us about forty-five minutes behind. I don't want to be late."

"It won't take long." Clearly Stanley did not understand. I could not show up at his parents' house looking and smelling like this.

But despite my best efforts, I failed. Stanley wasn't even listening to my last sentence and had climbed into the car. He sat waiting for me. *I don't even get the door opened? He won't get my suitcase or open the door?* I stomped over to the passenger side, threw myself into the seat, and slammed his car door as hard as I could. Childish, yes, but I couldn't help it. He wasn't listening.

I was starting to have a bad feeling about this weekend.

I leaned my head back against the passenger seat and closed my eyes for a moment. This was not part of my plan. I did not look glamourous. I did not smell pretty. I was fairly certain I would not make a good first impression, and I really wanted Stanley's family to welcome and accept me. Instead, they would probably ask me to use the servant's entrance and help clean the ashes out of the fireplace.

If they had a servant's entrance.

To be honest, I didn't know much about Stanley's family. I knew that he had a sister, Victoria, and his father was a professor at a prestigious college in New London. I wasn't sure what his mother did, but I was fairly certain there was also an older brother that nobody talked about.

After twenty minutes of driving, I opened my eyes and stared out at the plant life dotting the interstate 95 corridor. Finally, the leaves were green and flowers were blooming, not just those yellow chrysanthemums that signaled the colder weather was almost, but not quite, gone. Tulips were out in full force and soon the lilacs would be bursting with fragrance. At this time of year, after an interminable winter and a half-hearted spring, any sign of life was more than welcome. Trucks and cars whipped past us, only to have to brake when someone in the left lane insisted on doing the speed limit. Stanley stayed in the right lane, cruising at a steady 62 miles per hour.

"Do you want to listen to the radio?" Stanley asked.

"Sure," I said. Maybe music would calm my nerves.

He wrinkled his nose. "What's that smell? Did something get wet in the car?"

I didn't want to tell him that the smell was my baby-puke shirt, and probably some of my hair, or remind him I needed to change. I could have mentioned that this was the result of his insistence that we leave without him digging out my suitcase. But I didn't want to bring attention to my dilemma. We were still new enough in our relationship that I felt like I always needed to look good, a feat I was failing at miserably at the moment. I said nothing as a wave of embarrassment flooded my body. Just as quickly annoyance flashed through me. Stanley hadn't helped the situation. At all.

"So, what station did you want to listen to?" Changing the subject might distract us both. I reached up and tried to pull my hair back, wondering if I should put it in a ponytail to hide the stringy look I was now sporting.

"Maybe I left the windows open on the car and it rained," he said. "Sometimes that happens, because I leave them down a little."

Was he really that dense, or was he trying to make me feel better? Neither option cheered me. "Mmmm," I said, trying to sound noncommittal. "I don't know what you usually listen to. Classic rock? Alternative?"

Stanley didn't even hesitate as he reached over and flipped on the radio. "Talk radio. Love those shows."

I settled into my seat and stared out the window again. It was going to be a long ride.

***

Our trip lasted forty-five minutes. To get to Stonington, Connecticut from our little town of Brewster Square we had to travel directly up the highway to the northern area of the state. Stonington was next to Mystic, the town that had been famous in the '80s because of the Julia Roberts movie. Mostly people remembered Mystic now for the shopping and tourist attractions.

Stanley's parents lived in a nice suburban area, a tree-lined neighborhood with what looked like upscale houses. He pulled into the driveway of an elegant colonial with a perfectly manicured lawn. I sat up and smoothed my hair back. I had surreptitiously put the window down on my side for the last fifteen minutes of the ride, hoping the baby Danny vomit smell would dissipate enough for me to meet the folks and get changed. Honestly, couldn't my brother be like the rest of the world and use regular formula instead of toxic strength super-yuck?

Stanley put the car in park, reached over, and squeezed my hand. "I'm glad you're here, Ava. This means a lot to me."

Stanley had invited me to come with him to his parents' anniversary dinner a couple of months ago. We had just started dating, and I'd been super excited at the idea that our relationship was going somewhere. My excitement hadn't changed, and even though we were still in the beginning stages—where everything is still new and wonderful—I felt like Stanley and I had something special.

Ping.

I rifled through my purse, trying to find my cell phone. That ping-ing noise meant I had a text.

Where R U?

"Who is it?" Stanley asked.

I didn't want to answer him, but I had no choice. Stanley and I had agreed to always be honest with each other, no matter what. "Oliver," I answered as I typed my answer.

Stonington. Dinner w/S parents.

Stanley let out a sigh. "The investigation is over. What does he want?"

Stanley was referring to the investigation into who had killed Ethel, a woman who lived in Brewster Square and had seemed to be routinely despised by all. I had been unfortunate enough to find her body, but I couldn't stand the thought that her killer would not be brought to justice. So I took it upon myself to investigate—caving to the demands from my brother that I find out what happened—and almost got myself killed by two people in the process.

When will u be back? U can have dinner w/me.

"Um, he wants to have dinner?" I couldn't help that my sentence came out sounding like a question. Oliver and I had not had the best of relationships, since he thought I was just being nosy and I thought he wasn't doing his job. We sort of patched things up by the time the killer was caught, but I wasn't sure why he was asking me to dinner.

"Didn't you have coffee with him already this week?" Stanley said, his voice almost sounding petulant.

"It wasn't like we arranged a date and met for coffee. He brought me some when I had to work late on Tuesday, that's all."

"With food, right?"

"Yes," I said, not sure what food had to do with anything. "And yes, I took him around Brewster Square last week, but that was because I thought he needed a history lesson. If he's going to work in this part of the world, he needs to understand what happened here and what people are like."

"So, you're the Brewster Square ambassador?"

I didn't like Stanley's tone, but I could understand it. He'd always felt threatened by Oliver, who was a former DEA agent and could pose for any month of the calendar.

"I'm sorry," he said. "I don't know what got into me."

"We agreed that we would be honest with each other, and I'll always do that," I said. "I'm not going to do something behind your back."

Stanley sighed and pushed his floppy blond hair back from his face. "I know. Please, bear with me. Being here..."

I wasn't sure where he was going with this, so I waited while he seemed to drift into space. Finally, he came back from wherever he was and said, "Being here brings up some bad memories. I don't mean to take it out on you."

I really wanted to explore that thought further, especially since I had no idea what he was talking about. Bad memories? I could guess all day, but hopefully he would tell me about it sometime soon. I wanted to know more about Stanley.

The ping of my cell phone distracted me again.

Dinner?

A flush crept up my face. Yes, I wanted to know more about Stanley. But I also wanted to know more about Oliver. Did that mean I was just nosy, or did it mean something more?

I didn't have time to think about it, because somehow a group of people had gathered in the driveway. I sent back a hasty "yes" to Oliver, got out of the car, and tried to project an air of confidence.

"Mom, Dad... good to see you." Stanley gave his parents a one-armed hug and ignored the other two people standing to the side. "I'd like you to meet my... friend, Ava. Ava, this is my mother, Birdie—"

Birdie was a small woman with a sharp face who looked a little bit like her name. Her face lit up in a smile when she saw me, but, cynic that I am, I couldn't tell if the smile was genuine or not.

"Beatrice," she said, extending her hand to me and staring at my shirt.

"Um, nice to meet you." I tried to angle myself so that my arm covered the front of my shirt, but I knew I wasn't fooling anyone. And what was with him calling me his friend? Hadn't he told his parents about me?

"We all call her Birdie," Stanley said, beaming at his mother. That was fine for Stanley and his family, but the jury was still out on what I would be calling this woman. Especially since I was a friend. "And this is my father, Chase."

Clearly Stanley had gotten his boyish good looks from his dad. Slightly taller than average, Chase had the same bright eyes and dimple. He stepped forward to shake my hand as well, and did a little bow as he clasped my hand in both of his. "It is a pleasure to meet you, my dear. Welcome."

"Thank you."

A silence hovered around us for a moment. *I'm guessing that's his sister standing off to the side with someone who just crash landed from the sixties.* The